PRAISE FOR THE BRO

For Better, For Murder

A finalist for the 2009 Agatha Award for Best First Novel.

"Bork juggles multiple puzzles deftly in her witty debut."
—*Kirkus Reviews*

"In this promising series debut, Bork has created an interesting cast of complex characters that readers will enjoy getting to know."—*Booklist*

"[A] lovely book."—*CrimeSpree*

"... a fun joy ride."—*Mystery Scene*

"Entertaining with subtle humor, [a] self-deprecating and complex heroine, and [an] engaging story."—CozyLibrary.com

"A fun, fast-paced mystery with both a great setting and a great cast of characters and plenty of twists and turns to keep readers engaged and coming back for more."—TheMysteryReader.com

"The series has promise and the book ends with a happy twist."
—*Bookpage*

For Richer, For Danger

"A winning second mystery."—*Publishers Weekly*

"The book is believable with all its U-turns and dead ends, which normally happen on life's road."—Kay Thomas, *Genesee Country Express*, Dansville, NY

"Readers will enjoy the hometown feel of this mystery."
—TheMysteryReader.com

"The characters are very interesting and very complex...a fun read with lots of twists that will keep you up reading."
—Once-UponARomance.net

In Sickness and In Death

"Bork packs in multiple story lines at a lively and humorous pace without overdoing it. It might be a standard cozy frame, but Bork's series pushes the envelope in a good way."—*Library Journal*

to Love and to Perish

A BROKEN VOWS MYSTERY

to
Love
and to
Perish

LISA BORK

MIDNIGHT INK
WOODBURY, MINNESOTA

FIRST EDITION
First Printing, 2012

Book design and format by Donna Burch
Cover design by Kevin R. Brown
Cover illustration: Michele Armatrula/The Drawing Room, Inc.
Editing by Connie Hill

Midnight Ink, an imprint of Llewellyn Worldwide Ltd.

Library of Congress Cataloging-in-Publication Data

Bork, Lisa, 1964–
 To love and to perish : a broken vows mystery / by Lisa Bork. — 1st ed.
   p.   cm.
 ISBN 978-0-7387-2337-2
 I. Title.
 PS3602.O755T6 2012
 813'.6—dc23   2012026529

Midnight Ink
Llewellyn Worldwide Ltd.
2143 Wooddale Drive
Woodbury, MN 55125-2989
www.midnightinkbooks.com

Printed in the United States of America

For the Ladysleuths:
Kathy, Kelly, Shelley, and Teresa.

ONE

"Look at that TR3 ... and that Porsche 914-6. Awesome!"

I grabbed Danny's elbow and steered him from the path of an oncoming golf cart. "I know you're excited, but please watch where you're going."

"I am, Jolene. I am." He yanked his arm from my grasp and darted over to a nearby Datsun Bluebird, bending down to get a closer look at the dashboard. "Ray, come look at this! It's right-side drive."

"Be right there." My husband, Ray Parker, shook his head in mock dismay. "Our boy takes after your side of the family, darlin.' He's got the fever."

Danny most certainly had the fever, but I suspected he'd come by it from his father, a wanted car thief of considerable skill and talent who had relieved me of a pre-owned but pristine F430 Ferrari Spider at the end of last year. Of course, I was forever indebted to Mr. Phillips. Not only had the Ferrari been tainted by the dead man found in it, but Mr. Phillips had left Danny behind with us when he took off with my unsalable car. Perhaps he'd known living on the run would be no life for his son. Regardless, Danny had filled Ray's and my childless void and brought us new joys daily.

I continued to follow Danny and Ray down the main drag in Watkins Glen as Danny shouted out the names of the vintage and classic sports cars lining both sides of the road, which was closed to all but golf cart and foot traffic. We had driven an hour and a half southeast from our hometown of Wachobe, New York, in order to see this Vintage Grand Prix Festival. Danny had revved his engine the whole drive here and the moment Ray put my Lexus in park, Danny leaped out and raced toward the cars on display. Ray and I had to hustle to catch up.

I understood his excitement. My father used to bring me to the Watkins Glen racetrack to watch all different kinds of cars race. It was our special time together, and one of the many reasons that added up to my opening Asdale Auto Imports, a boutique that sold pre-owned but pristine sports cars in Wachobe, our small but popular upscale tourist town located on the western edge of the Finger Lakes region. I hadn't thought twice about hanging the "Closed—Gone Racing" sign on the shop's front window for a three-day weekend. This race always drew a huge crowd from not only all over New York State but from points all over the country ... even the world.

The dark clouds overhead spit raindrops on the crowd, but no one seemed to mind. We passed by the beer tent where a crowd was enjoying the Miller Lite, Yuengling, and Samuel Adams offered. One light-haired man in a Binghamton sweatshirt stepped from the tent and off the curb right in front of me. I gave him an irritated glance. He looked to my left then my right, his dark eyes vacant, and made no move to get out of my way. I decided to go around him when it occurred to me that he might be too drunk to move any farther.

The scent of Philly cheese steaks and the tang of pulled BBQ pork made my stomach rumble. It was close to five o'clock, and we were supposed to meet my sister, Erica, and her husband, Maury, for dinner at the food tents in front of the courthouse in half an hour. Meantime, I'd spotted a sign for the Girls Varsity Soccer Bake Sale across the street by the store that sold Carhartt. Maybe a little brownie would tide me over to dinner. I started to move toward the treats.

"Jolene, come on. You're missing all the cars. Look at this three-wheel Morgan." Danny grabbed my forearm and dragged me away from the delicious cakes, cookies, and Rice Krispies treats. "Isn't it awesome?" He pointed to the dark blue, open-top race car with two wheels in front and one in back.

"Very. You know this is the 100th year anniversary of the Morgan. The company switched to manufacturing a four-wheeler around 1950 when no one outside of England really wanted to buy their three-wheeler. This is a rare car in the U.S., but Morgans have been racing at the Glen since 1954."

"Cool. Oh, wow, look at that Camaro." Danny crossed the street and disappeared into the throng.

"Hey, wait up." I looked for Ray, who was always easy to spot at six-foot-three, 220 pounds of masculine muscle. He was examining the interior of a 1957 black Corvette with silver coves. "Ray, Danny needs to stay close to us. There are a lot of people here. We don't want to lose him."

He straightened and put his arm around me. "What do you think this car would go for?"

"Around sixty thousand." I tugged on his sleeve. "We need to catch up to Danny."

With a look of regret, Ray pulled himself away from his dream car. "He's fine. He's having a good time. Leave him alone."

"He is alone, Ray. That's my point."

Ray's arm dropped from my shoulder. "Listen, Jolene, Danny is almost thirteen now. He needs his space. I know the word 'mother' is included in smother, but you've got to loosen the leash a little. He's not going to get lost. Let him enjoy himself."

Ray only called me by my given name when he was irritated—or in the mood, which wasn't likely at the moment. This wasn't the first time we hadn't seen eye to eye on how to care for Danny.

"Okay, if you say so." I continued down the street, pretending to look at the array of cars, but I didn't stop moving until I caught sight of Danny out of the corner of my eye. I needed to know he was safe.

A moment later, Ray appeared at Danny's side, and I breathed a sigh of relief. Danny was only twelve, and although he had many skills and experiences other children his age did not, he still needed to be protected from evil. Unfortunately, evil wasn't so easy to recognize or anticipate as one might think.

I walked across the street to join them. We continued on, reaching an intersection where the street was painted like a black and white checkerboard pattern. Danny pointed to it with glee. "It's a race flag."

"You know what else is cool?" I beckoned for him to follow me over to the sidewalk. "See this stone marker?"

"Yeah." Danny's gaze moved over the inscription.

"It's part of the Drivers Walk of Fame. The markers have the names of the greatest drivers who have competed at the Glen since 1948. They have them all up and down Franklin Street, beginning at the starting line of the original race course and heading north. This year, Paul Newman gets a marker." Posthumous. To match his stone on the Hollywood Walk of Fame, a place Danny had probably never heard of or been.

"The spaghetti sauce guy?"

Ah, the gap between generations. Approaching forty, both Ray and I remembered a slew of celebrities, politicians, and athletes Danny would never see. "He was also a famous actor and race car driver. I saw him win a race driving a Nissan at the Glen in 1985."

"Cool. Hey, Ray, look at this Mini Cooper. Think you could fit in it?"

I followed my boys as they took in the sights, bemused by the fact that even though I knew way more about cars and the Glen's history than Ray, Danny seemed more willing to stay by Ray's side. Of course, it was natural for a boy his age to prefer spending time with men, especially Ray, who had a more exciting career as a county deputy sheriff, an excellent poker face that I referred to as his "good-cop, bad-cop, whatever-you-need-me-to-be-cop face," and the ability to put a wicked spiral on a football. Even when Danny came to my shop after school, he always wanted to be out in the garage with my mechanic Cory, learning about engines, suspensions, brakes, and all the other technical stuff instead of my "boring" sales and bookkeeping.

Yes, Danny was definitely becoming a little man, as evidenced by his height, now an inch over my own five-foot-four, the smattering of acne on his forehead, and the frequent crack in his voice. He preferred to keep his dark hair long, but neither Ray nor I would allow it so long as to cover his face. I liked to see Danny's high cheekbones and even the little nick the size of a pinhead on his right cheek just underneath his eye. He never told us where he got that. We weren't sure we wanted to know. The knowledge might add more gray hair to Ray's already light temples and a deeper furrow to my brow.

It tickled me that both my boys had beautiful brown eyes and that our whole family had brown hair, Ray and Danny's both straighter and darker than my bobbed hair. To a stranger, Danny looked like our child, and that pleased me. I had no doubts that it pleased Ray, too. He'd do almost anything for that boy, as would I. Funny how quickly one can bond to a child.

I checked my watch. "Hey guys, it's time to meet Erica."

As usual, they didn't race to respond.

Ray and Danny checked out a few more cars while I tapped my toe to the beat of the four-piece rock band playing from a nearby bar's porch roof. I didn't mind keeping Erica waiting. She'd kept me waiting many a time; in fact, she was prone to disappearing altogether, both literally or just inside herself. But Maury was always on time or early. I didn't want to hurt his feelings.

"Come on, guys."

Reluctantly, they fell in step with me, and we headed over to the food tents, where hamburgers, sausages, fried dough, ice cream, and a whole slew of culinary treats waited. One vendor even had a "Weenie Wagon," which sent Danny into a fit of laughter.

I spotted Maury sitting at a table near the street. "Hey, Maury. Sorry to keep you waiting."

"No problem." Maury stood to shake Ray's hand and slap Danny on the back.

"So where's Erica? Is she in line for food?"

"No, she didn't want to come." Maury sat again and toyed with a discarded straw wrapper, his baby-cheeked face the epitome of despair.

Ray gave me a look that said "you deal with this." "What do you guys want to eat? Danny and I will get in line."

Maury didn't respond, so I told Ray to get everyone a cheeseburger, fries, and Coke. I seated myself across from Maury and wondered what my sister saw in him. True, at a well-built five-eleven and one hundred-seventy pounds with a shiny head of dark hair, he had a certain physical appeal but his wimpy personality detracted from that significantly. All he needed was the horn-rimmed glasses he'd worn in high school to complete his geek image.

"Is something wrong with Erica?"

"She said she didn't feel like it."

Immediately I was on alert. Erica was bipolar and had been in and out of the psych center for years, most often because of attempted suicides. "Is she taking her medicine?"

"Yeah. I see her. She's taking it." He squished the straw wrapper into a ball and pitched it into the grass.

"Is it a cold? The stomach flu?" I'd heard both were going around now that school had reopened last week, two days after Labor Day.

"No. She doesn't want to be with me."

"Oh."

"Yeah." He heaved a sigh. "I think we're in a rut."

I managed to choke back my laugh. The two of them hadn't been married a year and had rushed into marriage after only knowing each other a few weeks. How could they be in a rut? I wasn't sure they even knew each other's favorite color yet.

"Either that, or she's having an affair." He looked at me as if I might be able to confirm or deny it.

I tried to freeze my expression neutral so as not to give my thoughts away—my face can be entirely too readable. I hadn't talked to my younger sister in a week. A lot can change with Erica in the space of an hour. She had a long history of relationships, broken ones. This marriage could easily be the next casualty. She'd married Maury during a time when I'd been too busy wallowing in my own problems to pay attention to her. I had no idea if she was having an affair now. It wouldn't surprise me, but I wasn't going to say so . . . at least, not until I talked to Erica.

Maury didn't seem inclined to say more either. I sat with him in silence until Ray and Danny appeared with the food. Even in his defeated state, Maury managed to inhale his cheeseburger and fries faster than anyone else. Danny finished a close second.

"What time is the race?" Danny's gaze swept the street behind me, raring to move onto the next activity.

I licked the last of the French fry salt from my fingertips. "I think the cars will go up to the track for the start of the race a little after six and come down shortly thereafter."

The festival was known for its "race," which was really a parade lap or two around the 1948–1952 race car course. In those years, the racing took place on the streets and hills of Watkins Glen with hay bales lining the roads to protect the spectators. The town gave that up soon after a car lost control, plowing through the hay bales into a spectator and killing him. When the international track was built on top of the hill above the town, all the real racing moved there. But in the early 1990s the festival took advantage of growing nostalgia and asked the Sportscar Vintage Racing Association to bring their race cars down from the track to participate in tribute laps. Nowadays, different groups of car classes descended the hill from the Glen, raced up Franklin Street, and ascended the hill to the track with roaring engines, squealing brakes, puffs of exhaust and flashes of racing color. It was an exciting tribute and a beautiful setting, just steps from the base of Seneca Lake and the glorious gorge in Watkins Glen State Park.

Danny leapt up and took a few steps from the table. "Can we get a spot to watch the race? I don't want to miss anything."

I helped Ray gather our trash. "Sure. I think the best view will be near Milliken's Corner." The corner was an almost ninety-degree left-hand turn where my dad had witnessed a car plow into the hay bales many, many moons ago. It wasn't so easy to turn a race car after riding its brakes down the hill. With today's drizzle, it was going to be that much tougher on the cars and their drivers. Things could get a little squirrely—and exciting for the spectators.

The four of us retraced our previous path down Franklin Street and headed left onto Route 409. A white and blue sign marked the famous Milliken's Corner, courtesy of the Glen Region Sports Car Club of America. Several spectators had already taken seats on the few hay bales available. A handful of folding chairs were turned face down on the sidewalk, keeping the seats dry while waiting for dignitaries or local store owners, no doubt.

"Where should we stand?" Danny looked at me for guidance.

"Well, if we stand at the base of the hill, we can see the cars come down and make the turn. If we stand closer to the corner of Franklin, we could see them on both turns and as they roar up the street, too."

Danny moved his gaze to Ray for a decision.

Ray wasn't listening. He'd spotted a local county deputy sheriff he knew and was waving to him. "I want to say hello. Be right back."

Maury sidled closer to me. "I think I'm going home. I'm not that into the race."

I felt guilty for inviting them to join us. Clearly, he'd only shown up to be polite. Erica could take a lesson from him in that regard. "Okay, sorry, Maury. Tell Erica I'll call her tomorrow."

With a nod, Maury melted into the crowd.

The cars lining Franklin Street roared to life as the drivers revved their engines in preparation for heading uphill to begin the race. Danny and I decided to stand on the inside corner of 409 and Franklin. We had a view of Milliken's Corner and the main drag. The spectators started to get a little dense as everyone jockeyed for position. I lost sight of Ray.

My cell phone rang.

I answered, expecting to hear Ray's voice. Instead, it was my friend and mechanic, Cory Kempe.

"Have you seen Brennan?"

I glanced about in surprise. Cory and his boyfriend, Brennan Rowe, had entered Brennan's Mini Cooper in two events this weekend: tomorrow's sprint race and Sunday's endurance race. They also planned to drive in the tribute laps this evening.

"No. I thought he was driving with you in the parade lap."

"He told me to go ahead without him. He said he had something to do."

"In town? Not at the track?" Cory and Brennan had been at the track all day, prepping the Mini for the sprint race tomorrow. Brennan had driven in the qualifying race today and done well even though it was his first time on the track.

"I don't know where. He took off an hour ago. He didn't say where he was going. I thought you might have seen him."

"Sorry. I'll keep my eyes open, though."

"Please do. Let me know if you see him with another man."

I wasn't sure I'd heard Cory correctly. "What do you mean?"

"I think Brennan's having an affair."

That didn't sound like Brennan, who called the shop at least twice a day for almost a year now to talk to Cory. He was the most attentive boyfriend Cory had ever had, and, unlike my sister Erica, a stable and responsible person. "Why do you say that?"

"He's been weird and standoffish ever since we got here. He keeps disappearing with no reason or excuse. And the other night at home he got a phone call from a guy. He locked himself in his office and talked for over an hour, then got angry when I asked who it was."

All right, that would make me suspicious, too. I couldn't even think of a way to put a positive spin on it. "Are you still driving in the race?"

"I guess so. Maybe I'll see him on the sidewalk."

"Okay. Well, be careful and concentrate. It's pretty slick out."

"Yes, mom. Keep your eye out for Brennan."

"Done." I snapped my cell phone closed.

The noise of approaching engines drew our attention to the street. First a local sheriff's SUV appeared, lights flashing, then the official Chevrolet Camaro pace car, and finally the vintage and classic cars. First an Allard passed us, followed by a Bugeye Sprite, a Porsche 356 Bathtub, and an open-top Formula Junior, the driver wearing old-time leather headgear and goggles, his yellow scarf embroidered with his car number flapping in the wind. All the cars' passengers waved to the crowd as their drivers cleared the turns and gunned their engines up Franklin. Dozens of cars passed by, including the Mini Cooper with Cory, who didn't seem to notice Danny and me waving to him. It didn't seem like as many cars as in years past, but the weather conditions might have put some drivers off. Open-top cars and racing slicks mixed with rain didn't make things festive.

After the first parade lap ended and the roar of the engines faded into the hills, I noticed Danny was fidgeting. "What's wrong?"

"I have to go to the bathroom."

"We can go over to the store across the street. The cars won't come around again for a few minutes." I started to step off the curb.

Danny pushed ahead of me. "I can go by myself."

"Ah … okay. I'll wait right here. Come right back when you're done." I watched as he crossed the street and disappeared into the store, wondering when Ray would rejoin us. Danny would have let Ray accompany him. I wasn't certain I'd done the right thing in letting Danny go alone. This crowd was huge and filled with all sorts of unknowns. What was keeping Ray anyway?

The cars were approaching again. I hesitated, trying to decide if I should dash across the street ahead of their arrival to follow Danny.

As I checked the cars' locations, I spotted a sandy-haired man with a deep tan a few yards away from me. He seemed to be in a heated conversation with a red-haired man who had his back to me. The redheaded man's arms waved through the air and the sandy-haired man's face appeared flushed. All I could see of the redhead was his royal blue windbreaker and jeans. A woman in a bright pink raincoat, her face obscured by its hood, clung to the redhead's arm. It looked like she was trying to pull him away.

I recognized the sandy-haired guy. After all, not very many men had Robert Redford's movie star looks and charm. It was Brennan Rowe.

He had an expression on his face I'd seen last Thanksgiving when Danny got angry, stole my Porsche, and backed it into the rear quarter panel of Brennan's Mercedes by accident. It was a tolerant, patient, understanding expression. His flush may have related to anger from the redhead's words or embarrassment from the unwanted attention of the surrounding crowd who pretended not to listen as the redhead ranted, but, either way, Brennan seemed to be keeping his cool.

I tried to move a little closer to him to listen, all the while keeping one eye on the store entrance that had swallowed my boy.

The sheriff's car passed in front of us again, followed by the pace car. One after another, the vintage cars made the right turn off 409 and hit the gas to fly up Franklin, putting on a show for the admiring crowd.

Brennan broke off his conversation and headed toward me. I called to him but he didn't seem to hear. The cars were too loud.

The crowd closed in around him. Although the majority of spectators remained stationary roadside, a throng continually moved up and down the sidewalk, making it too difficult for me to grab Brennan as he passed. The man and woman he had been talking to disappeared in the mass.

I moved down the curb toward Brennan, who had gotten stalled by a woman trying to weave her wheelchair against the crowd. I turned to check again for Danny. No sign of him. Must be the store restroom had a line. The race had drawn one heck of a crowd.

Rising on my toes, I waved my arms like a crazy person, trying to catch Brennan's eye as he jockeyed around the woman. I was about to give up when he spotted me and waved back.

I motioned for him to come over. Cory hadn't passed by a second time yet, so maybe I could get Brennan positioned next to me in time to catch Cory's eye.

Brennan nodded and gave me the "there in one second" finger.

A brake squealed nearby. I turned to catch sight of a Triumph Spitfire rounding the corner in front of me.

Again, I checked on Brennan, who had started to move in my direction against the pedestrian traffic flow. The masses on the sidewalk surged, shifting him closer to the street.

I took my eyes off him and craned my neck in the opposite direction to look for Danny again.

A TR2 flew around the corner and hit the gas. The crowd cheered.

My gaze moved back to the store entrance. What was taking Danny so long? And where in the world was Ray? I started to sidle back up the curb toward the store, trusting Brennan to find me.

The next car took the corner even faster, brakes squealing in protest, before accelerating on the straight. Applause broke out.

A BMW 2002 rounded the corner, almost on two wheels, squealing. The spectators let out an appreciative gasp.

The Cobra behind it took the curve still faster. Too fast.

Brakes squealed. I heard a sickening thump.

A woman started screaming.

I swung around. I couldn't see the screamer or determine the reason for her screams. I couldn't spot Brennan anymore either. The mass of people was too thick.

I turned back to check for Danny again and watched in horror as the oncoming line of race cars slammed on their brakes, the ones coming around Milliken's Corner struggling for control. For a second, it looked like one of the Porsches was headed into the crowd. But no, all the cars came to a safe, if off kilter and herring-bone shaped, stop.

People poured into the street. Sheriff's deputies appeared. Ray was with them.

Then I heard, "Oh my God, is he all right?"

"Call 911. Somebody call 911."

"Is he dead?"

"Did he fall?"

"Did anyone call 911?"

A woman shrieked, "That guy pushed him. He pushed him!"

The other deputies cleared the crowd from the street. I held my ground on the curb. Danny would never find me if I moved now.

I was left with an almost unobstructed view of the road. The redheaded man lay in the street a few yards away, his legs bent at an impossible angle and a pool of blood beneath his head, soaking the shoulders of his royal blue jacket. The spectators were now silent, eyes wide, as the sheriff's deputies moved fast to secure the area.

I choked back my cheeseburger and fries as they rose in my throat. I scanned the other side of the street, fearing Danny would see the man.

A sheriff's deputy approached the group nearest the victim. "Are there any witnesses?"

A dark-haired woman tumbled off the sidewalk and grabbed the sheriff's deputy's arm. Tears streamed down her face. "That guy pushed him. He deliberately pushed him."

My gaze followed her finger.

She was pointing at Brennan Rowe.

TWO

SHOCK AND DISBELIEF CROSSED Brennan's face. He blanched and grimaced, giving the crowd a glimpse of his square white teeth. "The lady is mistaken. I tried to save him."

A couple men in the crowd started to mutter, one stepped toward Brennan with his arm raised. The sheriff's deputies were on him in an instant, herding him away. Ray stepped closer to Brennan, his gaze scanning the crowd until it came to rest on me. He looked all around me then mouthed, "Where's Danny?"

I gasped and spun around. The crowd in the street blocked my view of the store entrance. I started to push through, stepping on toes and bumping people out of my way. A hand grasped onto my forearm.

"Jolene?"

"Danny! What took you so long?"

"I was looking at the race car miniatures. They have 1:43 scales in there of tons of cars. Can I get one?"

I hugged his shoulders. "Sure, but later. We have a problem."

"What?"

I tugged him in the direction of the store and stopped next to the bake sale table, which was now surrounded by crying girls in red varsity sweatshirts. "A man got hit by one of the cars. He's dead." I said that with certainty.

An ambulance siren erupted, making me jump. The vehicle crept up the street, coming from the far end. The race organizers always had ambulances and flatbeds nearby, just in case. How unbelievably awful and surreal that this time they had been called into action.

My cell phone rang. It was Ray.

"Did you find Danny?"

"Yes, we're by the bake sale table."

"Can you come back over here?"

"What about Danny? I don't want him to see ... you know."

"Leave him at the table. Tell him I said not to move, not one inch."

"Okay."

I clicked my cell phone closed and instructed Danny. He didn't argue, taking up a position against the store wall. Then I wiggled my way across the street through the growing crowd, who were pointing, crying, explaining, speculating, or just plain standing with their jaws slack, expressing their own shock and dismay. I must have said, "Excuse me" a hundred times before I broke into the area cleared by the deputy sheriffs. One of them put his hand up to stop me, but Ray motioned to him to let me pass.

Cory now stood next to Brennan, pure panic on his porcelain-colored face. At a wiry five-foot-one with poodle-tight auburn hair and girly eyelashes, Cory was often tapped to play a teen in his

Finger Lakes Broadway-quality theater group, but the fear on his face today made him look all of his thirty-plus years.

Ray flanked Brennan's other side, along with the sheriff's deputy Ray had gone off to talk to earlier. The three kept a wary eye on the crowd, Brennan still pale beneath his summer tan but standing tall.

A few yards down the road, I could see a deputy taking the statement of the woman who'd accused Brennan of shoving the man into the street. Her arms waved as she described the scene, and the deputy had to step back to avoid being whacked.

Ray motioned me closer. I kept my eyes averted from where the ambulance workers and deputies surrounded the dead man. "Ken, this is my wife, Jolene Asdale Parker. Jolene, this is Ken Sampson. He's got a few questions for you."

Ken was an imposing man with a thick neck, crisp uniform, and no-nonsense aura. "Mr. Rowe said he was walking over to meet you when the victim was shoved off the curb. He said you might be able to confirm he reached out to save the guy."

My chest felt tight, my mouth dry. "Confirm?"

"Yes, ma'am. This gentleman"—Ken gestured to a white-haired man holding a camera with a telephoto lens—"has a picture of Mr. Rowe's arm extended out into the street as the victim is falling."

I swallowed. "A picture?"

Ray nodded. "It's Brennan's arm. Same gray shirt color. Same Rolex watch. What did you see, Jolene?"

This was not what I had expected. Ray looked at me, eyebrows raised.

Cory grabbed my bicep. "You saw Brennan try to save the guy, didn't you, Jo? Didn't you?"

I took in the tears sparkling in the corners of Cory's eyes, the dawning realization in Ray's, and the resignation in Brennan's. Now would not be the time to admit that my gaze wasn't on Brennan because I was watching the store entrance for my twelve-year-old boy who had gone to the bathroom and, if not there, then the other side of the street for my husband who'd disappeared in the crowd when he went to talk to his friend, this very officer standing before me and waiting for my answer.

"I'm sorry, Brennan. I'm sure you did try to save him, but I wasn't looking your way at that precise moment."

Always the gentleman, he dipped his head ever so slightly to acknowledge my apology.

Cory tightened his grip on my bicep. "Then what did you see, Jo?"

"I'm so sorry, Cory. I didn't see anything."

As I crossed the street to rejoin Danny, it occurred to me that what I had said wasn't quite the truth. I had seen Brennan in what appeared to be a rather heated conversation with the victim, minutes before he lay dead in the street. No one had asked me about that. I considered calling Ray's cell, then decided it should wait until we could discuss it in private. I didn't want to add to Brennan's trouble.

I reached Danny, who was biting into a cookie. "Where'd you get that?"

"The girls gave it to me. They gave everything away and went home."

The crowd had, in fact, thinned rapidly. The rain had dialed up to a full force downpour, killing any remnants of the spectators' curiosity about the accident, which I felt confident it was. While I didn't know Brennan all that well, I believed him incapable of violence. Cory wouldn't be attracted to him otherwise, that I knew for sure.

By now, the ambulance had driven away with the victim inside. No sirens this time, just flashing lights. A dozen sheriff's deputies had begun to take statements from the spectators on our side of the street, some of whom seemed excited to be questioned while others were more subdued. I wondered if any of them had been in the nearby bars or the beer tent earlier and how accurate their recollections might be. Hopefully one of them would be more helpful to Brennan than me.

Ken had asked Brennan to accompany him to the Sheriff's Department, placing him in the back of a department SUV that had arrived minutes after the ambulance. Cory had tried to go with him, but Ray blocked him and herded him back in the direction of the Mini Cooper, instructing him to return to the track and wait for him there. Cory put up an argument to go to the jail instead, but Ray convinced him otherwise. Ray then asked me to wait with Danny for a couple more minutes until he could rejoin us.

Danny offered me a chocolate chip cookie from the sandwich bag he held in his left hand.

"No, thanks, you enjoy them."

"Okay. What happened?"

I filled him in minus any details about the victim.

"They took Brennan?"

"Yes."

"And Ray's helping them?"

"Yes, but he'll be here soon."

"And you didn't see anything. Geez."

Again, I knew that wasn't quite the truth. I turned to watch for Ray.

THREE

I HAD RESERVED A room for us at the same motel—a family-owned, twelve-cabin basic close to the track—where Brennan and Cory were staying. Ray dropped Danny and me off, intending to meet Cory at the track and make a plan to obtain a lawyer for Brennan. I wanted to go with Ray to tell him about the redheaded man and to help Cory and Brennan, but at the same time, I didn't want Danny too involved in this whole mess. From the moment he joined our family, we'd treated the evening news and the details of Ray's job as X-rated. Danny didn't need to know more about the poor redheaded man's violent demise, and Ray was far better suited to deal with Brennan's arrest.

Trouble was, the motel room was dark and tiny—maybe thirteen by thirteen with most of that space taken up by two double beds—and had no television to keep Danny entertained with his beloved SpongeBob. The room didn't have a phone either. After one trip into the claustrophobic five by seven bathroom, I decided to take him across the street to the ice cream parlor, a popular spot in the town for many years.

When the vanilla scent of fresh-made waffle cones hit my nose, I thought I'd made a wise decision. The thirty-plus homemade ice cream flavors as well as a dozen fresh fudge choices were all enticing. An older couple in line ahead of us seemed to have difficulty choosing what to order. They taste tested a handful of flavors before ordering, giving Danny and me plenty of time to decide. I settled on a sugar cone of Southern Pecan Praline while Danny chose a double scoop waffle cone of Cake Batter and Triple Brownie.

Unfortunately, the deadly incident was bound to be the talk of the town, not to mention the flat-screen television mounted above the ice cream counter where we stood.

As pictures of the ambulance leaving the scene flashed, a newscaster's voice announced, "We have new details in today's tragic death in Watkins Glen. The Sheriff's Department has a prominent contractor from Wachobe, New York, Brennan Rowe" —Brennan's picture from his construction company's web site appeared on screen—"in custody at this time. According to the Sheriff's Department, Mr. Rowe is not under arrest, although an unidentified witness at the scene claims Mr. Rowe pushed the victim in front of the Cobra automobile that struck and killed him on impact in front of hundreds of race fans attending the Vintage Grand Prix Festival on the main street in Watkins Glen this evening. The name of the victim is not being released pending notification of his next of kin. When asked if the Sheriff's Department suspected foul play, the department declined further comment at this time."

As the newscast moved on to the day's next top story, Danny and I took seats at the table farthest from the television, next to the table where the couple had sat. I licked my cone with little enthusiasm and watched them enjoy theirs.

The man shook his head. "I'm not surprised. The way the two of them were going at it, I could tell there was going to be trouble."

"Did you tell the sheriff's deputy that the dead guy kept saying, 'You killed her, you bastard'?"

"I told him, Gladys."

"And that he said, 'You should have died, not her'?"

"Yes, Gladys."

"And that the woman with him said, 'Leave him be, Jimmy; it won't bring Monica back?"

"Yes, dear."

"Well, I guess that's all we can do. Sure looks like that Rowe killed him, though."

Danny ate his cone with gusto, seemingly oblivious to the discussion going on behind him. I tried to keep my eyes averted, but my gaze returned to the man's face over and over, hoping he'd say more.

I should have been relieved not to be the only witness to Brennan's and the redhead's argument on the street. Apparently this couple not only witnessed the scene but got an earful and had let the Sheriff's Department know. Instead, I feared evidence was mounting against Brennan, who I still believed incapable of murder. I did wonder what happened to the woman in the pink raincoat, who had been hanging from the redhead's arm, apparently pleading with him to leave Brennan be. She never appeared at the scene. Where could she have gone?

The man crunched up the last of his cone and wiped his lips.

"Are you ready to go, Gladys?"

She rose. "Yes, we have a long drive ahead of us."

The man hitched up his pants. "I can't say I'm all that eager to get behind the wheel. I keep seeing that man lying there on the road, when just minutes before he was so animated. I wonder how them fellas knew each other."

Gladys put her hand through the crook of his arm. "I'm sure it's all going to come out. We may not hear about it at home, though. This is local news."

I pondered the woman's statement as the bell on the ice cream shop door announced their departure. Was this going to be just local, small-town news? If the tragedy was deemed an accident by investigators, then probably so. But if investigators ruled this death a homicide, would the story get widespread press? I supposed it depended on other breaking stories and perhaps on how sensational this story might become. For Brennan Rowe's and Cory's sakes, I hoped it would all be cleared as an accident, but after hearing what appeared to be the couple's eyewitness account of the argument on the street and learning of the photographer's shot of Brennan's arm reaching out into the street near the fallen man, even I wondered about Brennan's involvement. Worse, I knew the residents in Wachobe had joked forever about what Brennan might have hidden in the poured cement basements of the homes and office buildings he erected there. After all these years, might the jokes have been more than that? Did Brennan really have something to hide? If so, had he hidden it from Cory as well?

Cory, I knew for a fact, did not appreciate having his partners hide things from him. He preferred honesty, even brutal honesty, perhaps the reason he and I were such close friends. Would this tragedy be the end of his relationship with Brennan, not to mention Brennan's days as a free man? And what about Cory's already existing fears that Brennan was having an affair?

My cell phone chirped. I flipped it open.

"Darlin', Cory and I are on our way to pick you up. He hasn't eaten and I think he should. I called the lodge. They can seat us at nine thirty."

I heard Cory say he wasn't hungry.

My ice cream cone stuck in my throat. Poor Cory. He was undoubtedly devastated, but Ray believed in "the show must go on" as did I. Most days Cory would have agreed with us. Today I wasn't so sure.

The local lodge Ray had referred to was known as the official racers' hangout. On its walls could be found the photographs and autographs of many of the greats, especially the race winners of year's past. The five of us would normally look forward to rubbing elbows there with this year's best drivers. Tonight it seemed like it could be a strain.

"What about Brennan?"

"He declined our assistance."

"What?"

"Let's talk about it later." Ray's tone implied he didn't want to talk now while Cory was sitting next to him in the car. "Meet us at the motel. We need to wash up."

Danny had finished his cone and was eyeing the remains of mine. He could eat more; he could always eat more.

I swallowed the last of my cone and my fears for Brennan. After all, now was the time to rally around Cory in support. No way did I want to be the one to suggest Brennan was anything other than innocent.

"It doesn't look good for Brennan."

Ray's voice was muffled as he pulled a clean polo shirt over his head and the fine hairs on his broad chest. At his suggestion, Danny sat outside on a woven lawn chair, listening to his iPod that he had retrieved from my Lexus. Cory had disappeared into the room next door without a word to anyone. I wasn't positive he would come out again.

Perched on the edge of the bed, I fiddled with the bedspread fringe. "Because of the photograph?"

"That and the eyewitness reports. A woman swears she saw Brennan shove this James Gleason into the road. A couple other people said they witnessed the two of them arguing near Milliken's Corner just prior, and some other woman was with Gleason at the time. They're looking for her, and the Department's interrogating Brennan now." Ray finished tucking his shirt into his jeans and started to re-buckle his belt.

"I saw them arguing. And I saw the woman."

Ray stopped buckling his belt. "What did she look like?"

"She had on a hot pink raincoat. I didn't see her face, just the raincoat. She was tugging on Gleason's arm. It looked like she was trying to pull him away from Brennan."

Ray resumed buckling. "The department knows all that. They need to identify her."

His tone said I made a disappointing witness, but how could I have known the woman was important at the time? "Doesn't Brennan know who she was?"

"No."

Well, he definitely knew the man with her. "What did you mean earlier when you said Brennan declined your help?"

"Cory and I drove over to the sheriff's office. I found Ken, and he went in and told Brennan we would arrange for an attorney for him. Brennan said 'Thanks, but no thanks. Tell them I'll take care of everything myself and to stay completely out of this.'"

"That's it?"

"Yep."

"What did Cory say?"

"He asked to see Brennan. Then he demanded. He got pretty worked up. I had to drag him out of there."

"Why couldn't he see Brennan?"

Ray eased onto the bed next to me, his weight pulling me against his side. "Brennan's in custody. The department doesn't want him talking to anybody, not to mention Brennan had already refused our help. We had no choice but to leave. I'm lucky they told me anything at all."

"Is Brennan under arrest?"

"I don't know if they've read him his rights yet, but I doubt he's walking out of there any time soon."

"Does Cory know about the witnesses?"

"I told him. I didn't see any reason not to. It'll be on the news soon enough."

"What did he say?"

Ray rubbed his hand over his chin, making his five o'clock shadow rasp. "He clammed up. I can't tell if he's pissed or scared shitless."

If I knew Cory, probably a little of both. Or maybe a lot. Brennan had gotten himself into a pretty big mess.

When we knocked on Cory's door a few minutes later for dinner, he appeared in his usual casual dress: a clean striped dress shirt, untucked of course, and khakis. He climbed into the car without comment.

The drive to the lodge was short and silent. Danny still had his headphones on and made no effort to remove them until Ray insisted he leave his iPod in the car.

Inside the log cabin lodge, the smell of prime rib and baked potatoes wafted over to greet us at the entryway. Dozens of men surrounded the bar in the center of the room, many of them still wearing their flat-soled leather racing shoes. Although the place was packed, our table was ready, and the hostess seated us immediately. The din of chatter was incredible, and the flat screens in the restaurant corners provided closed captioning. Danny and I took the seats facing the television while Cory and Ray had their backs to it.

Ordering proved difficult because we had to shout at the waitress, who asked us to repeat ourselves more than once. Conversation was impossible. Danny seemed engrossed by all the photos on the walls. I entertained myself by watching all the people, having seen all the photographs at least a dozen times before. Ray appeared to be enjoying his beer. Cory's gaze never left his placemat. I hated seeing him like this, so unlike his usual carefree, lighthearted self.

Just as the waitress delivered our sampling of appetizers—the only thing we could get Cory to agree to consider sharing—a breaking news story flashed onto the flat screen. Brennan's photo appeared again, followed by photos of a car wreck, a young woman, and what appeared to be Brennan's high school graduation picture. The closed captioning took longer than the live announcer and bled into the next story's pictures. I had no trouble following the gist of the newscast.

Thirteen years ago, Brennan Rowe had been driving a car that veered off the road into a tree, killing a passenger and leaving him in a coma. The two had just left their five-year high school reunion. The young woman who died in the crash was named Monica Gleason, sister of James Gleason, victim of today's tragedy. Worse, thirteen years ago, investigators believed Brennan Rowe had been driving drunk.

The gist: Brennan Rowe was already a convicted killer.

FOUR

I DIDN'T SHARE THE news story with Cory and Ray when we left the restaurant. The whole story had felt a little more *Inside Edition* than *CNN*, in line with the disturbing news trend toward sensationalism rather than fact. I hoped in the days ahead more information might come to light that would paint a different picture. This information wouldn't help Cory get through the night alone.

The news story hadn't said Brennan ever served time for Monica Gleason's death. In fact, the newscast said Brennan was not charged with Monica Gleason's death. Apparently, the crash occurred on country roads, was not discovered for several hours, and, by the time investigators requested tests of Brennan's alcohol levels, results inconclusive. But the news reporter allowed two of Brennan's fellow reunion goers—although certainly not his friends—to appear on screen. The men hinted the district attorney's reluctance to charge Brennan at the time might have had something to do with the significant campaign contributions Brennan's wealthy father had made throughout the years, and they did their best to refuel the rumors Brennan may have been drinking that night. The whole report implied the court of popular opinion had convicted him long ago. Perhaps this story was what had fueled all the jokes in Wachobe for all these years.

But somehow I doubted it. Brennan wasn't from Wachobe; he grew up in Albany, the state's capital, five hours southeast. Until today, I hadn't even known his father had money—or anything about his father at all. Granted, I didn't follow the news much and the local grapevine even less, but I would have heard this story about the car accident before now if it had made it to Wachobe. No, Brennan had arrived in our town ten years ago to start his contracting business untainted. The rumors that traveled the vine these days had to be linked to some other event. Perhaps now was the time to find out what it was. I could only hope it didn't paint Brennan in an even worse light.

After dinner, Ray had to drop us at the motel and head home for work, so I never got another word alone with him. He did tell Danny to stick close to me at the track the next day, a complete turnaround from earlier today. I wondered if that was for my protection or Danny's—or just Ray's theory of safety in numbers. Surely he didn't think we were at risk of being run down ourselves?

The next morning, Cory met Danny and me in the parking lot promptly at eight. His eyes appeared sunken into his head with dark circles highlighting his lack of sleep. He wore the same shirt and pants as last night, now creased and wrinkled after he apparently slept in them. I didn't remark on it, but for Cory, a failure to attend to his appearance was a major indication of just how understandably rattled he was. I hadn't slept all that well myself—visions of my loved ones being pushed in front of cars and crushed to death kept waking me. Danny, however, slept like a rock and needed to be prodded to awaken and get dressed.

"Let's grab some breakfast." I pointed to the motel office, where we'd been assured a continental breakfast would be available each morning.

Danny took off at a fast clip; Cory shuffled along three paces behind me.

The motel owner looked up with a frown when we entered the office. "Good morning. Are you in room nine?"

Cory glanced at his key fob and lifted his eyebrows. "Yes."

Her frown deepened. "These messages are for you. The press has been calling on and off all night. My husband and I didn't sleep a wink."

I peeked at the pink message slips over Cory's shoulder. The messages were addressed to Brennan Rowe, asking for interviews.

The manager fussed with some papers on the desk. "I don't know why they're calling here. It's clear from the news this morning that your friend has been arrested and will be arraigned Monday morning. But once I made the mistake of saying he was registered here, they wouldn't stop phoning."

A stricken look crossed Cory's face. He crumpled the messages in his hand. "I'm sorry you and your husband were disturbed. We'll be checking out this morning." He laid his key on the counter and turned to me, waiting.

I set my key down next to his, demonstrating my solidarity. "Can we have our bills please?"

Danny looked up from the table draped in a floral plastic tablecloth and covered with an assortment of juice boxes and packaged cheese and apple pastries that apparently passed for continental breakfast. "Aren't we staying for the races?"

Obviously Danny was more interested in the race than concerned about Brennan and Cory. I hated to do it, but this time their needs had to take priority over Danny's. "We'll get to see some racing this morning, but then we need to head out."

I hoped the disappointment on Danny's face wouldn't add to Cory's torment. He was too busy pulling his credit card from his wallet for me to read his emotions.

The motel manager laid our bills on the counter. They reflected a two-night stay.

I picked up my bill. "I'm sorry; we've only been here one night."

Her look was dismissive. "We only book for two-night stays on race weekends, when demand is so high. We charge for two nights whether you stay or not."

I forked over my credit card and sent a reassuring smile toward Cory. He didn't meet my eyes. I'd been his friend long enough to know that this whole situation was boring a hole in his heart and clouding his every thought. I trusted he knew that he had no need to feel any shame or embarrassment. And that I believed in Brennan just as much as he did. Trouble was, at this point, I wasn't certain how much Cory did believe in Brennan.

We made the drive up the hill to the track in silence. Cory had turned on the radio news, which confirmed the motel manager's statement. Brennan had in fact been charged in James Gleason's death and would be arraigned first thing Monday morning. I wanted to call Ray to see if he could learn more inside information from his friend Ken but decided to wait until later in the day when Ray's shift ended and we could talk freely The radio news didn't mention the connection to Monica Gleason's death. Perhaps that was old news already, even though I had yet to share it with Cory.

None of the other racers in the garage at the race track took much interest in us as we loaded the Mini into the trailer along with the easy-up tents, toolboxes, spare tires, racing slicks, jack stands, jacks, gasoline cans, and all the other paraphernalia associated with racing. The other drivers were all too busy and hyped for their own race to worry about or be interested in anyone else. Cars were already on the track, and the roar of their engines vibrated in the air, making my eardrums throb.

Danny may have been more affected by the whole situation than I thought. He didn't pay any attention to the other race cars nearby, even though some of them were premium. And more than once, as we loaded the truck, I turned around to find him right on my tail. In fact, he stepped on the heel of my sneaker twice, the second time stripping it from my foot.

"Danny!"

"Sorry, Jolene."

Yesterday, I'd been unable to keep him in sight. Now I couldn't keep him off me. I sat on a tire to put my sneaker back on my foot. "You're crowding me a little here, bud. What's the problem?"

"Ray said to stay close."

"Yes, he did. But that's too close."

Danny nodded and moved a few feet away, still glancing my way every few seconds. Again, I wondered who was keeping an eye on whom.

Cory worked in silence, not bothering to inform any race officials that they were withdrawing from the race. At this late date, no one would offer a refund on the few thousand he and Brennan had paid in registration and licensing fees to enter, and when the Mini Cooper failed to appear on track at the designated starting time, it would simply be marked "DNS"—Did Not Start—and they would be out the money, cash even a wealthy man like Brennan might need if he was now looking at a trial and attorney's fees.

When we finished packing, Cory wanted to leave for home immediately, although he acknowledged all he could do there was sit and wait for word from Brennan. Danny wanted to check out the racing. I preferred to stay until after the vintage auction, which had my 1957 MG MGA roadster in it. I hoped to make at least five grand off the sale. I also needed to know for sure if the MG sold, because if it didn't, Cory and I were going to have to come back to the track again to trailer it home.

Since the auction was at ten, only a half hour away, Cory reluctantly offered to take Danny around the track while I checked in with the auctioneers.

I reminded Danny to stay close to Cory. I watched them walk away.

As they reached the grandstand, Danny stepped on Cory's heel. Cory didn't seem to notice. Maybe we all should have just gone home.

I shook off my doubts and headed in the other direction toward where things were humming at the auction tent. After the rain last night, sellers were busy polishing their vehicles while the bidders registered.

Martin Feeder, the auctioneer, spotted me and waved.

I shook his hand. "Can you get me $18,000 for my MG?"

"I'll sure try. What's your reserve?"

"$13,000." I wouldn't make a profit if the car sold for anything less than that.

"Are you going to hang around for the auction?"

"Wouldn't miss it." This sale could make or break my month.

The auction area consisted of a large white tent with a podium and a strip of green carpet over the grass to form a runway for the cars to roll down. Dozens of people roamed the auction area including a few photographers, who were always prevalent at race events. The majority of photographers took pictures on spec, emailing the car owners pictures of their cars on and off the track after the event in hopes they might want to purchase some of the more spectacular shots to commemorate the race.

I spotted the white-haired photographer who had snapped the shot of Brennan's arm yesterday, the damning photo that got him arrested. The photographer caught me staring at him. Recognition crossed his face.

"You're Jolene Asdale."

"Yes."

"Howard Pint."

"Nice to meet you." I shook his cool, fleshy hand.

"I'm sorry about your friend."

I assumed he was referring to Brennan. "Thanks. He's in trouble, especially after the deputy sheriffs saw your photograph. Would you mind telling me exactly what you witnessed yesterday?"

Howard capped his camera, let it drop on his chest, and ran his fingers over the stubble on his chin. "Honestly, like you, I didn't really see anything. I was shooting the cars as they made the turn onto Franklin and came toward me, front end shots more than anything. When I heard the brakes squealing, I swung around and took a shot. The picture only caught that instant. I don't know if your friend was withdrawing his arm after pushing the guy or if he really was reaching out to save him, although that woman was adamant. The crowd was thick there, and they surged toward the road every time a car came around the bend. Gleason just could have been bumped off the sidewalk and fallen."

"The sheriff's department apparently doesn't think so."

"Well, the news reports have been feeding the flames, haven't they?"

"I'm afraid so. Did you take any other pictures that might be helpful?

Howard shrugged. "The sheriff's department took my memory card. The only other photos on the card were close-ups of cars. They asked about crowd shots, but I don't sell crowd shots. I sell car pictures."

I thanked Howard for the information then stepped closer to the podium to listen to the auctioneer start the bidding on a beautiful Lotus Super Seven. Normally, I'd be making notes on the level of interest in all the different types of cars and the final sale values for future reference in making my own purchase decisions as to which pre-owned but pristine cars I wanted to offer for sale through my dealership. But today, all I could think of was James Gleason and Brennan Rowe... and the news about them I had yet to share with Cory.

Yesterday James Gleason's life had ended in a split second. Either he'd been accidently bumped off the sidewalk or someone had pushed him. Hard to believe the crime could have been premeditated. How would anyone know he'd be on that corner in just the right position and at just the right time to shove him off the curb? I didn't see how Brennan could have known it, nor had Brennan ever struck me as one to act on impulse. Of course, I didn't know what the two of them had been arguing so hot and heavy about either. Maybe Brennan had been angrier than he appeared. Only the two of them would know—and maybe the woman in the hot pink raincoat. Perhaps she could provide answers. Maybe she'd seen something.

Then again, maybe she'd taken off in the other direction and, like me, witnessed absolutely nothing.

The one thing I did know was Brennan had been walking away from Gleason, not toward him, the last time I saw. I just didn't know if Gleason had chased after Brennan, enraging him or threatening him to the point where he'd decided to give Gleason a little shove. Could Brennan have killed Gleason by accident? Again, I liked to believe not, but I supposed Cory might be able to shed some light on whether Brennan had any sort of temper or not. He and I would have a long talk later at home.

The auctioneer's assistants rolled my MG in front of the podium. I started to edge closer, not wanting to miss a moment of the bidding.

My cell phone rang.

Annoyed at the interruption, I snapped it open, my thoughts and eyes on the auctioneer.

"I saw the news. What's going on with Brennan?"

It took me a second to recognize the voice of my close friend and college roommate, Isabelle Branch. Isabelle lived in the city an hour from Wachobe, where her husband, Jack, ran a jewelry store and she operated an advertising agency. She had created my sports car boutique's advertising campaign and even done some ads for Brennan recently. Her daughter, Cassidy, was my godchild.

"Nothing good." I sidled to the edge of the crowd and covered my other ear so I could hear her better. "What have you seen on TV?"

She recounted the contents of both broadcasts I had viewed. "They're saying a third person was injured in the accident that killed Monica Gleason."

"Really? Who?"

"Some woman who didn't want to be identified at the time."

"Interesting. I wonder if the press will out her now."

"No doubt if they can, they will. How's Cory holding up?"

"Not well. Brennan didn't want to see him or have him involved in any way. He wouldn't even let Cory get an attorney for him."

"Oh, he's got an attorney. I thought you guys called her."

"Who?"

"Catherine Thomas."

A sick feeling welled in my stomach. The beautiful Catherine Thomas was a highly respected defense attorney in New York State. She was also the woman Ray took up with during the last year of our three-year separation, attracted to her as he was to me because of our resemblance to his favorite actress, Valerie Bertinelli. She even had Valerie's same long hairstyle, while I had bobbed mine years ago. Although Catherine had been extremely helpful and supportive to us in the past, the thought of having her around again made me queasy. No one likes to be confronted with a woman her husband once slept with, especially a woman like Catherine, who I had to admit had it all goin' on, unlike me, who more often had it all goin' south.

"Wonderful."

"Sorry, thought you knew."

"I didn't." But now that I did, it was one more thing to worry about that was completely out of my control.

"Well, join the club. You're not the only one in the dark."

Martin Feeder chose that moment to slam his auction mallet down on the block. I jumped three inches in the air then frantically listened for the MG's final sale price. Naturally, he didn't repeat it. I'd have to wait until I hung up to find out. Besides, Isabelle's words had sounded bitter, quite unlike her usual personality. My antennae went up.

"What do you mean? Who else is in the dark?"

Silence.

I pulled the phone from my ear and checked the screen to make sure we were still connected.

"Isabelle? Is everything all right? How are Jack and Cassidy?"

At the other end of the line, I heard Isabelle burst into tears.

FIVE

I HAD TO ASK Isabelle to repeat herself three times before I clearly heard the words in between her sobs, "Jack is … having … an affair."

Was it something in the water? An epidemic?

My response was automatic and emphatic. "He is not."

Jack worshiped Isabelle. He bought her the finest jewels and the fanciest trips … and oh my god, had he just been making amends with gifts all these years? I reassured myself and her. "He loves you."

"Ray loves you, too, but he spent a whole year with Catherine."

Ouch. "We were separated for two years before he met her. The divorce papers were signed." Signed but never filed. Still, technically Ray was not a cheater. "Have you and Jack separated?"

"Not yet, but I'm thinking about it."

I moved farther away from the auctioneer as he geared up to sell the next car, not wanting to miss a word of what Isabelle had to say. "Why? What happened?"

"You remember my cousin, the one who thought her husband was having an affair. Remember, she figured out the password to his business AOL account and found out his only business was monkey business?"

"Yes."

"Well, Jack has a new AOL business account, and he didn't share the password with me. And he's acting all secretive, hanging the phone up when I come in the room. Plus we haven't had sex in two months."

"Is that all?"

"Isn't that enough?" She sounded outraged.

Not really. The whole world had gone nuts. At least, all the people significant to my universe were losing it. Me, well, I'd never been sure I had it in the first place.

"Two months is not that long, Isabelle. It's not unheard of, you know." I didn't care to elaborate, but I knew this for a fact.

"We used to do it every night."

"EVERY night?" I tried to imagine that level of … well … enthusiasm. Jack and Isabelle had been married almost ten years. They each owned a thriving business. They had an active five-year-old. Good grief, they had that kind of energy? I felt like a slacker.

"Yes."

"Well, even an Energizer battery needs recharging eventually." Silence.

"I'm sorry, Isabelle. I simply can't picture Jack with anyone but you. Have you asked him about all this?"

"Yes."

"What did he say?"

"He said he wasn't having an affair. That he would never love anyone but me. That he was too tired, too busy at work. That things will get back to normal soon. You know, all the lies a cheater would say."

I rolled my eyes, thankful she couldn't see me. "Isabelle, I know your cousin believed her husband's lies for a long time and felt like a fool afterwards, but I think Jack's telling the truth. I don't know anyone more in love with his wife than him."

"Then you ask him."

"What?"

"You ask him why he's hiding things from me. You ask him why he doesn't want me anymore."

"I can't do that."

"Why not? You're my best friend. You're his friend, too. You could ask him."

"I don't think so." I could, but I really didn't want to get involved. It was between the two of them. Isabelle and Jack were reasonable adults. They would sort it out on their own in no time, without any interference from anyone else.

"Then I guess I'll hire a private investigator."

Or not.

Cory and Danny reappeared outside the auction tent seconds after I hung up with Isabelle. Cory's fists were clenched, his lips flat lined. "Why didn't you tell me, Jo?"

"About what?" Danny averted his eyes as I spoke.

"About the news report. About the woman Brennan killed."

I caught Danny peeking at me out of the corner of his eye. Apparently, he'd been paying attention to the news report on television last night in the restaurant, too. Why he'd chosen to repeat the story now at the track, I'd never know.

"Cory, I was waiting until we were alone to discuss the whole situation." I raised my eyebrows and tipped my head toward Danny, who had turned away.

"Danny knows everything. He saw everything."

"What do you mean, everything?"

Danny glanced at me over his shoulder. "I saw the guy lying in the street."

"You were supposed to stay put."

"I did. He was right in front of me."

So much for protecting our boy from ugliness and evil. I wondered what else Danny had seen but didn't think now was the time to ask. Instead, I tried to calm Cory.

"The news said Brennan wasn't charged with killing anyone. It was ruled an accident."

"But a woman died in the car crash. And he was driving the car."

"The report did say that. But that's all."

"They said he was drunk."

"Two guys probably looking for their fifteen minutes of fame said 'everyone' at the reunion was drinking. No one said they specifically saw Brennan drinking or drunk."

"So why was it on the news?"

Good question. Why was half the stuff on the news? Or on magazine covers? Worse, why did anyone believe any of it anymore?

Had we all forgotten poor Richard Jewell, wrongly accused of the Olympic Park bombing and the poster child for law enforcement and media excess? Funny how we can remember a rumor forever while the facts fade fast.

"I don't know. But I don't think Brennan intentionally killed anyone, yesterday or thirteen years ago. Do you?"

Now Cory wouldn't meet my gaze. "Let's go home."

I let it go for now, wondering if Cory didn't share my conviction of Brennan's innocence. Did he know something more he wasn't sharing?

We stopped for a second at the auctioneer's table and learned the MG had gone for $17,500. I'd take it. They assured me the check would be in the mail as soon as the buyer's payment cleared.

The first hour of the ride home dragged. Cory didn't respond to my weak attempts at conversation, nor would he allow me to turn on the radio or even play a CD. Danny sat in the back seat of the truck with his iPod blasting. I watched the scenery go by, wondering what, if anything, I should have or could have done differently. Then all the silence made me feel drowsy. I closed my eyes against the sun.

An hour later, I snapped awake. Cory had pulled up alongside the patch of lawn fronting our yellow-sided, two-bedroom bungalow in Wachobe village. I let Danny run ahead with the key to the front door, not that he needed one. Lock picking was a skill his father had passed onto him, along with driving, hotwiring cars, and jimmying locks. A man had to have some skills, according to Danny's father. Seeing a dead man lying in the street and being able to sleep soundly the night afterward could now be added to

Danny's skills. Maybe he had more in common with Ray than dark hair. I wondered what else Danny might be capable of.

I, on the other hand, couldn't even let Cory drive away mad. "Can we talk about Brennan now?"

He nodded, his gaze focused on the windshield.

"What do you want to do? How can I help you … and Brennan?"

"He doesn't want our help. He wouldn't even see me." A tear sparkled in the corner of Cory's eye. He swiped at it angrily. "Why doesn't he want to see me? Why doesn't he want my help?"

"Maybe he's trying to protect you. And Ray said the department wouldn't let anyone see him until they finished questioning him anyway."

"I could have gotten him a lawyer."

"He's got a lawyer. Catherine Thomas."

His shoulders relaxed, showing his relief. "That's good. She's the best, right?"

"Right." The best lawyer, anyway. I didn't want to know if she was the best at anything else.

"What about the woman with James Gleason? Do they know who she was? Did she see anything?"

"The department is working to identify her. I'm sure she'll come forward soon."

Cory twisted to face me. "I have to know what's going on, Jo. I can't just sit here and wait. I can't let Brennan go through this alone. You're right. He needs help. He needs me."

I realized the error in my words too late. "He asked you to stay out of it."

"I don't care. I can't stay out of it. I love him."

"I know." I'd seen them together often enough to know this was true, but I didn't know what the right thing was for Cory to do. He seemed pretty convinced Brennan needed his help. I could certainly give him the time off in the event Brennan asked for him. I really didn't know what more I could do.

Cory did. "Jo, are you going to help me find out what's going on or not?"

SIX

Around seven o'clock that night, I sat out on our front porch, rocking in my white wicker rocker and enjoying the cooler evening air. Shouts and laughter from the neighbor's heated pool drifted over. Occasionally I could make out Danny's voice in the mix. Soon enough the temperatures would plummet, the leaves fall, and snow arrive. I wanted to breathe in as much fresh outdoor air as I could before that.

But mostly I was lying in wait for Ray.

He hadn't answered his phone all day, and I felt near frantic with the need to talk to him. I was in over my head with both Cory and Isabelle and not afraid to admit it. Hopefully Ray would be able to help. He tended to be the voice of reason, and, much as I hated to admit it, most often right.

I recognized the sound of his car engine before his vehicle even came into sight. Ray parked and strolled up our flagstone side-walk. "Hey, darlin.'"

He brushed his lips over mine and dropped onto his matching rocker, which creaked in protest. "I'm sorry I couldn't talk today."

"Something big happen?" I noticed smears of mud on his gray uniform and caught a whiff of ... evergreen?

"Major world crisis. A nine-year-old got his knee wedged in the crotch of an oak tree. He couldn't pull it out. I couldn't pull him out. His mom was hysterical, carrying on to the point where I actually considered slapping her. I had to call the fire department. Meantime, every yahoo in the county with a scanner showed up to watch. I needed Gumby and Max just for traffic and crowd control. It was a circus, and I was the ringmaster."

"Did you get him out?"

"We took down almost the whole tree after first cutting down the evergreen next to it, to get at the oak from the right angle. The kid's knee was swollen and twisted, but he'll be okay." Ray settled more comfortably in his chair and unbuttoned the top two buttons of his shirt. "So what's going on?"

Where to start? Murder accusations take precedence over adultery any day of the week.

I filled Ray in on the day's events and my last conversation with Cory. "He's really worked up about Brennan. He's got all kinds of wild ideas about investigating on his own." I left out the fact Cory had asked me to help, which was superfluous.

Ray snorted. "What's he think he's going to learn that the department doesn't know?"

"He's curious about the woman with James Gleason. He wants to talk to her, find out what James and Brennan were arguing about."

"She's Gleason's estranged wife. Ken spoke with her."

"And what was the argument about?"

"His sister's death. Both Brennan and the wife confirmed that."

"How did you know?"

"I talked to Catherine."

That sick feeling washed through my stomach again. "She called you?"

"I called her to see what we could do to help Brennan."

A nice gesture on his part. We were all friends, after all. "Did Gleason's wife say anything else helpful?"

"Not really. Apparently her son suggested the family attend the race. She and Gleason ran into Brennan by chance. Gleason accused Brennan of not caring about his sister and causing her death, and the two got into an argument. When they wouldn't stop arguing, his wife took off in the opposite direction, missed the whole crash, and didn't even hear about it until the sheriff's department showed up on her doorstep for next of kin notification. She and Gleason didn't come to the festival together, and they don't live together anymore either. Hard to say how broken up she is over his death."

Or if she told the truth regarding her whereabouts during the accident. "Did Catherine know anything else new?"

"Just that she thinks Brennan's going to have trouble with his bail."

"Why? He has ties to the area, no prior record. Surely no one believes he's going to go around pushing other people in front of cars."

"True. But right or wrong, the cloud of Gleason's sister's death is hanging over him now. The judge may not set bail at a figure Brennan can afford."

I wondered what amount would be unattainable for Brennan, who owned a million dollar, two-story contemporary house with a panoramic view of the lake and an in-ground swimming pool, plus a huge garage to house his car collection, a brand-new office building in the village, and a much-in-demand construction company. Very little got built on our lake or in the town without his involvement. "What can Brennan do?"

"I don't know. Catherine says it's unreasonable, but the bail amount may be enough to keep him locked up. She said to tell Cory to sit tight for now. That she's got it all under control."

I doubted Cory would be able to "sit tight," especially if Brennan remained in jail indefinitely. In fact, I wondered what Cory was doing right this minute. When I hadn't jumped on the idea of looking into things on our own, he'd gotten a wild look in his eye, a new and worrisome look for him. He wouldn't plan a jailbreak in this day and age, but he might do something equally crazy in the name of love. Though for the life of me, I couldn't imagine what that might be. The last thing Cory had said to me was he would see me at work on Tuesday, two whole days from today. At lot can happen in two days.

"I also got a disturbing call from Isabelle."

Ray's eyebrows shot up in surprise. He loves Isabelle. Everyone loves Isabelle, including her husband, Jack, no doubt. "How so?"

He listened patiently as I told him Isabelle's tale of woe, including a reminder about her cousin who believed in her husband for months until she walked in on him and his paramour in flagrante delicto. Ray's lips twitched a little bit when I got to that, but he agreed with me.

"Isabelle needs to give him some space. No way should she hire a private investigator."

"That's what I said."

"In a couple days, they'll have been back in the sack and it will all be over."

I could only hope. Still, Ray and I agreed. And maybe Isabelle had listened to reason.

This left me with only one other potential adulterer to worry about—my sister, Erica.

Our hometown of Wachobe sat at the head of a seven-mile, crystal-clear lake, the Mecca for boaters, bathers, and water sport enthusiasts. We were known as the western portal to the Finger Lakes region, and our town's population more than doubled in the summertime. Although the official tourist season had ended on Labor Day, the town still seemed bustling this bright and cheery Sunday morning.

At the edge of our village, a few yards beyond the quarter mile of original and picturesque brick and clapboard buildings lining the shopping district, a small but charming park offered visitors an area to swim under the careful watch of a lifeguard. The lush grass surrounding the area cried out for picnics. Yesterday I'd called and left a message for Erica to meet me there.

The park also showcased the loading dock for a paddleboat that offered luncheon and dinner cruises on the lake. With the sun shining at full blast and temperatures in the seventies, a line to board today's luncheon cruise wound across the park and around the white band gazebo. Through the crowd, I spotted Erica sitting on one of the gazebo benches, dressed in jeans, a V-neck T-shirt, and flip-flops, just like me, and holding a paper bag. If her V-neck hadn't revealed cleavage and her jeans had been a little less tight, holey or frayed, our clothing would have matched. As it was, even with only five years difference in age between us, I looked like the conservative mom and Erica, a teen on the prowl.

As soon as she spied me, Erica rose and pointed to the side-walk. I nodded in agreement, welcoming the exercise. My blue-eyed sister with her long, blond ringlets, who used to be a size four, was not so happy at her current size eight, a result in equal parts from her medications and the richer cuisine of married life. Still, she could give Kate Hudson a run for her money any day, in my humble opinion. The two looked quite a bit alike.

We fell into step and left the park, strolling down the sidewalk past the stately village homes dating as far back as the 1790s. Their magnificent porches decorated with overflowing hanging baskets of purple petunias, red geraniums, yellow marigolds, and fuchsia verbena made the view all the more spectacular. Blessed with a black thumb, I always admired other people's flowers.

Erica handed me the bag. "I made you something."

This was a first. Surprised, inordinately pleased, and curious, I reached inside the bag and pulled out a pillow. In uneven cross-stitch, it read, "I smile because you're my sister. I laugh because there is nothing you can do about it."

Never were words so true. We looked at each other and burst out giggling.

I shook the pillow at her. "If you only knew how many Finger Lakes gift shops have items with this saying on it. I think of you every time I see it."

She seemed pleased, always happy to be the center of the universe. "What do you think of my pillow?"

"I'm impressed. When did you take up cross-stitching?"

"Last week. I'm unemployed, you know."

A sobering fact. Erica spent most of her adulthood unemployed, able to get a job but always losing it when either the depression or the mania along with the phone calls to her coworkers at all hours of the night arrived. All the restaurants and shops in town flipped the "Closed" signs in her face now whenever she tried to apply, having learned either firsthand or through the grapevine just how unreliable or disruptive she could be.

"I'm glad you're putting your time to good use. I love the pillow. Thanks."

I broke our companionable silence after a few yards, beginning my ritual questioning. "So how are you?"

"Good."

"How are things going with Maury?"

"Okay."

"Are you happy with him?"

"Sure. He loves me."

I waited for Erica to say that she loved him, too. And waited. At least it didn't sound like she had another man. She would have told me. Discretion was not one of her virtues. And what a relief! Erica had taken up cross-stitching instead of with another man. It felt like real progress. If only it would last.

I moved on. "Are you taking your medication?"

Erica whipped her face away from me as though something interesting had caught her attention on the far side of the road. "Which one?"

She only takes two: one for her bipolar disorder and one to prevent... I'd never had to ask her about that one before. "What do you mean, 'Which one?'?"

A bottle cap lay in the road ahead of us. I watched as Erica stooped to pick it up and place it in her pocket. She'd been collecting them for years, some from beers she'd consumed, others from bars she'd frequented, and the rest from other people's discarded trash. The caps blended nicely with her enormous wine cork collection, and I didn't think she was even aware she was doing it anymore. She didn't seem about to answer my question, so I prompted her along.

"Let me be specific. Are you taking the medication Dr. Albert prescribes for you?" Dr. Albert was Erica's stud-muffin psychiatrist she saw once a month for her bipolar disorder. I'd considered developing a mental health issue just to spend some time with him alone myself.

"Yeah."

"And is it working?"

"It quiets the buzzing."

That was the best we could hope for because the buzzing would never completely disappear. "And are you taking your birth control pills?"

Erica started walking faster. She mumbled an answer.

I hustled to catch up to her. "I didn't hear you."

She stopped dead. "I'm taking them, but don't tell Maury."

I got that sick feeling in the pit of my stomach again, a feeling I could really live without. "Why not?"

"Because..." she heaved a huge sigh, "he thinks we're trying to get pregnant."

My blood turned to ice. "And are you... trying?"

"God, no. Never. Never ever."

I should have felt relieved. After all, Ray and I had split for three years after I refused to have a baby with him, fearing the family mental illness gene would be passed on to our child. It seemed far more likely that Erica could pass it on to a child. But instead of relief, I felt concern. A marriage built on lies wasn't going to last long.

"Why are you pretending otherwise?"

Erica kicked a pebble off the sidewalk. It zinged a nearby mailbox.

"Maury was all over me yesterday that we needed to do something together. He thinks we're growing apart. I never want to watch his stupid Japanese animated cartoons and I didn't go to the Glen with him. He says we need to find a hobby where we can"—she flicked quotation marks as she rolled her eyes—"bond. He wanted to take up canoeing. He's always wanted to take up canoeing, or so he says. Our landlord broke up with his girlfriend, and he offered Maury the use of his canoe, since he's not going to be taking her out of the lake anymore. Maury thinks it's the perfect time to"—her fingers flicked again— "get out on the lake. He's obsessed with the idea."

I loved how she referred to "our landlord." Erica and Maury lived in my old apartment, and I was pretty sure I was the only one regularly writing checks to the man who owned the 1870s Victorian and lived in the apartment above their first floor love nest.

"It's not such a bad idea. What's wrong with canoeing?"

"What do you think of when you hear the word 'canoe'?"

"Ah, Indians, birch bark, um … paddles? I don't know. Why?"

"I think 'tippy,' 'tippy canoe.' I can't even swim. I don't want to canoe."

Our mother had stayed on this earth long enough to enroll me in swim lessons. She committed suicide when I was twelve and Erica seven, leaving me to assume the role of surrogate mother to Erica. As a pre-teen and teenager, I could feed Erica, get her to and from school on time, make sure she had on clean clothes, and help her with her homework. My father, an automobile mechanic, was busy running his garage and holding our family together. Erica never got all the little extras like swim lessons.

On the other hand, we did grow up in a lakeside town, where most teenage activities revolved around the water during the summertime. I wouldn't dump her in the middle of the lake and expect her to swim to shore, but Erica had no genuine fear of the water and could do a decent doggy paddle, especially when in heat for a nearby dog.

But I didn't want to argue with her when she was being so forthcoming. "So just tell Maury that."

"I tried, but he brought me a dozen roses and told me he wanted to serenade me in the canoe on the lake."

Maury has a thing about roses. He used to give them to lots of women. In fact, he was so aggressive about it that one woman filed a complaint with the police. I guessed every woman didn't want roses ... or his attention. And with his current occupation as a floral delivery man, the roses remained plentiful, especially when he pulled the discarded, slightly defective ones out of the trash. But Erica had married him ten months ago, granted on the spur of the moment and in the throes of depression. She wasn't going to be able to opt out quite so easily.

"Where does the baby come into all this?"

"I told him we would have a baby together. I told him that would bond us. He got all excited."

"Oh, Erica." It was just like her to take the quick—yet completely absurd and bound to explode in her face—way out. How could the two of us ever have come from the same womb?

"I know, I know. It was dumb."

"You're going to have to tell him the truth. Now."

She bit her lip. "What if he leaves me?"

"He won't." I said this with great confidence. Maury looked at my sister like she was a goddess. Besides, any man with the urge to "bond" wasn't likely to leave, at least not right away. He probably liked the bonding notion of a child, but I doubted he really wanted to sign up for parenthood, both he and Erica being way too child-like themselves.

"He's going to be really, really upset, Jolene."

"Undoubtedly. You'll have to make it up to him pretty quick."

"How?"

The answer seemed obvious to me. I just looked at her, eyebrows raised.

Erica cringed. "No. Oh, no."

I nodded.

"I'm going to have to get in the freakin' canoe?"

"Wear a life jacket. It'll be fun."

"Oh, crap."

SEVEN

Monday morning rolled around without word from Cory. Given the sports car boutique's regular hours of nine to five Tuesday through Saturday, I wouldn't see him again until tomorrow. So I called him from home minutes after Danny climbed onto the school bus, curious to know if he planned on attending Brennan's bail hearing and arraignment. I had offered to go with him before we parted on Saturday. He said he'd let me know. When he didn't answer his phone at home, I tried his cell, only to go directly to voicemail. I didn't bother to leave a message; his phone would record the missed call. Cory could get back to me on his own time.

Ray called me around lunchtime. "Brennan's got bail trouble. The judge asked for cash bail of $100,000. Apparently Brennan's not that liquid."

"He's got a rich father."

"Really? Catherine didn't mention him."

"You talked to Catherine?" I tried not to let the green monster poke me. I failed. Ray had already chosen me over Catherine

61

a couple years ago now, but I still felt insecure. No wonder all my friends and relatives felt the same about their relationships—they actually had more reason than me.

"Yes. She's building his defense."

"Which is?"

"Flimsy. Brennan's word that he was reaching out to save Gleason, not pushing him, and the photograph itself."

"How does that help Brennan? It's part of the evidence against him."

"Catherine's going to contend that the picture shows Brennan's hand reaching out in a position like he was about to shake hands or grab something. She said if he was pushing Gleason his hand would have been in an upright 'Halt' or shoving angle."

I considered this notion. "Is that all she's got?"

"She thinks it's enough. She's confident she can discredit the one female witness, and knowing Catherine, she can. Eyewitness reports are notorious for inaccuracy, and no other witnesses have come forward to say anything other than the crowd surged toward the street. She's going to contend it's simply unbelievable that no one else witnessed Brennan shove Gleason into the road with so many others close by. She doesn't even think it will go to trial."

Catherine was good, but she might have to be Perry Mason to make that one work. "Did she say what the prosecutor contends?"

"He says Gleason held Brennan responsible for the death of his sister, that the two of them argued bitterly, and that Gleason threatened to kill Brennan. He said the eyewitness saw Brennan shove Gleason into the road, most likely in retaliation for that threat."

I wondered what a jury would think. Truthfully, with the way the story appeared on the news, if I hadn't known Brennan, I might believe he had pushed Gleason. I certainly wouldn't brush it off without wanting to hear all the testimony myself. Apparently, the judge agreed.

"Did she say if Cory was at the hearing, by chance?"

"That's why she called me. She needs us to throw a net over him. Brennan does not want him around, and he kept trying to speak to Brennan during the hearing. We have to keep an eye on Cory. He's not taking the hint."

And that task apparently fell to me. Wonderful. "Does Catherine know why Brennan feels that way?"

"If she does, she didn't tell me. She's not repeating anything Brennan said except to keep Cory out of this."

A nasty thought wiggled its way into my head. Brennan liked to keep a low profile as to his sexual orientation. In fact, he once asked Catherine on a date, misleading her as to his intentions by omission. For years, I'd had no idea he preferred men, although I hadn't known him well then. I'd thought he'd become more open of late, especially since he and Cory could be seen together frequently. Of course, I'd never seen them hold hands or exchange any sort of public affection. Maybe Brennan didn't want to admit his relationship with Cory. If so, their relationship would be over quickly. Cory didn't like being kept in the closet. He'd burst through that door a long time ago.

"Darlin', I got a call. Can you get the net out and use it on Cory?"

Ray hung up before I could tell him that Cory wasn't returning my calls. So I hit the speed dial button for Cory's cell again—and went right to voicemail. Now he'd apparently turned his phone off altogether. I left an urgent message for him to call me immediately.

When Ray and I went to bed that night, Cory still hadn't called me back.

∽◦

Tuesday I left for work right after Danny got on the bus at 7:45 a.m. I visited the donut shop on the way, bought a newspaper from the machine in front of the store next door to it, and parked my Lexus around 8:10 a.m. behind Asdale Auto Imports, a cedar-shingled, white-trimmed building that stuck out like a sore thumb in among the historic, more picturesque and stately buildings that made up downtown Wachobe, causing the town mucketymucks no end of angst. Of course, now they could sweat the bad publicity of being the hometown of an accused murderer. Wouldn't that do wonders for tourism? My building would be the least of their worries.

I unlocked the doors, turned off the alarm, flipped the light switches, checked the messages and my emails, then dusted and straightened my desk. Afterward I wandered into the showroom to inspect the Austin Healey, Mercedes, and Mazda under the pin lights, checking for any fingerprints that might be marring their shine. I didn't find a one. Nor could I find any scuff marks or dirt on the black and white checkered tiles covering my showroom floor.

Seated at my desk with not much more work to do, I couldn't find any mention of Brennan's case in our local paper either. From the looks of the world news in the paper, reporters had plenty of other violent things to report.

Cory arrived for work on time at nine a.m., properly groomed with his stainless steel travel mug of coffee in hand. I sat waiting for him in my office. He called out "Good morning, Jo" from the showroom and disappeared into the garage.

Never once in the last four years had he failed to come in my office to sit and chat for a while, nor in all the years prior when he'd worked for my dad. Most days he even had a few jokes to tell. No way was he going to get away from me today.

My heels rapped the floor as I marched through the showroom and entered the orderly three-bay garage. Cory had a Volvo on the lift and a Mercedes on jacks. I didn't know what he was doing to either of them. The garage was his domain, and he was a certified mechanic for at least a dozen common foreign manufacturers.

"I got donuts."

"Awesome." With his back to me, Cory stepped into a pair of overalls and pulled surgical gloves over his hands. He'd learned a long time ago that grease under the fingernails didn't work for a man who liked to be on stage, not to mention he was a bit of a clean freak. No oily floors or smelly rags in his garage.

"Want to come in the office and have one?"

"Maybe later. The Volvo's due at eleven."

I leaned against his workbench, determined not to be driven away. "I called you twice yesterday."

He grabbed a wrench and stepped under the Volvo to work one of its bolts. "I know. I'm sorry I didn't call you back. I had a busy day."

"I heard you attended Brennan's hearing. How'd that go?"

"As expected."

"Really? I was surprised Brennan doesn't have the cash to post bail. He must be worth millions."

Cory's shoulders slumped. "Most of his money is in real estate, and he has expenses."

"Like what?"

Cory sprang from underneath the Volvo and tossed the wrench on his workbench, where it clattered to a halt inches from the far edge of the bench. "I'm not sure, Jo. I'm not sure about anything, okay? Brennan won't talk to me. He doesn't want me around. And you won't help me. Everything I find out just makes me more worried."

I studied his face. Dark circles and a pinkish tinge to the whites of his eyes suggested Cory hadn't slept much since I saw him last. "Why? What have you found out?"

"Nothing." His face was the picture of innocence.

Of course, Cory was an accomplished actor, but he'd given the answer Danny always gave Ray and me when we caught him doing something he shouldn't. Nothing, my sweet fanny.

I decided to try a new route. "Where were you the rest of yesterday?"

"Nowhere."

Another of Danny's favorite answers. I burst out laughing. "Cory, you're lying to me, and you're not even doing a very good job of it."

He had the good graces to blush. "Then stop asking me questions and I won't have to lie anymore."

"Cory!"

He stripped his gloves off and tossed them in the nearby plastic garbage can. "Okay, okay, let's go in your office and sit down."

We settled in the black leather office chairs, Cory in front of the laminated desk and me behind it. I handed him a donut. He ate it in two bites and washed it down with his coffee. I slid another one in front of him. It disappeared. I wondered when he'd eaten last.

He waved off the third, mine. "What do you think Brennan had for breakfast this morning?"

The bite of donut I had taken wedged in my throat. All I could do was shrug.

Cory didn't seem to notice. He was too busy looking toward the floor. "I did something I probably shouldn't have. You're not going to be proud of me."

I'd managed to dislodge the donut and swallow it. "What did you do, Cory?"

His gaze met mine. "You can't tell Ray."

This presented a problem. It wasn't that I told Ray everything. Heavens, no. Although Ray was the first person I wanted to tell anything and truly my best friend, some things he didn't want or need to know. Often in the past, the most significant of these things had related to Erica. But if Cory had done something illegal or found out something pertinent to the case, my obligation would be to tell Ray, even though another county altogether had charge of this investigation and he wasn't really involved. I wasn't going to pretend any different.

"No promises until I hear what you did."

Cory signed. "First I drove to Albany and went through the newspaper archives at the library."

No harm there. "What did you find out?"

Cory's eyes lit up. "Brennan was a track star in high school, a long distance runner. He won a lot of medals."

Not the answer I expected, nor the one Cory really wanted to tell me, I suspected. "That's cool." I waited for him to continue.

"He was in Torque Club, too, just like me."

I smiled. The club for gear heads. For some boys, it was all about the toys, and cars were one of the best toys of all, lucky for my business.

Cory's shoulders sagged. "And I found articles about the crash. The car left the road and hit a tree around eleven o'clock at night. A passing motorist found them an hour later. Monica Gleason died on impact. The other girl sustained serious injuries and spent months in the hospital. At her family's request, she wasn't named in any of the articles. Brennan sustained head injuries and was in a coma for a couple days after the accident. When he woke up, the last thing he remembered was leaving his home to go to the reunion picnic in the park around noon. He claimed he didn't have any memory of anything after that."

Interesting. "Anything else?"

"James Gleason attacked him the day he was released from the hospital. He jumped him in front of his house. Brennan didn't press any charges."

A vision of Gleason's waving arms on Friday night flashed through my mind. I could picture him attacking Brennan, frustrated and enraged at the legal system's failure to punish the man he believed responsible for his sister's death.

"Did you learn anything else from the papers?"

Cory swigged his coffee. "Not really."

I still hadn't heard anything I couldn't tell Ray. "There must be more."

He sipped of his coffee and licked his lips. "Lots more."

Oh boy. "Go on."

"I went over to Brennan's house. I just wanted to be ... to feel ... close to him. I started thinking about the weird phone call from that guy and how Brennan doesn't want me around now ... about how sometimes I think I don't know him as well as I should. I remembered all the jokes about the skeletons in Brennan's closet."

Cory sucked in a deep breath. "Anyway, I went through all his stuff."

"Huh!" I couldn't help it—the gasp just burst from my lips. It sounded judgmental, even to me.

Cory hung his head in shame.

I didn't know what to say. It was a huge breach of trust, certainly not the foundation upon which to build a solid, lifelong relationship. In fact, it sounded too much like Isabelle's crazy notion to hire a private detective. I didn't approve. But I had to admit I was curious as to what Cory found. Did that make me guilty by association?

"You didn't break in, did you?" Ray would want to know about that; Brennan's residence was in his territory.

"Of course not! Brennan gave me a set of house keys months ago, and the alarm codes."

Well, that made it all better, didn't it?

I still wasn't grasping the problem. If Ray knew about all this, he might lose respect for Cory, but nothing more.

"You found something you don't want me to tell Ray about?"

"Sort of, but not exactly."

"Then what is it?"

Cory laid his hands flat on my desk and leaned forward to whisper his confidence.

"I don't want you to tell him about the evidence I took out of there."

EIGHT

THE PULL OF UNANSWERED questions was like quick sand—deadly and impossible to escape.

I leaned forward and breathed my reply, "What evidence?"

Cory pointed at me. "Wait here!"

He leapt from his chair and raced across the showroom floor, narrowly missing a collision with the spoiler on the Mazda when his dress shoes slid out from under him on the ceramic floor. The bells jingled as Cory slammed through the front door and disappeared toward the parking lot. Clearly he'd taken my question as the green light to share all. I hoped I wouldn't find myself in an awkward position with Ray or any other lawman once he'd finished.

A minute later he reappeared, out of breath, briefcase in hand, the contents of which he dumped on my desk after furtively closing and locking my office door.

I assessed the check registers and high school yearbook, wondering if they technically constituted stolen property and what the legal ramifications might be of having possession of them, seeing as they were laid out on my desk.

"Cory—"

He cut me off. "Look at these registers, Jo. Starting six months after the crash and lasting for eleven and half years, Brennan wrote a check on the first of every month to "Cash" for five thousand dollars. He stopped a year ago. I think someone was blackmailing him."

"That's a huge leap. Maybe it was to pay monthly bills."

Cory dismissed my notion with a wave of his hand. "His monthly bills were paid by check, too, and he made cash withdrawals throughout the months that look like spending money. His business records don't reflect this money, either."

I grabbed my calculator and did the math. $690,000. Wow! "I don't know, Cory. Who would be blackmailing him?"

"Maybe the other passenger in the car. She would know if he was drunk."

"I'm sure the police must have spoken to her after the crash, before they decided not to charge Brennan."

"Maybe she lied for him."

Cory had veered into wanton speculation now. Or had he? Impossible to know without further investigation. "I'm not sure this all adds up to blackmail."

"I think it does. I asked Brennan once why everyone jokes about skeletons in his closet. He got all embarrassed, then he said, 'I guess I didn't pay off enough people.' I thought he was kidding, but now that I think back, he seemed serious."

That would make me think blackmail, too. "What else did you find?"

He dropped the check register and reached for the yearbook. Three pictures fell from it as he lifted it in the air: two of young women and one, a young man. "This is Brennan's senior yearbook. I read all the notes his friends wrote in it. It looks like he and Monica were going steady. Her best friend was Elizabeth Potter, and his was Wayne Engle, who was also on the track team and in Torque Club. The four of them planned to go to the senior ball together. They wrote about it." Cory whipped the book open, flipped through the pages and pointed the entries out. "See?"

I did. "So who's who?"

Cory pointed to the two by three photo of a stunning blond girl with startlingly blue eyes and dimples that had fallen on my desk. "That's Monica. The other is Elizabeth. And this is Wayne."

Elizabeth had dark hair teased into an incredible pouf, heavy eye shadow that made her eyes disappear, and a crooked but friendly smile. Wayne was another blond Adonis, dark eyes sparkling and a loopy, happy grin. No wonder he and Brennan were friends. He looked a little familiar, too. I wondered if we'd ever sold him a car.

"Did Wayne and Elizabeth date?"

Cory shook his head. "Doesn't seem like it."

I leaned back in my executive chair, which squeaked in protest. I'd have to find the oil can later. "What do you make of Brennan going steady with Monica?"

Cory's smile was rueful. "I went steady with a girl in high school, too. The heterosexual pressure is pretty tough to ignore, you know."

I could imagine. "Not to get too personal, but were you intimate?"

Cory burst out laughing. "I never even kissed her. All we did was hold hands. We still send each other Christmas cards every year. She has three kids now with her husband. I wished she'd been the one. She was a really nice girl."

I glanced over the spoils on the desk. "So you took this stuff because you're afraid Brennan was paying Elizabeth to keep her mouth shut?"

"Yes."

"I think the statute of limitations would have run out by now, don't you?"

"The court of popular opinion is in session every day. Brennan's reputation and his business could be ruined by this if it's true."

"Why did the payments stop a year ago?"

"I don't know, but I'd like to find out."

Something else bothered me. I decided not to keep it to myself. "You don't seem to have much faith in Brennan, Cory. Have you known him to be impulsive or violent?"

He shook his head. "Never."

"Then why are you so convinced he's guilty of something?"

Cory rubbed his hands together and cracked his knuckles. "You know my track record. Mr. Right has been Mr. Wrong every time. I don't have that much confidence in my judgment anymore."

"What about Brennan? What do you really think of him?"

A wistful expression crossed Cory's face. "I'm afraid he's too good to be true."

I contemplated Cory's statements the rest of the day and into the evening, so much so that I failed to pay attention to my pot of chili on the stove, heating it to the point where the smoke alarms went off in the house. Danny proved quite adept at removing the batteries to kill the noise. We must have aired the house out enough before Ray got home because he didn't comment on any lingering burnt smell. I skimmed the top of the pot to serve with cornbread. No one complained.

But keeping Cory's confidence proved challenging. Ray asked me if I'd talked with Cory and gotten him under control. I said, "yes" but really thought "no." Cory had asked me to help him look into the thirteen-year-old accident, believing it would offer insights into Gleason's death. It seemed possible. And I wanted to help. I wanted to know the truth about the accident and the huge checks Brennan wrote, but more importantly, I wanted to know if Cory and I had been wrong about Brennan. We both had thought he was a prize until now. On the other hand, Ray was not likely to be pleased to have me aiding and abetting Cory's investigation. Ray and Catherine might want to lock up both of us.

I tossed and turned all night, to the point where Ray threw his arm over me and pinned me between his chest and the mattress so he could get some rest. I got up with my head feeling clouded, still uncertain of the right course of action.

Ray and I dressed side by side in the walk-in closet, Ray donning his gray sheriff's deputy uniform and me, tan slacks and a summer-weight blouse. "Darlin', what was on your mind last night? You were like a jumping bean."

"Cory asked me to help him find out more about Monica Gleason's accident. It's eating at him that Brennan might have been responsible for her death. He wants to see if we can find the other passenger in the car and talk to her." I hoped Ray wouldn't ask how we planned to do that.

He didn't. Instead, he laid his hands on my shoulders and leaned down to look me in the eye. "Darlin', Brennan asked Cory to stay out of it. Catherine asked him, too. Ken will look into it as part of the investigation. The two of you will only create problems."

I resented his immediate dismissal of our capabilities. "We're only trying to help."

"Help with what?"

I shook him off and answered through the pink silk blouse I pulled over my head. "Finding the truth."

My head popped through the neckline in time for me to catch Ray's frown.

"Jolene, I hate to say it, but I think you're both only going to learn the truth when it comes out in court. Until then, just keep Cory busy at the shop."

I pondered Ray's advice after he left for work. Keeping Cory busy could prove problematic. With Cory's attention divided because of Brennan, our customers might be in danger. Yesterday, Cory had pulled the Volvo out of the bay for the customer, who drove off only to return minutes later to say the car was acting "funny." Turned out Cory didn't release the parking brake when he backed the Volvo out of the garage. Our customer never thought to check something as simple as that. Normally Cory never would have overlooked something like that either. I had to worry what else he might overlook. Things could get deadly.

Cory was waiting for me when I arrived at the shop around 8:50 a.m. This time, he brought the donuts. The scent of fried cakes and cinnamon filled the showroom. Maybe if we opened the door, the aroma might entice car buyers in off the street like it did at the donut shop. Probably not, though. Labor Day marked the end of the tourist traffic and sales would be slow from now until April. Cory's business picked up with the first snowfall, when the ice turned driving into bumper cars and everyone worried their engines wouldn't turn over. Too bad today's weather report said, "Indian summer." My business' cash flow was about to lull.

Cory let me finish my donut before he brought up the subject of investigating Brennan's crash. "Do you want to go with me to look up Elizabeth Potter or not?"

"Today?"

"Tomorrow. I have an appointment for a transmission and a brake job today, but everyone else is going to have to wait."

I opened my mouth to object, then closed it again. Cory had vacation time coming. Besides, our maintenance customers were a loyal bunch. "Where do you propose to start looking?"

"Her parents still live at the Albany address listed in the yearbook. I found them online last night. I thought about calling them, but I think they might be more forthcoming if we show up on their doorstep."

He was right. Plus, body language gives away so much, and we'd have the element of surprise. On the other hand, Albany was hours away. Given Danny's school schedule and his football practices, I wasn't going to be able to disappear without telling Ray where I was going so he could pick up the slack. "Ray's not going to like it."

"Since when does that stop you?"

True, I liked to make up my own mind. I'd even been referred to as stubborn. Stubborn can work to one's advantage, especially with a sister like Erica. Cory knew that, but shame on him for playing me that way. I took it as a sign of his desperation.

"This is a legal matter. Ray's the expert on legal matters, he and Catherine. And he said his friend Ken would look into it as part of the investigation." Of course, Ken would be looking to make his case, not get Brennan off, and he didn't know about the strange monthly payments and all of Brennan's old friends who might be hiding something.

Cory scraped some crumbs off my desk and into his hand. "I wasn't going to tell you, but Brennan called me last night."

"From jail?"

"Yep." Cory flicked the crumbs into the trash can and brushed his hands on his coveralls.

"What did he say?"

"That he missed me and not to worry. And not to do anything. He thinks Catherine has everything under control."

"But he's still in jail."

"He's working on the bail money, calling in a few favors. He said it wasn't all that bad in jail anyway."

"Really?" I had pictured Brennan lying on a thin mattress with a stainless steel toilet and sink two feet from his head and jail bars tickling his toes.

"It's a county lockup, not prison, you know." Cory said the words as though quoting Brennan.

"I don't understand why he doesn't call his father. The news reports said he's loaded."

"He is, but they don't talk. His father doesn't like what he refers to as Brennan's 'lifestyle.' He wrote him out of the will a long time ago. That's why Brennan moved here, to get away from his father."

"What about his mom?"

"She's dead, remember? She left Brennan her family money, though. That's how he got his business started."

I did recall Brennan mentioning his mother was dead when he joined us for Thanksgiving last year. Now I knew why he hadn't mentioned his father.

"Did Brennan say anything about the crash, like if his father bought his way out of being charged?"

"I tried to ask him about the crash. He said he was out of time to talk and had to hang up. But I heard a guy in the background say that he still had two minutes left on his time." Cory raised his eyebrows.

"Okay, I agree that's suspicious. You're onto something."

Cory flourished his hand. "Exactly. So you're in?"

Truthfully, I wanted in. I was curious and would go stir-crazy sitting here alone in our quiet shop, listening for the phone to ring, surfing the Internet for car deals, and waiting for Cory to investigate alone and report back. On the other hand, I felt like a hypocrite. I'd told Isabelle it was wrong to have a private investigator follow Jack around, invading his privacy and undermining trust, and now here I thought it might be a good idea to snoop. What was the difference in this situation? The fact that Brennan was in jail, facing a trial and prison perhaps? Or that I believed Cory's theory might actually have some merit?

My doubts and concerns must have flashed across my face, because Cory started to look worried, too. "Aren't you going to help me, Jo?"

Ray would not be happy. I could hear him saying "Jolene" in that tone of voice he gets when he's annoyed. Was it really worth agitating him, particularly when the luscious and agreeable Catherine was back in the picture and only a phone call away?

Cory slumped in his chair. "It's okay. I understand. I don't want to cause trouble between you and Ray. In fact, Brennan may never speak to me again. But I just can't let him sit there alone in jail and do nothing. I'd rather have him out of jail, never speaking to me again, than visit him in prison every Sunday."

I made my decision. "No, I'm in."

After all, Ray was used to me making up my own mind and doing my own thing. It was one of the things he loved about me, wasn't it?

If not, this would be one way to find out pretty quick.

NINE

CORY SUGGESTED I TELL Ray that he and I had to go to look at a car in Albany tomorrow. Since we'd taken that trip more than once in the past, Ray might buy the story. But I didn't want to sell him lies. Of course, I wasn't going to let on we suspected anyone of blackmail, either. So I told Ray about Cory's continued turmoil over Brennan's questionable past and the Volvo incident, hinting that Cory would not rest until he knew the truth about the alleged drunk driving incident.

"I knew the two of you weren't going to leave it alone." Ray tossed his holster onto the top of the refrigerator and took a seat on the stool at our granite breakfast bar. "Brennan probably knows it, too."

I turned down the heat under the stir fry to avoid burning another dinner and rested my arms on the bar opposite him, leaning in so we were almost nose to nose. Danny was doing his homework in the living room nearby and I didn't want him to hear us.

"Cory spoke to Brennan last night. Brennan hung up on him when he tried to ask about the crash. I saw how heated James Gleason got about it before he died. There's something there, Ray."

Ray's gaze met mine and held it, his "good-cop, bad-cop, who-ever-you-need-me-to-be cop" expression in place. It felt like we were having a contest to see who blinks first. I let him win.

He sighed and rested his forehead against mine for a moment before pulling away. "You're not going to learn anything new. I called the Albany police and spoke to the lead detective from the case. Brennan's father didn't buy anyone off. The guy said there was not enough evidence to make a case."

"Did he say anything else?"

"Just that Gleason is a bit of a hothead. His wife called them a couple times before she left him last year. He never hit her, but he wouldn't let her out of the house. She felt intimidated."

"So maybe she had reason to kill him? We can't be sure she didn't give him a little shove, can we?"

Ray shook his head. "I don't think so. Their kid was with her. He vouched for the fact she was nowhere near the scene."

"How old is the kid?"

"High school age."

I tried to visualize the crowd in the minutes before the accident. "I don't remember seeing him."

"He met up with her right after she walked away from Gleason and Brennan's argument."

Or so he says. "Is he their only child?"

Ray scratched his chest. "That I don't know, darlin.'"

It surprised me Ray had taken the time to call Albany. I wondered if Catherine had put him up to it. "What made you decide to call the detective down there?"

He grinned. "Just trying to save you a trip. I knew after our conversation this morning that you and Cory might want to head down there."

At least it didn't sound like Catherine had put him up to the call. "Actually Cory and I are more interested in talking to the other passenger injured in the crash." Too late, I realized her name had been withheld. Did Ray know that?

From the way his eyes narrowed, I thought he did, but if so, he chose not to question me, perhaps preferring simply not to know. Often for him, ignorance really was bliss, particularly as it related to my concerns. "She didn't remember the crash. Last thing she recalls is getting in the car. She wasn't buckled in, and from her injuries, they think she may have been lying down on the back seat, asleep at the time of impact."

So she told the police she didn't recall the accident. That didn't mean it was the truth. Maybe she said that at first to protect Brennan then later to blackmail him. "What were her injuries?"

Ray got up and walked over to lift the lid off the pan and sniff the stir fry. "Extensive. She needed rehabilitation for her legs, which were partially paralyzed, and plastic surgery. The passenger side of the car hit the tree, killing Monica on impact. Elizabeth Potter went through the windshield. She's lucky to still be alive."

Ray replaced the lid and got the plates out from the cupboard, bent on eating and not the least bit distressed over the image of the poor girl flying through glass. It seemed to me the girl might think she was entitled to a few dollars from Brennan after enduring all that.

"Where is she now?"

Ray dealt the plates onto our oak table. "It's been twelve, almost thirteen years. She could be anywhere."

"You didn't ask the detective?"

"He didn't know."

Hah. Ray had asked, which meant we were sniffing down the right path. Cory and I could never match a hound dog like Ray, but it pleased me to know we were only a few yards behind him.

I gathered silverware from the kitchen drawer and walked around the table, setting each place. Ray followed me with paper napkins and glassware.

I took a deep breath and plunged. "Cory isn't going to be satisfied unless he can ask a few questions himself. He wants to go to Albany tomorrow, and he asked me to go with him. I agreed to go, if you can get Danny on the bus and home from football practice." I didn't say, "Is that okay with you?" because I had promised to go. No need to ask permission—it was more like I was calling for back up. "Let's keep this between the three of us for now. Catherine and Brennan don't need to know unless we come up with something."

Ray got the milk out of the refrigerator and filled our glasses. Even after he returned the gallon to the refrigerator and bellied up to the table, he hadn't replied.

I spooned rice and stir fry onto everyone's plate then set a loaf of bread in the center. I guessed we'd be talking more about this later. "Danny, dinner."

Danny appeared in a flash, dropped into his chair, and started shoveling food into his mouth.

I sat down and watched him. Ray's gaze was on him, too.

After a few mouthfuls, Danny looked up and caught us staring at him. He glanced back and forth between us. "What? What I'd do?" A few grains of rice fell out of his mouth and onto his plate.

I smiled and shook my head, always amused by his insatiable appetite.

Ray's massive hand reached out to muss Danny's hair. "Nothing. Jolene's going to Albany with Cory tomorrow. I'm going to get you on the bus and pick you up from practice, okay?"

Danny's eyes lit up. "Great." He forked another load of rice into his mouth with gusto.

I mouthed "thank you" to Ray.

He picked up his fork. "I just hope Cory knows what he's risking."

I kissed Ray and Danny goodbye at six a.m. Both were still in bed, with another half hour of sleep to go before Danny had to get up to be ready for the bus. When I bent over Ray, he slid his hand behind my head and pulled me in tight. "Be careful."

I inhaled his warm scent and brushed my lips over his neck, pulling back to Eskimo kiss him. "We will." My tone was light, belying the fear his words struck in me. Ray must think we might be onto something, too.

This early in the morning my breath made clouds in front of me as I jogged down the sidewalk and climbed into Cory's navy BMW. The radio blasted the news.

"Hey, Cory, did you hear anything from Brennan last night?"

Cory pulled away from the curb and hit the gas. "Nope."

"Hear any more about him on the news?"

He shook his head. "Nothing."

I clicked my seat belt into place and fussed with my beige suit jacket, trying to avoid wrinkling it. "Where are we headed first? To see Elizabeth Potter's parents?"

"That's the address I put in the GPS"

Ah, the GPS Ray referred to it as the greatest marital aid known to mankind. Since I used to be the map reader, I tried hard not to take offense.

"What are we going to say to them to explain why we landed on their doorstep?" I glanced around the interior of the car, looking for clues. All I saw was Brennan's yearbook, but with Cory's background in theater, he'd been known to write entire scripts and insist I learn my lines before we tried to purchase a car. Although the last time he did, it ended tragically for me. Hopefully this time I would be spared.

"I looked on the high school's website last night. Brennan's class is coming up on their twentieth reunion and the alumni news said the class wants volunteers now to start planning the festivities. No one is named yet as chair of the reunion committee or signed on as a volunteer. I thought we could pretend to be involved in the planning, looking for more participants."

"I thought reunion committees only went door to door in Wachobe." I'd lived in the same small town all my life. My class of fifty-two could meet up at the soda shop. In fact, we often bumped into each other at the grocery store, coffee shop, or bakery. We had a twentieth reunion a few years back, just for kicks, arranged through a sort of phone tree and knocks at the front door. No one but the twenty-seven locals and their significant others showed up.

Once members of our class left town for bigger and better opportunities, they ticked Wachobe off their list of vacation destinations.

"Yeah, well, Elizabeth's not registered online as alumni of the school, nor is the majority of the class. I don't know how anyone else would find her, except to call or write. Do you have a better suggestion?"

"No. How many kids were in the graduating class?"

"Five hundred and twenty-eight."

"Wow. How many were in your graduation class?"

"Three hundred and sixty-five."

"Did you know all of them?"

"Not even a fifth. I checked Brennan's yearbook. Neither he nor his friends were involved in student government. Those are the kids who always know about class reunions. Chances are Elizabeth Potter won't know a thing until we tell her."

I grabbed the yearbook and started reading through the notes. As I read the scribble from Wayne Engle, a thought occurred to me. "Cory, if the four of them were such good buddies, how come he wasn't in the car with them at the time of the accident?"

Cory downshifted to take the curve of the access ramp to the thruway. "Good question. After Elizabeth's house, We can pay a visit to the address listed with his name in the yearbook."

"Sounds like a plan." I snapped the yearbook closed and laid my head back against the headrest, feeling tired already. The New York State Thruway would be miles of pavement, grass, and trees, broken up by sedimentary rock in the areas where they had blasted through the hills left behind by the glaciers. I'd seen every crest and valley hundreds of times. Listening to the newscaster drone sports scores wouldn't keep me awake either, especially since I

hadn't slept much last night. My worries about this whole plan—
or more specifically, lack of plan—had kept me awake. Car travel
always puts me to sleep.

∽◌

I was back in high school with an English paper due and a test in
calculus. I wasn't ready for either, and if I didn't hand the paper
in on time as well as pass the test, I wouldn't graduate. My father
woke me for school twenty minutes late. I'd slept through the
alarm, which still beeped, and ...

Cory nudged my shoulder. "Jo, wake up. Your cell phone's ringing and I can't reach it."

I jerked upright, fumbling for my purse. "Hello?"

"Jolene, it's Isabelle. I don't know what to do."

I straightened up in the seat. "Why? What's going on?"

"It's Thursday. Every Thursday for the last two years, I've taken
Cassidy to dance class at ten o'clock. This morning, Jack offered to
take her. He said he knew I had an ad shoot and he wanted to help
me."

"That's nice."

"It would be if he didn't offer right after he got off the phone
with someone. I don't know who. I heard him say he would try to
get away this morning. I followed him."

My brain still felt fuzzy from my dream. I almost thought this
conversation might be a dream, too, but Cory looked too real in
the seat next to me, maneuvering his sun visor to block the glare.
Unfortunately, Albany lay southeast of Wachobe—the poor guy
had been driving into the sun's rays all morning while I slept.

I wiped a little dampness from the corner of my mouth. Had I been drooling, too? "Okay, what happened?"

Isabelle spoke quickly. "He dropped Cassidy off at dance class, then he drove to this new bed and breakfast in an early 1800s colonial. He went inside. He's been in there for half an hour. What should I do?"

"I don't know. Could he be showing someone a piece of jewelry?"

"No. He might be looking to buy an heirloom piece, though."

I seized on that possibility, preferring it to other images in my head. "That makes sense."

"Or he could be having a rendezvous with another woman."

"Oh, Isabelle. Why don't you just go inside and find out?"

"Be … cause … I don't … want … to know."

"You could look the bed and breakfast up on the Internet. A nice old lady and her husband probably own it."

"May … be." Isabelle hiccupped.

"Maybe he's getting you a gift certificate. You guys love to go to bed and breakfasts."

"Not … near here. This one's only seven miles from our house."

"I don't know what to tell you, Izzy. I don't think it's a good idea for him to catch you following him, though, in case you've got this all wrong."

Isabelle blew her nose softly. "You're right. You're right." She sounded as if she was trying to convince herself. "I have a commercial shoot in half an hour anyway. I spent weeks begging all the local politicians, big business owners, and newscasters to participate in for free. It's for the United Way campaign. I can't be late.

Whatever's he's doing, I can't wait around to find out. I have more important things to do than worry about losing that man."

That's the Isabelle I knew and loved, more or less. I heard her car ignition turn over.

"I'll call you, Jolene."

I snapped my cell phone shut and looked at Cory.

He turned down the volume on the radio. "What's up with Isabelle?"

"She thinks Jack might be cheating on her."

Cory's grip tightened on the steering wheel. "I thought they had the model marriage."

I used to think that, too.

TEN

We made good time, due to Cory's lead foot, and arrived at
Elizabeth Potter's parents' suburban Albany home twenty minutes later, just prior to eleven o'clock. The home was a 1920s
colonial with a tall, pointy roof, white siding and green shutters.
Its trim needed to be sanded and repainted, and their blacktop
driveway lay cracked and in chunks, tufts of grass waving in the
gentle breeze. A lone bedraggled pot of red geraniums decorated
the front steps, which creaked as Cory and I mounted them. The
garage door stood open, an enormous collection of junk inside,
including what looked to be a wheelchair and a walker.

Cory hit the doorbell. No one responded. I hadn't heard a
doorbell ring on the other side of the door.

"I think it's broken." I rapped my knuckles on a pane of glass
next to the door.

Moments later, a sixtyish woman in a pink velour jogging suit
shuffled into the hallway. She squinted at me through the window
and opened the door halfway. I noticed she had fuzzy pink rabbit

slippers on her feet. One rabbit had lost half his ear. The other, his plastic eyeball.

"Can I help you?"

Cory took the lead, naturally. "Are you Mrs. Potter?"

"Yes."

Cory held out the yearbook, face down, most likely because Brennan's name was embossed in gold on the front cover. "Elizabeth's mother?"

Mrs. Potter wrinkled her brow. "Yes."

"Excellent. My name is Cory and this is Jolene. Elizabeth's twentieth class reunion is coming up soon, and we'd like to speak with her. The alumni association is forming a committee to plan the reunion. We wondered if she might like to get involved."

She opened the door up all the way. "Elizabeth lives in Binghamton now. I can give you her address and phone number if you like. You could call her." Mrs. Potter sounded doubtful, as though calling Elizabeth wouldn't do much good. "Wait here."

She scuffed over to a table, extracted a sheet of paper and pen, and jotted down the information.

I accepted the piece of paper when she returned to the door. "Does Elizabeth have a family?"

Mrs. Potter rubbed her chest. "Married and divorced. Twice. She's dating a boy now."

I smiled as though that were wonderful news. "Do you think Elizabeth would enjoy working on the planning committee?"

"Honestly, honey, Elizabeth doesn't even like to come to visit. This town has bad memories for her."

"I'm sorry to hear that. I didn't know."

Mrs. Potter nodded. "We kept it quiet. Elizabeth had a car accident after your class's five-year reunion. It took her years to learn to walk again. She had to have all kinds of reconstructive surgery." She pointed to the book in Cory's hand. "She's not that girl in the yearbook picture anymore."

I tried to smile sympathetically. "Now that you mention it, I remember something about that crash. Wasn't Brennan Rowe the driver in that accident?"

She stiffened. "It wasn't his fault. He was a good boy."

I exchanged a look with Cory. "I would have thought you'd be angry with him. Didn't the police think he was driving under the influence?"

Mrs. Potter waved the suggestion off. "Elizabeth was asleep when the crash occurred, but she said none of them were drunk."

Hard to know if her statement was true or if the "kids" had kept their vices hidden from their parents. "Does Elizabeth still see Brennan?"

"No, he moved away years ago. He sends a Christmas card every year, though."

A dog barked and snarled behind us. Startled, I turned to find a miniature brown and black Doberman straining at its leash, held by a white-haired man in a navy jogging suit and white sneakers.

"Bill, this is . . ." Mrs. Potter broke off, frowning.

"Cory." He shook Mr. Potter's hand.

"Jolene." Mr. Potter's hand felt like ice. I wondered how long he and the dog had been walking, but now I knew who had eaten Mrs. Potter's bunny slippers. The tiny monster looked ready to take a chunk out of us, too.

"They were looking for Elizabeth. Her twentieth class reunion's coming up, and they wondered if she wanted to be on the planning committee. I told them I didn't think she'd be interested."

Mr. Potter eyed both Cory and me up and down. "Not likely."

I gestured to his wife. "Mrs. Potter was explaining about Elizabeth's accident. We didn't know."

Mr. Potter brushed by us, yanking the dog away from our ankles, and entered the house. "We don't like to talk about that. What's done is done."

"Yes, of course. We won't intrude on your time anymore."

Nor would that be an option. Mr. Potter had closed the door right in our faces.

Wayne Engle's childhood home lay four miles from Elizabeth's parents, a large blue colonial with black shutters, a red door, a three-car garage, and a white picket fence. The well-manicured lawn covered at least two acres, a covered in-ground pool visible in the backyard.

I glanced at Cory over the roof of the BMW as we climbed out. "We're moving on up."

He grinned in response. "It is the eastside."

A woman around Cory's age answered the doorbell. She had blond hair and light brown eyes as well as a distinct resemblance to Wayne's yearbook picture. His sister? Again, Cory took the lead. "Hi, I'm Cory and this is Jolene. Is Wayne Engle home?"

"Wayne doesn't live here anymore, not for years." Her gaze swept over the two of us, measuring, assessing then dismissing.

"I see." Cory waved the yearbook. "His twentieth class reunion is coming up. The alumni association is looking for volunteers to plan the event. Any idea if he would be interested?"

"I doubt it." She moved to close the door.

Cory stepped forward. "Would you have his current address or phone number? I'm sure he'd at least like an invitation to the reunion."

She hesitated.

I spoke up. "We're trying to locate the whole class and make this the best-attended reunion ever." With my smile, I tried to channel pep rally spirit, flying in the face of my true long and happy history of nonparticipation.

The blond frowned, perhaps not a school spirit kind of girl either. "He lives in Binghamton. He owns an insurance company, Wayne Engle Insurance. You could try him there."

For the second time that day, a door closed in our faces.

"Friendly, wasn't she?"

Cory didn't seem phased by the woman's behavior. "We got what we came for, maybe more. Don't you think it's weird both he and Elizabeth live in Binghamton?"

"It's a big city, close by. I like it better than Albany. Maybe they do, too."

Cory glanced at his watch. "Should we swing by his office on the way home?"

We'd driven across the state and approached Albany from the north this morning. It would be easy to return home to Wachobe from the south, driving through Binghamton and Watkins Glen on the way.

"We could, but it's definitely weird for us to drive all the way there to tell him about a class reunion. We look like hometown cheerleaders here in Albany. But there, we'd look like fanatics, tracking down the man to discuss a reunion that's more than a year and a half away, especially after his sister said he wouldn't be interested. I think he would expect to get a phone call or a letter about the reunion, now that we've talked to her. If she calls him to say we stopped by his parent's house, he's going to be suspicious."

"Okay. Let me think."

Back in the car, Cory fiddled with the GPS, typing in Wayne Engle's company name and city. The street address popped up on the screen and the system plotted a two hour and twenty minute drive for us. At least it was in the general direction of home. He repositioned the GPS on his dash and turned to face me. "I got it. Wayne Engle sells insurance. We sell cars. Cars and insurance go together."

"That's true, but how are we going to segue into talking about Brennan's crash? How are we going to ask him why he wasn't in the car at the time of the accident?"

Cory slapped his palm against the steering wheel. "I don't know, Jo. We may just have to tell him the truth. He was Brennan's best friend. Don't you think he'd want to help him, if he could?"

"It's hard to say. If he thinks, or worse, he knows that Brennan was drunk that night, he might not want to help him. He might want to see him punished, even if it is all these years later."

Cory swallowed. "Maybe he knew Brennan was drunk, so he didn't get in the car."

"I hadn't thought that far through it, but that makes sense. Imagine the guilt if you're the only one who didn't get in the car.

Imagine the survivor guilt after learning Monica Gleason died in the crash. Imagine if he knew Brennan was drunk and did nothing to prevent him from driving those two girls home."

The stricken expression on Cory's face made me stop. His imagination was pretty damn good—what actor's wouldn't be? My words horrified him.

I laid my hand on his arm in comfort. "Then again, we don't even know if he was supposed to be in the car. He could have a different story altogether. Why don't we go with telling the truth and see what he says?"

Cory nodded and turned the key in the ignition.

I thought I'd reassured him, but as the estimated drive time on the GPS inched upward with each passing mile, I realized Cory was no longer in such a hurry to find out the truth.

ELEVEN

A TINY CAPE COD on a rabid thoroughfare housed Wayne Engle Insurance. The road had one of those irritating meridians dividing the eastbound and westbound lanes, and Cory had to make a U-turn at a busy four-way intersection in order to swoop back around to the company's driveway entrance. Four other cars occupied the lot: a Civic, an Accord, and a Geo—all popular economy cars—and a brand spanking new Mercedes convertible.

I offered to bet Cory that the Mercedes belonged to Wayne. He passed.

Inside the office, the phone lines rang incessantly as two women tried to keep pace with the volume of incoming calls. Both women wore heavy makeup, short skirts, high heels, and less than adequate tops revealing plenty of cleavage. It was impossible to determine their age, but quite obvious what they were selling. Two other desks sat empty, but leftover coffee cups with bright red and pink lipstick indicated women had occupied the desks earlier in the day. Each desk had a name placard. Pam and Missy answered the phones; Beth and Silvia were missing, perhaps still at lunch?

Cory and I waited for a couple minutes while the women dealt with their callers. Finally, Pam placed her call on hold to greet us. "Can I help you?"

"We'd like to speak to Wayne Engle, if he's available." Cory flashed his pearly whites, turning on the charm.

Pam glanced at the closed office door. "Do you have an appointment?"

"I'm sorry, we don't. We'll only need a minute of his time."

Her lacquered fingernail pressed a button on her phone. "What can I tell Mr. Engle it's regarding?"

Cory glanced at me.

I shrugged. "Go for it."

"Brennan Rowe."

Wayne Engle opened the door of his office five minutes later. Dressed in a navy business suit, a white shirt, red tie, and wingtips, he looked spiffy enough to be running for president. His handshake was firm, but his eyes wary as he ushered us inside the office, which held an oak desk, multiple chairs, a credenza, bookshelves, and a conference table. A single photograph of a teenaged boy with blond hair and blue eyes adorned the top of the credenza. Diplomas, certificates, licenses, and registrations covered one wall. I spotted a S.U.N.Y. Binghamton business administration diploma among them, which explained his connection to this city.

He offered us a seat at the round oak table and sat, legs crossed, with his profile to us.

Something about his face seemed familiar. Maybe it was because I'd seen his yearbook photo, although his face had aged and his hairline receded. His hair color seemed a bit sandier. Maybe Wayne colored it now to hide some gray. No, I'd definitely seen him somewhere more recently than that. I wondered if we'd sold a car to him or if he frequented our tourist town.

He got the conversation rolling. "You're friends of Brennan's?"

Now that we'd made it into the inner sanctum, Cory didn't seem inclined to engage. Wayne looked between us, politely waiting.

I took the lead this time. "Mr. Engle—"

"Please, call me Wayne."

"Thank you, Wayne. Cory and I are friends of Brennan Rowe's, and we're very concerned about him. Have you spoken to him recently?"

"Not for years."

I decided to charge ahead.

"Did you know Brennan is in jail?"

Wayne's head jerked ever so slightly. "No. Since when?"

"Friday. He's accused of pushing a man in front of a car."

Wayne licked his lips. "What man?"

"James Gleason."

Wayne shot forward, shifting to face us. "What?"

"On Friday night, we all attended the Vintage Grand Prix in Watkins Glen. Are you familiar with it?"

"Quite."

"Brennan and James ran into each other there. They argued over Monica Gleason. Apparently James thought Brennan was responsible for the crash and her subsequent death. When the two stopped arguing, they separated, but a few minutes later, Gleason was killed on impact by one of the cars as they raced through town. A witness says Brennan pushed Gleason in front of the car. Obviously, we think the witness was mistaken, but the news reports say the two men had a long history with James angry and threatening Brennan over his sister's death. We're wondering what, if anything, you remember about the crash."

Wayne rubbed his forehead. "Did Brennan send you?"

"No." I looked at Cory, who wouldn't meet my eyes. "Brennan is in jail and unable to make bail. We thought because you two were best friends in high school, you might be able to help us."

Wayne leaned back in his chair again. "In what way?"

"The news reports have had a couple of your fellow alumni on camera, stating everyone was drinking at the reunion and implying Brennan might have been driving drunk. Do you know if he drank at the reunion?"

"He had a beer or two over the course of several hours. He was not drunk."

A sound exploded from Cory's mouth, like a cutoff sob. Wayne gave him the once over and narrowed his eyes.

I tried not to lose momentum. "Did you tell the police that at the time of the crash?"

"No one asked me."

Surprised, it took me a second to recover. "At the time, you must have known the police were investigating the crash. They thought he was driving under the influence. You didn't tell them differently?"

"No."

"Why not?" Cory's anger showed in his tone of voice.

Wayne hesitated ever so slightly before answering. "Brennan and I had an argument the night of the reunion. We said a lot of things we could never take back. We weren't ever going to be friends again, but I would have come forward if he got charged."

"Brennan says he doesn't remember what happened that night."

"That's what I read in the papers at the time."

"Did you believe it?"

"Yes."

"He doesn't remember anything about that night, so he wouldn't recall your argument either."

"Probably not."

I didn't know what to say next. What could have happened between them to ruin their friendship, especially after losing Monica and almost Elizabeth, too?

"You, Brennan, Monica, and Elizabeth were quite close, weren't you?"

A hint of a smile touched his lips. "We were the four Musketeers in high school."

"What about afterward?"

"We got together on school breaks. Over time, we didn't see each other as much. It happens naturally." He looked between us as though waiting for us to agree.

My closest friend in high school was Ray. No comparison. "Did you all ride to the reunion together?"

"No, we wanted to, but I had to work. I met them there a little late." A flicker of something like regret or guilt crossed his face.

"Was Elizabeth ever able to provide any insights into what caused the crash?"

"Not really. The police thought she might have been asleep in the back seat."

"Are you still close to Elizabeth?"

Something else flickered across Wayne's face. This time I thought it was anger. "No."

Wayne's response matched the information Ray had gathered from the detective. I felt as though we were at a dead end. Still, Wayne's attitude toward Brennan made me uncomfortable—and curious. What had they argued about?

I decided to go for broke and ask.

"Wayne, if you don't mind my asking, what did you and Brennan argue about that cost your friendship?"

Wayne stood up. "I'm sorry. I have another appointment. If the police need a statement now that Brennan was not drunk the night of the accident, I'll give them one."

I didn't know if that would be helpful at all. The police had long ago ruled out alcohol as a cause of the accident.

Cory and I rose. As we walked to the door, I glanced at the pictures on Wayne's credenza again. "Handsome boy. Your son?"

"Godson. He's a great kid." Wayne opened his office door. "I'm sorry I couldn't be more helpful."

I doubted he was sorry at all. "Just one more question, Wayne."

"Yes, Jolene?"

He said "Jolene" like Ray did when he was mad at me. Annoyed, I managed to smile in an effort to keep things friendly. "Do you think Brennan would push James Gleason in front of a car?"

Wayne's response was immediate. "No. Brennan wouldn't intentionally hurt anyone."

He emphasized the word "intentionally," leaving unspoken thoughts hanging in the air.

Brennan had hurt people, Wayne included. And apparently they hadn't forgiven him.

TWELVE

Throughout the day, temperatures had risen. When we opened the doors to the BMW in the insurance office's parking lot, clouds of hot air billowed out. I took off my suit jacket, laid it across the back seat of the car, and rolled down my window before climbing in to singe my butt on the hot leather. Cory already had the engine running and the air conditioning turned up full blast.

I twisted in my seat to face him. "What did you make of all that?"

Cory grabbed the yearbook and flipped through the pages. "I'm relieved and overjoyed to hear he didn't think Brennan was guilty of drunk driving or pushing Gleason into the street, but he didn't seem to like Brennan much. I didn't feel like he was all that forthcoming with information, either. I'm not even sure he was telling the truth. He definitely wasn't looking you in the eye."

"I want to see . . . I knew it." He turned the book around to show it to me. "Wayne was in drama club. Look, there he is playing a villain."

The black outfit was a dead giveaway, as was the dark, vacant look in Wayne's eyes. A giveaway in more ways than one.

"Oh my god, it's him." I pointed at Wayne's picture. "That's the guy."

"Of course it's him, Jo. His name is right under the photo."

"No, no, no. Wayne's the man I saw at the vintage festival. He stepped right in front of me, coming out of the beer tent. He wouldn't get out of my way. I had to go around him, but not before I got a good look at him. It was him. Wayne. He even had on a Binghamton sweatshirt."

"What's the sweatshirt got to do with anything?"

"He had a diploma on his office wall from the university. He's an alumnus. I know I saw him at the festival, Cory. I know it was him."

Cory snapped the yearbook shut. "Should we go back in and ask him about it?"

"No." I didn't see where that would help us. Wayne had closed the door on us, both literally and figuratively when he escorted us out of his office. "It's strange he didn't know anything about Gleason's death or Brennan's arrest."

"Yeah, well, the guy has acting experience, and he's a salesman."

"Oh, yeah, we all know what a bunch of slippery liars salespeople are."

"Especially those car salespeople." Cory grinned and, for a moment, I caught a glimpse of the guy I'd worked with for fourteen years. Then the shadow returned to his eyes. "I'd really like to ask Brennan if he saw him there, not that I think he would tell me."

"Cory, did Brennan ever talk to you about high school or his friends or anything that might provide any insight into what's going on here?"

He shook his head. "I knew he didn't speak to his father. I knew his mom left him the money he used to start his company. Otherwise, we pretty much talked about the here and now—and sometimes about our future, you know, together."

I wanted to hear more about their future together, but not right now. Something was bothering me. Brennan, Wayne, Elizabeth, and Monica had kept in touch enough to attend the reunion together, and only after that did their relationships end. "Wayne said the four of them were inseparable in high school. They even went to the reunion together. I don't understand what could have happened to erase their friendship in one night."

"You don't? I do."

"What?"

"Brennan must have told them he was gay. How would you like to be the high school girlfriend of a gay guy? Or his best friend, who never knew and shared a locker room with him? Even if your friends accept you, you're not the person they thought you were. Everything changes."

I considered Cory's statement. "So you think, during the reunion, Brennan told them he was gay, causing Wayne to say unkind things to him and ruin their friendship?"

"It's possible."

"And maybe Brennan was so upset that his driving was effected on the way home?"

Cory frowned. "Maybe, but in that case, the accident would still be his fault."

"It would be an accident, not illegally driving under the influence."

"True."

"The girls couldn't have been too upset with Brennan about everything because they got in the car with him."

"Right." Cory's expression turned sheepish. "I have to say when I told my high school girlfriend that I was gay, she said, 'Well that explains everything.' Brennan's girlfriend must have suspected."

"So Monica might not be angry. She'd be relieved to know why he wasn't all over her."

"Exactly."

I leaned back against the headrest. "This is all great conjecture, but even if we'd guessed correctly, it doesn't help Brennan's current situation, other than to lift the stigma of the drunken driving rumor. In fact, it leaves us with no motive for Elizabeth to blackmail Brennan."

"Unless she planned to lie and say Brennan was drinking."

"Wayne would have denied it."

"That's what he said today, but he never came forward back then. They could have been in on it together." Cory tapped the yearbook's cover. "You saw Wayne at the festival, which means two people Brennan angered were at the festival. When and where did you see Wayne?"

"I saw him right when we arrived, a little after five o'clock, over an hour before the accident. He stepped out of the beer tent, which was a hundred yards or so down Franklin Street from where the car struck and killed Gleason a little over an hour later. I didn't see Wayne in the crowd at the time of the crash, but he could have been there. I thought he was drunk earlier when he walked right in front of me and didn't even notice. He could have just been preoccupied."

"He could have pushed Gleason into the road."

I laughed. "Anyone could have pushed him, Cory. Anyone could have pushed Brennan or me or anyone else standing there on the edge of the curb into the road, too. Wayne could as easily have been half a mile down the road or inside a bar and missed the whole thing."

"But not anyone could have been right at the same spot on the road. The only people who could be pushed at that spot on the curb were Brennan and Gleason. They had to be next to each other, right?"

"I assume so."

"Everyone said the crowd surged a second before Gleason fell into the road."

"Right."

Cory's knee bobbed up and down, a sure sign of his excitement. "Do you think there's a chance Wayne pushed Gleason into the road?"

"Why would he want to do that?"

"Maybe Gleason's been harassing him about the reunion and drinking and letting his sister get in the car with Brennan. Or maybe he was aiming for Brennan, but he hit Gleason instead?"

"Wow, Cory, that's a huge leap."

"But it's possible."

I tried to get Cory to regain his perspective. "We don't even know if Wayne was close enough to do that. We'd never be able to prove it either way, not without photos of the crowd."

"Does the sheriff's office have any photos of the crowd?"

I thought about it. "I know the photographer, Howard Pint, had to give them his memory card, but he didn't have any crowd pictures, except for the shot of Brennan's arm. I don't know if the sheriff's deputies took other people's memory cards, too. They could have. Ray's friend Ken would know."

"Okay, so call Ray." Cory pointed to my purse.

"Right now?"

Cory waved his hand as if to say, why not? I pulled my cell phone out and hit the speed dial button.

Ray answered before I heard a ring. "You're psychic."

"Why?"

"I was just picking up the phone to call you. Brennan got his bail money together, and he wanted Cory to pick him up from the jail."

"Why didn't he call Cory directly?"

"He did."

"His phone hasn't rung." I raised my eyebrows at Cory.

He pulled his cell phone from his pocket, snapped it open, pushed a few buttons, and frowned. He showed me the dark screen.

"I take that back. Cory's cell phone needs charging. Where's Brennan now?"

"When he couldn't reach Cory at your shop or on his cell phone, he called here and asked where you two were."

"What did you tell him?"

"I told him you were on a scouting expedition for the day."

"Did he buy that?"

"Hard to say."

"Can we pick him up now?"

"His construction foreman is on his way down to pick him up."

"Well, we're in Binghamton. We won't be home for another couple hours or so." I wanted to stop by Elizabeth Potter's home and ask her a few questions before we headed back to Wachobe.

"Did you learn anything new?"

"Yes." I proceeded to fill Ray in on our meeting with Wayne Engle and the fact that I saw him at the Watkins Glen festival. "Can you call your friend Ken and ask him if he has any pictures of the crowd so we can try to spot Wayne?"

"I can call him. He's not going to appreciate your interference in his investigation. And he'll want to know everything you've learned. Are you prepared to tell him?"

Yikes! "Never mind. Maybe we can get pictures from another source."

I hung up with Ray and looked at Cory. "Brennan got his bail money together. His foreman's on his way to pick him up."

"Good."

I looked at the yearbook still clutched in Cory's hand and thought about the check registers he'd spread on my desk yesterday. "Not good."

"Why?"

"Cory, if you think the check registers and this yearbook are evidence that needs to be hidden from the sheriff's department, don't you think Brennan will be thinking the same thing, too?"

The puzzled expression on Cory's face quickly changed to horrified.

"When he finds them missing, what's he going to think?"

Cory's eyes closed. "Oh my god, I'm dead."

THIRTEEN

CORY WANTED TO RACE home and replace the items he'd taken from Brennan's. I knew we wouldn't make it in time without risking a serious accident. Instead, I convinced Cory to plug Elizabeth Potter's home address into his GPS and follow the directions over there, hoping we'd learn something of use.

But minutes later when he pulled out in front of an oncoming car that swerved to narrowly miss us, I realized just how dangerous it was to ride with an agitated driver. "Cory!"

He pulled over to the side of the road. "You drive. I can't concentrate."

We hopped out and ran around the car. I slid in and adjusted the driver's seat position. Cory put the passenger seat all the way back so he was almost lying flat. I pulled out and continued to follow the instructions from the GPS.

"What am I going to tell Brennan when he realizes that I took his stuff?"

"The truth."

"What if he never speaks to me again?"

Any answer I thought of would be nothing more than empty reassurances. I opted for silence. When we arrived at Elizabeth's townhouse fifteen minutes later, Cory asked to remain in the car, claiming he felt sick.

I walked up the sparkling white gravel sidewalk to the front stoop, taking in the old-fashioned orange brick townhouse and cracked cement porch, trying to guess her rent. I estimated it at the lower end of the scale.

No one answered when I rang the front bell. I shouldn't have been surprised. Elizabeth, no doubt, had a day job.

Across the street, a row of mailboxes sat, numbered to correspond to the townhouses. I considered leaving her a note. As I hesitated, the neighbor's door opened and an elderly woman in a light blue housedress poked her head out.

"Are you looking for her?" She jerked her finger at Elizabeth's door.

"I am. Is she at work?"

The woman nodded.

"Do you know where she works? I could call her there." I smiled, hoping to convey I was worthy of this woman's trust.

Her blue-veined hand on the door knob trembled as she thought. I wondered if she had Parkinson's or the like. "In an office downtown. She used to come home every night around five thirty, but now she's got a young man. She might not come home at all. Would you like me to give her a message?"

"No, thank you. I'll call her instead."

"Suit yourself." She closed her door.

Another dead end. Frustrated, I couldn't resist kicking some of that sparkling white gravel all over the lawn on my way back to the car.

∽

Cory remained silent for most of our ride back to Wachobe. We stopped in Watkins Glen to get gasoline, drinks, and a few snacks. I purchased the area newspaper, curious to see what, if anything, it had reported lately about Gleason's death. Although Cory offered to drive when we got back in the car, I refused. He didn't seem any less agitated than he had earlier. In fact, his knee bounced up and down the whole ride home.

As soon as we reached my house, I relinquished the wheel to Cory, who pulled away from the curb with a screech of his wheels, hell bent on seeing Brennan as soon as possible. I could only hope their reunion would be a happy one.

Danny and his friends were in the middle of a heated pickup game of football two houses down from ours. He called "hello" and waved to me.

I stopped to watch a few plays. Danny's passing arm was true. All his practice with Ray had paid off. Danny's football team had their first game this Sunday. He couldn't wait. Ray couldn't wait either. Ray never got to play football in high school. His fireman father had died a hero on the job, and Ray had assumed responsibility for the care of his little brother after school while his mother worked, just as I took care of Erica for my dad. It was one of the life experiences that brought the two of us closer. But now Ray could have his football vicariously again through Danny, who had the makings of a star athlete, as had Ray's younger brother. Pride and happiness flowed through me. I headed into the house.

The aroma of beef stew greeted me at the front door. I kicked off my pumps and carried them across the living room and into the kitchen, where Ray stood at the counter making a salad.

I rose up on my toes to kiss him. He barely gave me a peck, clearly preoccupied. I dropped my heels to the floor with a thud. "What's wrong?"

"We had two phone calls. The first was Danny's father."

Danny's father called once a week and the two of them talked for five minutes or so each time. If Ray was home when he called, Ray always found something to do outside. I suspected he felt conflicted over law enforcement's failure to put Danny's father in jail for car theft, especially since he'd made off with the Ferrari from my showroom right under Ray's nose. I knew allowing Mr. Phillips to contact Danny without any effort to discern his location and arrest him violated Ray's code, although he never said a word, perhaps not wanting to risk losing Danny. It was in the back of both our minds that Mr. Phillips could pick Danny up from school or off the street at any time and disappear with him, but we counted on Mr. Phillips' continued desire for us to provide stability for Danny. After all, he stole my Ferrari in order to get money for Danny's college fund.

"Did Danny talk to him?"

"He did." Ray tossed the knife he'd been using to slice a cucumber onto the counter. He turned to face me, folding his arms across his chest. "Did you know they met up at the vintage festival?"

Surprised, I dropped onto one of the stools at the breakfast bar. "No, when?"

The moment I asked, I knew the answer. Danny never bugged me to go back and buy the 1:43 scale car model he'd asked for when he came out of the store. If he'd really wanted it, he would have. His father had been in the store. I should have known he wouldn't miss a moment of the parade laps for anything as insignificant as a miniature car.

"That's what I want to know. I didn't see his dad. Did you?"

"No, but Danny went in the store to use their bathroom. He didn't want me to go with him." Now I wondered if he'd known his father was inside or if it had been a delightful surprise. Last week, I had overheard him tell his father we were going to the festival, but it didn't seem like they'd made any plans to meet up.

Ray stared at me, his good-cop, bad-cop, whatever-you-need-me-to-be-cop expression in place. God, I hated that expression, completely unreadable and oh so frustrating!

He turned back around and started slicing the cucumber again.

I sidled over next to him. "Ray, does it bother you that Danny saw his father?"

"The man's a wanted felon."

"He's also Danny's father."

Ray stopped slicing. "I know." He sighed. "I know."

"It's important for Danny to know his father loves him, as important as it is for you and I to both love him and provide a good example."

Ray slid his arms around me and buried his face in my hair. "You are the only mother figure in Danny's life. You don't feel the constant tug of war."

I understood. Ray needed reassurance and, since he'd probably been stewing about this issue for hours, a diversion. "Remember

Mr. Phillips gave us Danny because he thought we'd be best for him, and you're doing a great job. Danny's got a wicked spiral. I saw him outside playing with the boys."

Ray chuckled. "I know. He's awesome. I can't wait to see the game." He pulled me a little closer. "Hey, we're alone here." His lips ran up and down my neck, sending shivers up my spine. "We could take advantage of this opportunity."

I slid my fingers underneath the back of his shirt. "We could."

His lips slid to mine. My heart started beating faster. I pressed closer.

Footsteps pounded up the stairs. The front door flew open. "What's for dinner?"

Danny's steps pounded across the living room. His bedroom door crashed into the wall. "I need a second to change for dinner then I'll be right there."

Ray sucked on my bottom lip and pulled away, a rueful expression on his face. "I need more than one second."

I smiled. "Yes, you're always very thorough."

He resumed slicing the cucumber. "The other call was from your sister."

"What did she want?" I went to the cupboard to get plates for the table.

"She wanted you to know your mother thinks canoeing is a really bad idea." The sardonic tone of Ray's voice let me know what he thought, too. "Your mother said if your sister was meant to float, she'd be a hippopotamus."

Although our mother died more than twenty-five years ago, Erica claimed the two of them still were in communication. I didn't know quite how that worked, nor did I want to. However, often when Erica got an idea in her head, she attributed it to Mom. "So she's not going canoeing?"

"On the contrary, she and Maury are going first thing in the morning on Saturday. She just wanted to let you know."

Strange, but then we were talking about Erica. "Am I supposed to call her?"

"No, she said she'd call you afterward."

Oh, I couldn't wait for that conversation.

After dinner, Ray went outside to mow the lawn. Danny sat at the dining table to do his math and social studies homework. I spread out the newspaper I'd picked up in Watkins Glen and perused it from cover to cover. I found one tiny article about James Gleason's death, accompanied by an equally tiny snapshot of a woman and a man. The man had his arm around the woman. Both had their heads bent, obscuring their faces.

According to the article, Gleason had been buried in Albany on Wednesday morning, following an autopsy performed by the county medical examiner for the Watkins Glen area. The photo was a shot of Gleason's estranged wife and his son, leaving the medical examiner's office on Tuesday with a bag probably containing the personal items found in his pockets. I could tell from the photograph that the wife was dark-haired, his son blondish. Her name was Suzanne Gleason, the son's Matthew, both of Albany. The article also said Brennan remained in the county jail, pending his ability to make bail. That was old news.

I refolded the paper and went out to the garage to toss it in the recycling bin, wondering if Cory and I should pay a condolence call on Gleason's wife and son to see what more information we could ferret out about Gleason's anger at Brennan. It would be tricky to make such a call. We'd have to admit to being at the scene and perhaps knowing Brennan, which meant they might not speak to us. We might also agitate them during their time of grief, which would be cruel, perhaps even unnecessary. Now that Brennan had made bail, he might be more forthcoming with information. Our investigation might be over. Cory had certainly planned to ask him about all the news reports of Monica Gleason's death.

Assuming nothing, I entered the house and fired up the computer in our office to search for pictures from the Watkins Glen festival. Hundreds of photos were available and for sale, the majority featuring cars on the actual racetrack. After forty minutes of clicking through photographs, I began to despair. No one had been standing on the opposite side of the street from us. I couldn't find a single shot of the cars coming around the Franklin Street corner where we'd been standing.

Then I found the YouTube video.

Granted, it was fuzzy and a little bit shaky. The parade of cars passing by was clearly visible, though. The crowd beyond on the other side of the road had featureless faces but their clothing, hair, and forms were easy to make out. I spotted my own yellow raincoat, jeans, and brown hair, curled from the humidity. The corner where Brennan and Gleason argued was outside the frame.

The accompanying audiotape included the roar of the race cars engines as the parade passed by the photographer, overridden by a child pestering over and over, "Dad, can I have money for a brownie?" His father, the cameraman, kept saying, "In a minute. Look at the cars."

I watched as Brennan entered the frame from the right and as I tried to get his attention. As he passed me by. His stopping. His head turn. His wave to acknowledge me. His approach toward me. The redheaded man in the royal windbreaker—two beacons in a sea of darker colors—entering the frame from the right, his wife's pink raincoat nowhere in sight. My search for Danny, my face looking into the camera as I swung around to look for Brennan again. Howard Pint leaning low to take his shots of the oncoming cars. A surge of the crowd. Brennan and Gleason shifting toward the camera, converging on a collision course, now side-by-side.

The BMW 2002 took the corner, brakes squealing.

I leaned forward, trying to magnify my view.

The Cobra rounded the bend, seconds before the incident.

I held my breath, hoping to have all my questions answered.

A child screamed, "I want a brownie, Dad. I want a brownie right NOW."

The YouTube video ended.

Tears welled in my eyes. So close. Still, I couldn't really blame the kid. Those brownies had looked good.

I replayed the video ten times, trying to spot Wayne Engle in the mass. Two men with light hair had passed behind Brennan and Gleason, along with a dozen others. One might have been wearing a gray sweatshirt. The angle and definition on the video made it impossible to tell for sure. The dark-haired woman who fingered Brennan arrived seconds before the BMW came into the frame. I recognized her hairstyle, although, honestly, I couldn't remember her face. No wonder Ray didn't think much of me as a witness.

The dark-haired woman was closest to Brennan and Gleason. I supposed she had had the best view of the two of them. All the other spectators' heads were turned toward the disappearing BMW or toward the oncoming Cobra. She seemed to be looking at the street directly in front of her, perhaps trying to figure where to stand to get an unobstructed view. Brennan and Gleason blocked her view and appeared to be speaking to one another. No arms were raised. Not yet, at least. But a crowd surged past them. At any second a different person passed behind them, even some blond men, one of whom seemed to hover in the background right before the video ended. Could that have been Wayne Engle?

I picked up the phone to dial Cory's cell. He answered on the fifth ring. "Are you with Brennan?"

"I'm home. We had an argument."

"He noticed his stuff was missing?"

"No. We had dinner together. I managed to put it all back when he was outside grilling. Everything was fine until I asked him about Monica and James Gleason. He clammed up. Wouldn't say a word. Refused to tell me anything we didn't already know. Wouldn't tell me anything about the reunion, the accident, or his high school friends. I got mad. He got mad. I told him if he didn't trust me enough to confide in me, we were through."

"How did he respond to that?"

"He didn't say anything. So I left."

"Oh, Cory, I'm sorry."

"I'm sure we're on the right track, Jo. He's hiding something. I know it."

Only problem, Brennan might be hiding something to save himself from prison. He and Cory would definitely be through if that was the case, especially if Cory helped put him there, which remained possible.

I filled Cory in on the article from the newspaper and the You-Tube video. I emailed him the URL. He watched it a couple times while I waited on the line. He didn't spot anything new. The video confirmed nothing—but it would make a great advertisement for brownies.

"The only people involved that we didn't talk to are Suzanne and Matthew Gleason. I'd love to hear firsthand what her husband and Brennan argued about, wouldn't you, Jo?"

"It might give us a clue as to why Brennan is being so secretive."

"Can we afford another day off?"

I'd checked the messages on the shop's answering machine before our family sat down to dinner. Only five calls all day, three for oil changes before winter, two for inspections. Cory could get them done early in the day. "Maybe an afternoon."

"Can you stand another drive to Albany so we can visit the Gleasons?"

"I'll bake them some chocolate chip cookies."

FOURTEEN

FRIDAY MORNING I MADE Danny and Ray instant oatmeal for breakfast, while the cookies browned in the oven. Ray appeared in the kitchen first, dressed in his gray uniform and looking hot. I love a man in uniform, especially this man.

He didn't notice me staring. He was too intent on inhaling his oatmeal. "Who are the cookies for?"

"Some are for us, but I'm taking a couple dozen to James Gleason's family."

He stopped chewing. "When did you decide to go see them?"

"Last night."

"I was home last night."

Meaning, why didn't you tell me then? I didn't mention it because I didn't want him to try to dissuade us. I had enough doubts and concerns without his adding to them. "I know. I just didn't want to hear again about how Ken would investigate. Brennan's home and he still won't talk to Cory about the car crash."

Ray spoke slowly. "Maybe he thinks it's none of Cory's business." His patronizing tone implied it was none of my business either.

"You're right, but now inquiring minds want to know."

"Brennan isn't going to appreciate your interference any more than Ken." He carried his dish to the dishwasher and inserted it. "Now that he's out of jail, it may get back to him that the two of you are snooping around."

"I think Cory's willing to risk it to keep him out of prison."

Ray ran his hand over his face. "Okay, have it your way. But don't call me when you two get arrested for impeding an investigation."

"Do you even know for sure your friend Ken is investigating ties to the crash?"

"No." Ray's response was curt. He hated to acknowledge even the possibility that the sheriff's department in any county would leave the smallest stone unturned.

I raised my face to his. "We may be a little late. Can you pick Danny up from football practice?"

"Done." Ray's lips brushed over mine. "Be careful."

After Ray left, I checked the clock and panicked. "Danny, you're going to miss the bus."

He appeared from around the corner. "Is Ray gone?"

"Yes, but he's picking you up from practice tonight. Cory and I are going to Albany again."

"Oh." Danny climbed onto a stool at the breakfast bar. He didn't pick up his spoon.

"What's the matter? You don't want oatmeal?"

His gaze remained fixed on the bowl. "I want it."

He made no move to eat.

I leaned against the bar. "Is something wrong?"

"My dad called last night."

"Ray told me. How is your dad?"

"Good. I saw him at the vintage festival. I didn't know he was coming. He followed me into the store when I went to use the bathroom." Danny glanced up at me from underneath the hair hanging in this face.

"That was a nice surprise, I bet."

He sat up eagerly, a huge smile on his face. "Yeah. He's been to Washington, D.C. and Boston. He saw a Red Sox game."

"Cool." I wondered if Mr. Phillips had stolen a few cars while he was there, too. Frankly, I was surprised he hadn't made off with any from the vintage festival, a Mecca for car fans. Maybe he'd been assessing future possibilities.

"My dad never takes cars people love."

For a minute, I thought I'd spoken my thoughts aloud. "What?"

"Ray asked me if my dad was at the festival to steal a car."

"He did?" I couldn't believe it. Well, I could, but I didn't want to. It was one thing to think it and quite another to say it out loud. Deliberately undermining Danny's image of his father was unacceptable.

"He wasn't. He came to see me."

"I'm sure you were glad to see him."

Danny nodded. "I know stealing any car is wrong, like Ray said, but my dad would never take one of those cars, ever."

"Why not?"

"Because those cars are loved."

"What?"

"All those cars. The people spend tons of time and money fixing them up to take to races and car shows. They love their cars. My dad would never take their cars. He only takes cars from people who drive them for show, or from the dealerships. They don't care. They don't love their cars."

I thought about the black Porsche 944 S2 my dad had restored and presented to me as a graduation present. I loved that car. My sister had it now. She didn't love it. She didn't even appreciate it, but I couldn't take it back from her. Maybe someday, but not now.

"How can your dad tell who loves their cars?"

Danny picked up his spoon. "I don't know, but he can. Ray doesn't understand." He started eating, apparently content to have gotten that information off his chest.

And right onto mine.

Cory and I arrived in the suburbs of Albany around four o'clock, planning to stay late, if necessary, to find Suzanne Gleason and Elizabeth Potter at home. We sure didn't want to have to drive back here again. If we couldn't unearth any new information this time, Cory planned to confess to Brennan about searching his home and to demand to know where the five thousand dollar a month payments went. Brennan hadn't called since their fight Wednesday night, Cory felt like he had nothing more to lose. I wasn't so sure.

Suzanne Gleason lived in a modest colonial dwarfed by two enormous pines in the front yard, the kind of evergreens that said White House or Rockefeller Center Christmas tree. The garage door stood open.

Cory spotted a navy car inside. "Hey, that's a 1972 Gran Torino. I had one of those in high school." He headed toward the garage.

I grabbed his shirt at the shoulder and tugged him toward the front door. "Focus."

We rang the doorbell. A blond young man opened the door, the same handsome boy with the startling blue eyes in the photograph on Wayne Engle's credenza—only aged a couple years. Shocked, I gaped at him, then glanced at Cory, trying to determine if he recognized him, too.

"Can I help you?" He smiled, revealing adorable dimples.

I recovered first. "We're looking for Suzanne and Matthew Gleason."

"I'm Matthew." He looked from me to Cory and back again, waiting.

Cory stood with his head tipped to one side, studying Matthew. I waited for Cory to jump into the conversation, but he didn't.

I thrust the tin of cookies forward. "We're so sorry about your father. I brought you some chocolate chip cookies."

Matthew accepted the tin. "Thank you. Did you know my dad?"

Cory came out of his reverie. "No, we didn't, but we were at the vintage festival on Friday night. I was actually in the parade of racecars. Jolene was at the corner where your father was ..." He stopped, obviously uncertain as to what to say next.

Matthew's eyes narrowed. "We were told only one woman came forward as a witness. Was that you?"

I shook my head. "We were more bystanders than witnesses." I held out my hand. "I'm Jolene Asdale. And this is Cory Kempe."

Matthew shifted the cookie tin to his left hand so that he could shake hands with us, his brow wrinkled, his gaze questioning.

I tried to think of something to put him at ease. "Forgive me for asking, but aren't you Wayne Engle's godson?"

Matthew blinked in surprise, his brow smoothing. "Yeah, I am. Do you know Wayne?"

"We visited him earlier this week. Your photograph is on his office credenza."

"Yeah. That's my freshman yearbook picture. I graduated last year. I'm looking for a job." He looked between Cory and me again. "So you're friends of Wayne?"

Cory smiled. "He's a great guy."

Fortunately, Matthew didn't seem to notice his question went unanswered. "Yeah." He looked at the tin of cookies. "Listen, my mom's not home, but I know she'll want to thank you for the cookies. Would you mind writing down your name and number for me?"

"Not at all." We stepped into the foyer at his invitation.

Matthew disappeared down the hall. "I'll be right back. We have a pad in the kitchen."

The foyer looked into the living room area, which was decorated in shades of gray, black, and red. Very contemporary and not my style. A chrome frame held a photo of Matthew and his mother. She had dark hair and funky fashion glasses, an average looking woman. Another photo held a picture of Matthew and his dad with his unmistakable red hair. No family shots, but then the couple had been separated.

Matthew returned with the pen and paper.

I wrote down my name and cell number and handed it back to him. "Will your mother be home soon?"

"She has to work late to catch up. She took a few days off this week to arrange for the funeral and stuff."

"I'm sorry we missed her. Please give her our condolences."

"I will."

I stepped back outside to join Cory. Matthew followed us to the edge of the drive.

Cory pointed at the Gran Torino in the garage. "Great car. I used to have one."

Matthew's eyes lit up. "Really? I love this car. It's got power."

"Mind if we take a look?" Cory headed for the garage without waiting for a response. Matthew didn't seem to mind, tagging right along behind him. I brought up the rear.

Cory admired the car and asked questions. Matthew opened the hood. Cory stuck his head under it.

Matthew smiled at me, happy to show off his wheels.

I returned his smile. "I own an import auto dealership in Wachobe. Cory is my mechanic. We're big car people. Is your whole family into cars?"

The light in Matthew's eyes faded. "Just me really. My dad's sister was killed in a car crash. He didn't even want to go to the festival. I talked him into meeting us there."

"You and your mom?"

"Yeah, and my girlfriend. We were all going to have dinner and see the fireworks in the Glen after the race. But then my dad ran into Brennan, and they fought. My mom took off to find me. We decided to head home. We didn't know about my dad until the sheriff notified us."

I noticed he referred to Brennan by his first name, as though he knew him. "Were you and your dad close?"

Matthew shrugged. "I'm closer to my mom. She and my dad fought a lot. We fought a lot, too. He liked to tell everyone what to do. We moved out when I started high school. It made things easier."

It didn't sound like they were going to miss him much. "Do you know Brennan?"

Matthew hesitated. "I met him once. He seemed like a nice guy."

His words caught me off guard. What boy thinks the man accused of killing his father was a "nice guy"? I glanced at Cory, who was studying Matthew again like a sports car he couldn't decide whether to buy. "Brennan's accused of killing your dad."

"Yeah, I know. Believe me, Dad and I got into it a few times. I could understand if Brennan got pissed and gave him a shove, but I don't think he killed him on purpose."

Matthew backed away toward his front door. "Truthfully, my dad had a way of pushing people's buttons. I loved him, but he's not going to be missed."

On the drive over to Elizabeth Potter's townhouse, I considered Matthew's words. How sad that James Gleason would not be missed. Had he always been an unpleasant fellow or had his sister's death taken a toll on him? I know my mother's death changed our family forever in some very obvious and many other subtle ways, including the loss of Erica's and my carefree childhood. Had James become angry and demanding after his sister's death? What a price to pay to lose his son's love and respect.

Cory interrupted my thoughts. "What do you make of Wayne Engle being Matthew's godfather?

"I don't know what to make of it. I wish you still had Brennan's yearbook. Maybe Suzanne Gleason was another one of the four Musketeers' friends that we overlooked. Do you remember any Suzannes in the book?"

"I'm sure there were some. I don't remember any specifically."

"Or maybe she's Wayne's sister."

Cory slowed for the stoplight. "Didn't you see the picture of his mom in the living room? She doesn't look anything like Wayne Engle."

"I saw it, but you know Erica doesn't look anything like me, either. Siblings can take after one or the other parent or be a mix of both. Or look like Aunt Fanny or Grandpa Mortimer. She looked familiar. She could be his sister."

The light changed to green and Cory hit the gas. "Well, I thought Matthew resembled someone we've seen, but I can't remember who. Everyone's starting to blend together."

I had to agree. Too many faces and too few answers. Maybe our next stop, Elizabeth Potter, would finally bring some closure.

Unfortunately, her townhouse appeared as uninhabited as the last time we visited. Cory accompanied me up the sparkling white gravel path and surveyed the lawn while I rang the doorbell. No one responded.

Cory checked his watch. "It's five thirty. Should we wait a half hour or so?"

"We could, but I'm hungry. We could go eat and then come back around again. Problem is, if she comes home to change and head out for the night, we'll miss her."

"There was a convenience store two blocks back. I could walk down and get subs while you wait here in the car."

"Sounds like a plan."

I climbed into the BMW and watched as Cory sauntered away, hands in his pockets, head bowed. Normally, his head would be held high, giving him the illusion of height even though he stood at five-three. This whole situation with Brennan had diminished him, both literally and figuratively. If Brennan knew how much Cory cared, would he be more forthcoming with the truth?

A tap on the window sent me jumping into the air. I whipped my head around. It was Elizabeth Potter's neighbor, wearing another stylish housedress, this time in orange.

I smiled and got out. "Hello again."

The tremble in the woman's right arm never ceased. Her lower lip moved up and down ever so slightly today as well. She pointed toward Elizabeth's door.

"If you're here for her, she got home at six last night."

Ah, the neighborhood watch. The elderly people in our neighborhood probably clocked Ray and my comings and goings, too. "Good, then I'll wait."

She pointed in the direction Cory had walked. "That man with you?"

"Yes."

"Is he coming back?"

"Yes."

She nodded. "Suit yourself."

A Honda Accord approached and pulled into Elizabeth Potter's driveway. The car door opened. A woman in a tight black pencil skirt, thick black tights, low-heeled black patent leather pumps, and a sexy red silk blouse slid out. She had one of those short, funky asymmetrical hairstyles, brown with blond highlights.

She waved in our direction. "Hi, Evie."

Evie didn't wave back. She scrunched her forehead instead.

I gestured toward our new arrival. "Would that be Elizabeth?"

Evie didn't respond. Her gaze never left the woman, who now approached us.

She limped ever so slightly. "How are you today, Evie?"

No response.

I started to wonder if Evie had Alzheimer's.

"What did you do to your hair?" Evie pointed at the woman, her finger shaking.

The woman fluffed her hair. "It's new. Do you like it?"

"No." Evie started up the sidewalk. "This woman's been waiting for you."

Elizabeth Potter flushed, then laughed. "She's an honest old bird, isn't she?"

I smiled. "I like your haircut, if that makes you feel better."

"Thank you, it does."

"You must be Elizabeth Potter." I held out her hand. "I'm Jolene Parker."

She took a step back. Her countenance changed to suspicious. "What can I do for you?"

I wished Cory would reappear, but he wasn't anywhere in sight. For a woman who made her living talking to people, I wasn't very good at ad-libbing. My sales presentations were well practiced, full of facts and information. Cory was the spontaneous one, used to filling in the gaps when someone else forgot their lines on stage. He and I should have discussed how we planned to approach this woman, who was scarred from the crash and not likely to welcome us.

I opted for honesty. "I'm friends with Brennan Rowe. I was hoping to ask you a few questions about him."

"Why?"

"Brennan has been arrested on suspicion of pushing James Gleason in front of a car, killing him."

"So I hear." Her tone sounded like she didn't care—about either of them.

I pressed on. "The news reports have brought up the relationship between James and his sister and the car crash that killed her. I understand you were also involved in that crash."

"I don't talk to reporters." She turned and started to walk away.

I chased after her, rounding her and cutting off her path. "I'm not a reporter. I'm a personal friend of Brennan's. I understand the two of you were once very close, too. You, Brennan, Monica, and Wayne Engle. The Four Musketeers, I believe."

Her face softened at that. "Monica was my best friend. She dated Brennan. Wayne was Brennan's best friend. We all hung out together."

"And you went to your five-year class reunion together?"

"Yes."

"Wayne Engle said he fought with Brennan that night. Do you know what the fight was about?"

She tried to get around me. I stepped back to give her some room while remaining directly in her path. I didn't want to be accused of menacing her.

She gave up and locked eyes with me. "Look, I don't know what you want. I can't tell you what they fought about. I don't want to talk about that night. I was in the car accident. I almost died. You have no right to come here, no right at all. Go away." She lifted her arms as if to shove me. "Go away."

I moved out of her path.

She walked quickly, her limp amplified.

I felt like crap. I called after her, "I'm sorry, Elizabeth. It's just hard to believe Brennan would kill anyone."

She spun around. "He killed Monica. He almost killed me. Is that so hard to believe?"

"I know that's true. Was he driving drunk?"

"No."

"Then how did the crash happen?"

"I don't know. I was asleep. Ask Brennan. Just leave, and don't come back."

She walked to her front door, unlocked it and slammed it closed behind her.

"You're really working the charm, Jo."

I turned to find Cory behind me, holding a plastic sack. "Now you come back. Where were you when I needed you?"

He lifted the sack in the air. "Hey, you wanted food."

Well, now all I wanted was to go home.

FIFTEEN

Saturday morning was a slow day at work, especially since we hadn't been in the shop for the last two days to answer calls and set up any appointments. Cory and I sat in the Austin Healey around ten thirty, pretending to drive the hills of Monaco with the sun—the overhead showroom pin light—on our faces. We did that sometimes. It felt peaceful, a little mini mind vacation. Of course I had the cordless in my lap and spent part my vacation time willing a customer to call in need of a pre-owned but pristine Austin Healey.

And part of the time I processed our trip to Albany.

Elizabeth Potter hadn't said she didn't *know* what Brennan and Wayne Engle fought about. She said she couldn't *tell*. Why not? We thought they'd argued about Brennan's homosexuality, which wasn't a secret now, by any means. She could have told me that. So Cory's theory had to be incorrect. We'd agreed on that during our drive back to Wachobe last night. We just hadn't agreed on a new theory regarding the argument.

She had also said to ask Brennan about the crash. But Brennan supposedly had no memory of that night. Was he lying to protect himself? If so, what would get him to tell the truth now?

Cory and I also hadn't agreed on approaching Brennan to ask him. Cory feared it would lead to him having to admit he'd gone through Brennan's stuff, a sure-fire way to not only make Brennan clam up more but also to terminate their relationship forever. I thought it might be time to confess we'd at least asked a few questions in Albany, based on the disturbing news reports, in the hopes Brennan would be more forthcoming with information once he realized how much Cory cared.

Cory didn't want to bank on that. This whole situation had shaken his confidence.

Hence, our little mini mind vacation.

I focused on relaxing. Breathe in, breathe out. Visualize. Was that the royal family waving to us?

Sirens interrupted our peaceful drive through the hills.

We watched as Ray's patrol car flew past the showroom window. The volunteer ambulance roared past a few minutes later, followed closely by county rescue.

It was the standard response team for a boating incident. A little unusual for this late in the year though. I wondered who was out on the lake.

Cory glanced at me. "Didn't you say your sister was going canoeing this morning?"

"They would hug the shoreline. I'm sure she's fine." Almost sure. I considered calling her cell phone. If she was fine and my call intruded on Maury's serenade, would she be happy or mad? Worse, would the canoe tip over as she fumbled for her cell? I convinced myself the brouhaha had nothing to do with her.

I settled back in my seat and tried to recapture Monaco.

Ten minutes later, Cory hit my shoulder and pointed as the medical examiner's vehicle flew past our window.

"You don't think—" I picked the cordless up off my lap.

It rang as if on cue. Cory and I exchanged fearful glances.

"Darlin', I need you to get over here and throw a net over your sister."

Relief washed through my veins. Erica must be safe, safe enough to be causing trouble. I covered the mouthpiece and asked at Cory. "Do I look like a butterfly keeper to you?"

Cory's eyebrows flew up. He wisely chose to shake his head.

"Thank you." I uncovered the mouthpiece. "Why, Ray, what's going on? Are Erica and Maury okay?"

"They're fine." Ray's emphasis on the word "they're" made me nervous. Who else could be involved?

"I'll let your sister explain. Hold on."

Before the cell phone exchanged hands, I heard Erica in the background, talking about hippopotamuses.

"You and your great ideas. Go canoeing. You'll be fine. I'm not fine, Jolene."

I didn't bother to point out canoeing wasn't my idea. I did get a mental picture of her bedraggled and soaked to the skin, wrapped in a Red Cross blanket. "You fell in, didn't you?"

"Only after I spotted the body and dropped my paddle. I couldn't reach it. It's not my fault I have short arms. Mom said she had short arms, too. It's not my fault the canoe tipped over when I lunged for my paddle. I told you canoes are tippy, but you wouldn't listen. I told you I didn't want to go canoeing. I told Maury I didn't want to go. No one ever listens to me, except Mom."

Only my sister would gloss over a body. "I'm definitely listening now, Erica. What body are you talking about?"

"The dead guy floating facedown in the lake. Actually, he was rolling with the waves on the shoreline, with a big gash in his forehead. Now he's on shore, like a beached whale. Poor guy, I think it's going to be a closed casket funeral."

I cringed. "Who is he?"

"I don't know. I've never seen him before. He looks like a politician. Blue suit, white shirt, maroon striped tie. He's wearing black shoes, wingtips."

That oh-so-familiar sick feeling washed through me. "Where did you find him?"

"He was lodged under a low-lying branch a few yards north of Brennan's place. We were paddling down to say hello to Brennan. You know, to cheer him up." Her voice lowered. "Actually, I was hoping he'd invite us out on his speedboat. This paddling stuff is for the birds.

"Hey, here comes Brennan now."

"Ah, Erica, could you keep Brennan away from the body?" I didn't want him to remember his old friend after being pulled from the water.

"The sheriff's deputies won't let anyone over there. Brennan's right here. You want to talk to him?"

"Not right now. Where's Ray?"

"He's coming this way, too. He doesn't look happy...

"Hey, what's he doing? Oh my god, he's pulling out his handcuffs...

"He's putting them on Brennan. He's reading him his rights...

"Suspected murder? Brennan?

"Jolene, who the hell is Wayne Engle?"

SIXTEEN

CORY BROKE ALL THE speed limits as we raced over to Brennan's house. It didn't matter because we found almost every Wachobe police officer and county sheriff's deputy there at the scene, along with an ample crowd of interested spectators, those yahoos with the scanners Ray loved so much.

Yellow crime scene tape surrounded the entire acre of Brennan's lakeside retreat, stopping at the shoreline. At the edge of the lake, a group of uniformed and suited men huddled around a black bag on a gurney. The medical examiner's wagon was parked within the perimeter, doors open, as though ready to receive its precious cargo. My sister, her husband, and a uniformed officer waited in the shade of a willow tree whose branches swept the surface of the lake, creating ripples.

The Wachobe police chief, whose everyday primary duties involved traffic control and metered parking, allowed us under the tape with strict instructions to see Ray and only Ray.

Cory, of course, wanted to see Brennan and only Brennan. We couldn't spot him anywhere.

Ray saw us and broke from the huddle.

Cory gestured frantically. "Where's Brennan?"

"He's under arrest. Max took him over to the sheriff's department for questioning."

"Why?" Cory's anguished cry caught the attention of the huddle. They swung around to study us for a moment, then went back to their own conversation.

Ray folded his arms across his chest, frowning. "Engle had an urgent message slip from his office in his wallet, with Brennan's address on it. When I called his office to find out his next of kin, the woman who answered said he didn't have anyone except his godson. I asked who his godson was. Imagine my surprise when I learned it's James Gleason's son. Then I asked her if she knew Engle's plans for last night. She said they got a call around six thirty, right before they locked up for the night, from a Brennan Rowe, asking to meet with him last night. She said Engle seemed surprised, but indicated he would drive up here. Now he's dead."

I had to admit Brennan would make my suspect list, too, but an arrest? "Ray, I don't see how you can arrest Brennan for his murder. Someone else could have called, using Brennan's name."

"That's true, but there's blood on Brennan's dock. There's blood on Brennan's oar. It all points to Brennan."

"What oar?"

Cory sighed. "He keeps one on his boat, in case the engine quits in the middle of the lake or he needs to push off something."

Ray nodded. "That's the one. He admitted it was his."

I swung around to look at Brennan's ski boat, sitting in its hoist at the end of the dock with the sun glinting off it. Beyond, in the middle of the lake, I saw another glint of metal, too, unrecognizable at this distance. I didn't let it distract me. "So you think Brennan lured Wayne here, hit him with the oar, and shoved him in the water, hoping he would sink and disappear?"

"That's the theory we're working."

"Someone else could have lured Wayne here just as easily."

"True, but all the evidence points directly to Brennan at the moment."

I let it go for now, having faith in my husband. Ray wouldn't railroad Brennan into prison. He would ask all the right questions, or at least ensure that they were asked. "It would have taken Wayne at least three hours to drive here last night. He probably got here around ten." I scanned the areas beyond either side of Brennan's home. "Did any of the neighbors see anything?"

"Engle's Mercedes is parked on the road at the corner of Brennan's lot. We're still canvassing, but the only neighbors with a clear view of Brennan's dock are seasonal. Their docks are out of the water and their places are locked up tight."

"What did Brennan say?"

"He said he worked in his office until eleven o'clock, then went to bed. He didn't see or hear anything last night or this morning when he got up. He didn't see the Mercedes parked on the county road when he pulled out of the driveway to go to work. A member of his construction crew heard the call to this address on the scanner and notified him. That's why he came back here."

Ray unfolded his arms, dropping his bad cop stance. "You need to take Erica and Maury home. They fell out of their canoe. It's in the middle of the lake. Someone from the department will take the patrol boat out and tow it in later today."

That explained the glinting metal I spotted earlier. Trust Erica to lose the canoe. Hopefully it wouldn't capsize in the meantime, forcing me to reimburse our landlord for its loss.

Ray continued, "You'll be getting a call from the department later today to come in for an interview. We're going to need to know about everyone you two met when you went to Albany and Binghamton, and what was said. And anything else you might be holding back. Understand?"

I glanced at Cory, immediately giving it away to Ray that we were in fact holding something back.

He shook his head in disgust and walked away.

Cory's panicky gaze met mine. "What are we going to do?"

I knew he was asking me if he had to tell about going through Brennan's stuff and the record of payment he found. I gave him the only answer I felt confident about.

"We're going to drive Erica and Maury home."

"Brennan's mouth just dropped open when Ray said he was under arrest for killing Wayne Engle. He even teetered a little bit. I thought he was going to faint, didn't you, Maury?" Erica whacked her husband on the shoulder.

"He definitely didn't know what hit him." Maury emphasized the word "him."

Erica missed the hint. "That's right."

Cory's gaze never left the road as he steered his BMW toward Erica's house, but I knew he was taking in our conversation. "Did he say anything when Ray put the cuffs on him?"

"No. He couldn't take his eyes off the area where Wayne Engle was lying on the beach. I thought Brennan looked sad, didn't you, Maury?" She whacked him again.

"Yes, Erica, I did." Maury raised his gaze to mine, silently asking for mercy. I twisted back around in the passenger seat to face the windshield, trying to end the conversation for the time being.

Erica chattered on, oblivious. "I can't believe you just met Wayne, and now he's dead. You must have stumbled onto something. Why else would someone kill him? I don't believe for one second Brennan killed him. He's too nice a guy. No way. Right, Maury?"

I heard her palm connect with Maury's shoulder again. This time he didn't respond.

Cory made the right turn onto Wells Street, and the 1870 white Victorian where Erica and Maury resided came into sight. Cory pulled up in front and put the car in park. He left the engine idling.

Erica leaned forward, thrusting her torso into the front seat between us. "Call me later and let me know what happens at your interrogation."

"I will call you later, Erica." Much later, if and when I could take her manic chatter.

Maury waited until Erica had slammed the car door to say, "Let me know if there's anything we can do to help Brennan. I don't think he killed anyone either."

"Thank you, Maury."

He nodded, a sober expression on his face.

As soon as Maury climbed out of the back seat, Cory pulled away from the curb. "None of Brennan's friends think he killed anyone. I guess that's good to know. He'll have lots of character witnesses. But you know what's bothering me?"

Cory didn't wait for my answer before continuing, "Like Erica said, we must have stumbled onto something. Someone killed Wayne Engle; someone we met. If I'd listened to Brennan in the first place and stayed out of all of this, maybe Engle would still be alive. So, no, Brennan didn't kill anyone, but apparently, I did."

Once again, I didn't respond.

I was too busy feeling guilty myself.

SEVENTEEN

SURE ENOUGH, AS RAY promised, my cell phone rang minutes after Cory and I returned to the shop. A terse and unfamiliar voice issued an invitation to come on down to the county sheriff's department and answer a few questions. I could bring one guest, Cory.

We didn't talk on the drive over to the county's public safety building. The building was about thirty minutes outside of Wachobe, in a much less touristy town. It housed the sheriff's office, county court, and a forty-cell jail. Flanked by a hospital and a convenience store, the imposing brick and cement facility seemed impervious to the hustle of traffic outside. I'd been there before several times, but every time I entered the place, I got the creeps. Jail was on my list of places I never wanted to go. Yet here I was.

The officer at the reception desk pointed us to the waiting room chairs. Cory picked the closest and sat with his knee bobbing up and down. He hadn't asked me again if he should admit to finding Brennan's financial records, and I hadn't brought it up either. As far as I was concerned, it was his story to tell. I would join in only if he asked me.

But they separated us. Cory got called in first, leaving me alone in the waiting room. We hadn't expected that, although we should have. I knew for sure Ray wouldn't be the one asking me questions now. I just didn't know who would be.

Twenty minutes later, I remained alone in the waiting room. When the door to the sheriff's department's inner sanctum opened, my head snapped up from the magazine pages I'd been idly turning. I expected to see an officer coming for me, but instead Catherine Thomas appeared.

She wore a striking red skirt and jacket, her hair pulled into a sleek ponytail. The leather of her black stilettos matched her briefcase perfectly and made her seem like a giant, since she stood quite tall barefoot. Three gold bangles adorned her wrist. They seemed to jingle "I'm so pretty." Once again, she reminded me that she had it all goin' on.

"Jolene. I'd say it was nice to see you, but I'm representing Brennan. I understand you and Cory are here to provide information about his latest arrest."

"Unfortunately."

She shot a glance at the deputy behind the desk, who was fielding a phone call, and settled into the chair beside me, leaning in conspiratorially. "Any chance you want to fill me in?"

"I would, but it might get back to Ray." Now that Brennan had been arrested in his county, I knew I'd better not talk to anyone until I talked to him or his fellow officers.

She heaved a huge sigh. "Ray won't tell me anything either. He's not assigned to the case because you're involved, and that only makes him that much more uncooperative. He hates it when he's not assigned to the big cases."

Our sheriff's department was small, though our county was relatively large. The sheriff had long ago decided that, in order to keep his tenured deputies motivated, they would rotate assignments between patrol and investigation. This method worked wonders for morale and employee retention, except really interesting cases didn't come along all that often, a murder almost never. Catherine was right. Ray was irritated to be left out of this one because of me and Cory. I hated that Catherine knew I'd affected my husband's career negatively.

But a brief burst of happiness flowed through me, knowing my husband wasn't talking to his ex-lover.

Guilt followed. Call me naïve, but I still believed in Brennan Rowe—and Catherine's ability to save him from the big, bad sheriff, not to mention the district attorney.

Catherine drummed her red manicured nails on the wooden chair arm. "I can't believe anyone really thinks Brennan is a murderer. It's obvious to me this whole thing is a setup. I couldn't get Ray to admit it, but I'm sure he thinks so, too."

I remained silent.

She popped up from her chair, still clutching her briefcase. "I'm going out to the car to make a few phone calls. They're through questioning Brennan until they get Cory's story and yours. Then they'll start in on Brennan again. I'm going to line up an investigator for whatever comes to light here today."

She leaned down toward me. "Listen, Jolene, just tell them the good, the bad, and the ugly. I can't help Brennan if I don't know the whole story. Neither can Ray or anyone else. Will you do that for me?"

She didn't wait for my answer. Maybe she already knew what it was. I wished I did.

The bad and the ugly could cost Cory his relationship with Brennan. It could cost Cory and me our friendship. My business might need to hire a new mechanic. On the other hand, a killer was definitely on the loose in our hometown. Again. Last time he might have been caught sooner if I'd been more open with Ray during the investigation.

When the door opened forty minutes later and they called me in, I felt like I was walking the plank. The sheriff himself, who bears a great resemblance to a most familiar and right jolly old elf, interviewed me along with Max, Ray's peer. They simply asked for my story.

And I told them the truth, the whole truth, and nothing but the truth.

So help all of us.

Ray was nowhere in sight when I left the department. I wondered if he'd been dispatched to interview any one of the people I'd named or perhaps to get a search warrant signed for Brennan's home. The sheriff's eyes had sparkled at the mention of the yearbook and the check registers. Brennan and Catherine were in for a long night. I wouldn't expect Ray home on time.

Cory was in the waiting room. We walked out to his car in silence. Only after we were safely inside its cocoon did we speak—simultaneously. "I told them about the check registers."

We both laughed with relief.

Cory leaned back against the headrest. "I was afraid you wouldn't tell and you'd get in trouble."

"I was afraid if I told and you didn't, you'd hate me."

"No way, Jo. We go back too far." He sighed. "I feel like a huge weight has been lifted off my chest. I don't think Brennan is guilty, and the only way they're ever going to find Wayne Engle's killer now is to know all the facts. If Brennan hates me forever, then so be it. And if by some bizarre twist of fate, he is a killer then I'm just lucky to find out now before I invest any more in our relationship. The truth will set you free."

I smiled at the all-too-familiar gift shop quote. We all spent too much time in our tourist town, which had its share of clichés for sale. "I have to admit I feel better, too. Let the professionals handle it. I'm happy to sit this one out."

"I doubt they're finished with us yet."

"I saw Catherine Thomas before I met with the sheriff. She wanted me to tell her the whole story. I wasn't comfortable telling her then, but now, hey, the sheriff didn't tell me to keep quiet. He did ask me to stay away from everyone we spoke to. What about you?"

"The same. If Catherine asks again, I don't see why we can't talk to her. It's in the interest of learning the truth, right?"

"Right." Still, I wondered what Ray would say about that. I'd ask him later.

Cory and I drove back to the shop, stopping to pick up submarines for a late lunch. The answering machine light wasn't blinking when we entered the shop. We set up lunch on my desk.

I bit into my tuna submarine.

Cory's roast beef remained wrapped.

"What's wrong?"

"They're probably talking to Brennan now, interrogating him."

I chewed and swallowed. "I'm sure they are. But they'll figure this out. We were just the catalyst."

"We must know the killer."

"I'm sure we do, but for the life of me, I don't know which person it is."

Cory shook his head. "We don't even know for sure if we're looking for one killer or two. And James Gleason's death could still have been an accident."

"The sheriff wanted to get the original of that YouTube video I found on the Internet. He said maybe they could enhance it to see the crowd behind James and Brennan better. Before he let me leave, I had to bring the video up on screen for Max."

Cory unwrapped his sub and took a bite, mayonnaise dribbling on his chin. "Who do you think killed Wayne Engle?"

"I have no idea." I reviewed the people we'd met in my head. "I doubt it was Elizabeth Potter's parents. They're too old, and the mother seemed to like Brennan. I don't think she'd want to frame him."

"Mr. Potter might want to. He seemed miserable—and so did his dog."

I laughed, trying not to spew tuna.

Cory picked up a tomato slice that had fallen out of his sub and popped it in his mouth, swallowing it in one gulp. "But they were pretty old. What about Matthew Gleason? He was young and strong. We know he was at the race."

"Why would he kill his godfather? He seemed to like him."

"I don't know. I'm sorry we didn't get to meet his mother."

"Me, too. She's my number one suspect. James Gleason was a hothead. They fought all the time. He could have been giving her a hard time about the divorce. Maybe she was having an affair with Wayne, who saw her at the Glen and realized she was the killer after we talked to him."

"Or maybe Matthew killed his father to protect his mother. We've read about cases like that in the paper before." Cory hesitated. "Do you think the guys at the sheriff's department are coming up with theories like this?"

"I have no doubt. They probably have even more fertile imaginations than we do." I chewed my sub. "Matthew admitted he wouldn't miss his dad. Maybe he didn't want Wayne as a replacement dad."

Cory pointed his index finger at me. "Another good theory. Keep going."

"Elizabeth Potter might want revenge on Brennan for the car crash years ago, but I don't know why she'd want to kill Wayne Engle, unless he knew she was blackmailing Brennan and threatened to expose her."

"Why expose her now? The blackmail payments stopped more than a year ago." Cory swigged his soda.

"If they even were blackmail payments." I crumpled the sub wrapper and made a basket. "We're going to drive ourselves crazy trying to piece this all together. Let's leave it to the professionals for now."

"I'll bet you one thing for sure."

"What?"

"It wasn't Evie."

I burst into laughter as my cell phone rang. I fumbled for it in my purse and answered, still grinning.

"Jolene, it's Isabelle. Are you busy right now?"

"Not really."

"Can you come give me a lift? Please?"

An odd request, considering Isabelle lived an hour away. I thought I detected a note of desperation in her voice, too. "What's going on?"

"Can you just come? I'll tell you when you get here."

I checked the digital readout on my office wall clock. A little less than two more hours to closing time. Danny was at football practice right now, and he had a birthday sleepover party immediately following. I'd dropped the gift and his things off at his friend's house this morning, promising to pick him up at nine a.m. tomorrow. Ray could be at work for hours.

Cory was slumped in his chair again, his brow furrowed, eyes clouded. He could use a trip to the gym to release some stress.

"We just decided to close up early today. I'll leave now. Where are you?"

"Sitting outside the jail."

EIGHTEEN

Two visits to jail in one day—an all-time high for me. I pressed the gas pedal of my Lexus to the floor and made it to Isabelle's town within forty-five minutes, worried and fearful after her call.

I found Isabelle sitting in the lobby of the police department on a scarred wooden bench. She did not look herself. On most work days, she wore form-fitting suits with fashionable shoes and elegant jewelry from her husband's jewelry store, attracting attention everywhere she went with the fine gems and her brilliant smile, two excellent assets. Isabelle's flat face and mousy brown hair tended toward homely, but those assets gave her the illusion of radiance.

Today, however, her flowered skirt had a tear in it, revealing the red slip she wore beneath. Her lightweight white sweater had a three-inch pull culminated by a hangman's loop, and her hair held leaves. Scratches on her skin were visible at her wrists. Pink pumps in her hand matched the flowers on her skirt. In her other hand, she clutched her open purse. Gold jewelry gleamed inside it.

Isabelle threw her arms around me and choked back tears. She and I had roomed together for six years at college while we pursued our undergraduate and master's degrees in business. She'd been brave enough never to question me about my mother's death and to stay at my house with Erica and my dad, who defined eccentric. She was also the only one in my life who never called me by a nickname. I liked to think that meant she took me seriously.

I hugged her tight, then pulled back to assess the damage again. The most dreadful thought popped into my mind. "Isabelle, have you been"—I lowered my voice to a whisper—"raped?"

She burst into laughter. "Oh, thank God you came. No, I have not."

"Then what happened?"

A uniformed officer passed by us, glanced at Isabelle, and shook his head with a smile.

She looped her arm through mine. "Let's go outside to your car, shall we?"

Once we settled comfortably in my bucket seats, she fussed with the rip in her skirt, trying to smooth the two raw edges together. "I did something really stupid. Promise not to tell even Ray."

I thought of how much trouble that same promise to Cory had created. Then I went ahead and made it anyway.

Isabelle sucked in a deep breath. "This afternoon I decided to take time off to do some yard work with Jack. Put away the patio furniture for the winter, stuff like that. He'd been home all morning, and I had just gotten home and was going upstairs to get changed when the phone rang. I heard him tell someone that he'd come by, just like last time. Then he came upstairs to tell me he needed to get fertilizer for the grass. He took off. I got in the car and followed him.

"He went to another bed and breakfast, not too far from our house. I waited for him to come out. A half hour went by. I decided to park a ways down and peek in the windows to see if I could spot him. I went around the house, looking in all the windows. One room was a bedroom and two people were in the bed … ah … doing it. I couldn't see their faces, but, of course, I thought it was Jack and another woman. I pressed my nose right up against the window." She closed her eyes.

I tried to wait patiently. I couldn't. "And?"

Her eyes flew open. "And it wasn't him. It was some other couple. She saw me first and screamed. Then the guy saw me and leapt out of bed. And I saw … well … all of him. I tried to run, but I got caught in the shrubs. It slowed me down. By the time I got around to the driveway, a man had come out on the porch. Not the naked one. I think it was the owner. He came running after me. I got in my car and peeled out, but he must have gotten my license number because the police pulled me over a few blocks down the road. They arrested me for peeping. They fingerprinted me and everything. It was awful and embarrassing."

A tear rolled down Isabelle's cheek and dripped off her chin. She didn't seem to notice.

I wanted to hug her again, but I was afraid she wouldn't make it through the rest of her story.

She breathed deep again. "I explained what happened. I apologized up and down. I offered to pay for any damages to their shrubbery. The officer couldn't keep a straight face. He left me sitting in the interrogation room for a while, then he came back and said no one wanted to press any charges. The officer said I could go home.

"My car was towed to impound. I asked for a ride over there. He refused. He said I should call my husband. He said we needed to talk and now would be the perfect time."

She wrung her hands. "Oh, Jolene, I couldn't call Jack. I've been arrested. I have an arrest record. What if my clients find out? What if they hear why I was arrested?"

I took her hands in mine, stilling them. "I don't think anyone will find out, since you weren't charged or arraigned. We can go get your car. It'll be okay."

Isabelle's tears flowed freely. "I'm acting like a crazy person."

I fumbled in my purse for tissues and handed them to her. "Love will do that to you."

She blew her nose and dried her eyes. "I thought everything was going to be okay. Jack and I did it the other night. Twice. I thought maybe he had just been under stress or maybe he was just getting older."

"Was he still at the bed and breakfast when you left?"

"I don't know. It all happened so fast. I don't know if his car was still there or not. But I already talked to him. He called and left a message while I was at the jail, wanting to know where I went. I called him back and told him I had an emergency at work. He seemed to buy my story. He offered to pick up Cassidy and make dinner." She buried her face in her hands. "God, I am such an idiot."

"You are not an idiot."

"And that officer. The way he talked to me. He was so patronizing. I felt like a two-year-old."

"He's just glad you're not a real peeper. It would blow their profiling to have women in flowered skirts and pink pumps take up peeping."

Isabelle's smile was weak, but a smile nonetheless. "Don't ever tell anyone, okay?"

"I swear."

"What am I going to tell Jack when he sees me like this?"

I thought for a second. "Let's get your car, then we'll stop by the mall. I'll go in and buy you a new outfit while you pick the leaves out of your hair. Jack won't notice a new outfit, will he?"

"God, no." She glanced at her scratched wrists. "Just make sure it's long-sleeved."

I arrived home around seven thirty. Ray's patrol car was parked in the driveway. He was in the living room, dressed in jeans and a T-shirt, watching the sports channel on the flat screen over the fireplace while eating leftover stir fry.

He didn't acknowledge my arrival, a sure sign he was angry. I eased onto the couch beside him, picking up the pillow Erica made to hold to my chest. I fingered the words on it, thinking Isabelle was like another sister to me.

I contemplated the best way to approach Ray and settled on a neutral course. "Are you in for the night?"

His gaze never left the television. "I'm on patrol tomorrow. Max and Gumby are going to Albany. They have appointments with the Potters, the Gleasons, and even Brennan's father, who is apparently half dead in a hospice."

"Really? What's wrong with him?"

"Pancreatic cancer."

"Does Brennan know that?"

"I don't know what Brennan knows, and Catherine won't let him tell me." Ray scraped the bottom of his bowl with a piece of cornbread, soaking up the remaining stir fry sauce.

He was mad, all right. I tried to make amends. "I saw Catherine today. She wanted me to tell her everything I planned to tell the sheriff."

"Did you?"

"No, I wanted to tell him first. Is it okay if Cory and I talk to her?"

"Now you're checking with me?" Ray gathered his dishes. "Now that I'm not the one to ask?"

"Because you're not assigned to the case?"

"Yes."

"And you're disappointed?" I wanted to say "angry," but why fuel the fire?

Ray rose off the couch and disappeared into the kitchen. "I'm the errand boy. I got the warrant to search Brennan's house. We collected the yearbook and check registers."

I followed Ray. "Does Brennan know you took all that?"

"Yes. The sheriff and Max asked him about the payments."

"What did he say?"

"I don't know. I'm not assigned to the case."

I didn't know what to say. It was highly unusual that the department wasn't talking among themselves, sharing information and theories. Ray must be devastated to be left out—and it was all my doing.

I focused on the facts he did know. "So Max and Gumby are going to talk to everyone tomorrow? Cory and I never got to meet Suzanne Gleason."

"She's on the appointment list. They'll probe into the divorce and try to map out exactly where she was when her husband ended up in the street. Ask about insurance money, that kind of thing."

"And her son?"

"Again, probe into their relationship. Ask if he benefits from insurance policies."

"That's a lot for one day."

Ray rinsed his empty beer bottle and set it in the bin under the sink. "It's a start. The guy who shot the YouTube video is in Europe for the next month working. His wife can't find the original. She's waiting for him to call her."

"Will Brennan have to sit in jail all that time?"

"I don't know if a judge will let him out on bail now that two deaths are linked to him. I'm guessing his fingerprints will be all over the oar used to knock Engle into the water. It's his dock. The message makes it look like he called the office and lured Engle to his house. Catherine is good, though. She might work it."

Ray leaned his back against the kitchen countertop. "Not to change the subject, but Danny called to remind me that it was our turn to bring the team snacks. I doubt if I'm going to be able to make the game tomorrow, but I can run over to the grocery store and pick up some sports drinks and granola bars now. Do we need anything else?"

"Nothing I can think of. Do you think Brennan—"

Ray held up his hand. "Enough. I'm not going to talk about this with you anymore. You know if you and Cory weren't involved, I'd be on this case."

"I know, Ray. I'm sorry. I really am." If Cory and I hadn't gotten involved, Wayne Engle might still be with us, too. That would be tougher for me to forgive and forget.

My dismay must have shown on my face, because Ray's expression softened. He moved closer to run his thumb over my lower lip then brought his lips close to my ear. "Hey, we're definitely home alone tonight. While I'm out, maybe you'll think of ways to make it up to me."

His hot breath sent chills through me. My mouth felt dry. "I'll wear your Christmas present from last year."

He pulled away and smiled wickedly. "I forgive you already."

I admired the view his tight jeans provided as he headed for the front door. God, I loved following the man through the grocery store, taking in that view. How fortunate that he still loved and wanted me, too—even if I did cost him a big case. Ray was never one to hold a grudge.

He paused before leaving the house. "Check the mail. I think you'll find it interesting."

I went over to the wicker basket we kept by the back door and flipped through all the unsolicited catalogs, bank card offers, postcards for oil changes and new mufflers, the request for a water meter read, and a few unwanted bills. A single blue envelope was left.

I flipped open the already torn flap and pulled out the card from inside. Confetti spilled from it to my floor.

Balloons decorated its face. The card cover read, "A Really, Really Big Surprise!"

Inside in blue script, the card said, "You're invited to a surprise party of monumental proportions. Isabelle and Jack are celebrating their ten-year wedding anniversary. Please join us for the celebration to end all celebrations." A popular party house near their home was the site for the celebration, on a Friday night two weeks away.

A list of local bed and breakfasts was included for out of town guests with a handwritten note from Jack, indicating he had blocked rooms at all of them. I felt certain the one he visited today was included.

Another handwritten note fell to the floor. I picked it up. It said, "Jolene, please, please keep this party a secret from Isabelle. She does so much for me, and I really want to surprise her. I didn't give you that much notice about the party so you won't have to keep the secret as long. I can't wait to see Isabelle's face! Thanks, Jack."

I couldn't wait to see it either.

NINETEEN

SUNDAY I STOOD ON the sidelines of Danny's first football game, surrounded by a group of parents who were even more excited than their kids. The fathers analyzed every play and call, yelling out advice to their sons. Mothers shrieked words of encouragement and triumph every time a play went off successfully and groaned each time the opposite was true. For the most part, the players ignored them, undoubtedly playing their best and hoping not to be the one who messed up during the game. They all wanted to be the one to make the winning touchdown and be carried away on the shoulders of their peers. I knew Danny did.

He'd chattered nonstop on the drive over. Every topic started with, "You know what, Jolene?" Then he'd proceed to tell me about his team or the coach or the professional football games he watched with Ray and how his team tried to emulate some of the plays. He talked about the different football positions and why he was a running back. He repeated dozens of things Ray had told him, making me feel all the more guilty to be the one with him at the game instead of Ray, stuck on patrol because of me.

Although I'd done my best to make everything up to Ray last night, he'd left for work this morning with a dejected look on his face. It wasn't even the patrol duty so much as missing this very important game. So far, though, he hadn't missed much.

Danny spent the first quarter on the bench. Apparently his team had a lot of players and the coach was making sure every player got in the game. But Danny cheered on his teammates, whooping when plays went well and screaming, "Shake it off" when they didn't.

The opposing team's players never changed, although they had plenty of benchwarmers. It was clear all their superstars were in the game. They scored two touchdowns, including one following a fumble by one of Danny's teammates. His failure turned out to be good luck for Danny. The coach sent him in to replace the other boy, who sat on the bench and hung his head. His shame was almost palpable.

The next couple of plays, the ball was carried by or thrown to other players, not Danny. He still bounded up to the huddle and listened intently to the quarterback each time, nodding with enthusiasm as they broke and hustling to his position on the line.

On the final snap before the end of the first half, Danny got the ball. He froze for a moment, seeming shocked that he'd caught it, then turned and headed for the goal line. His legs pumped, ball tucked tight to his chest, his other arm outstretched to ward off a tackle. With a final burst of speed, he crossed the line.

Touchdown.

My eyes filled with tears. I clapped until my hands stung.

Danny danced, his knees knocking and arms whirling. His teammates jumped on top of him.

"Yeah, Danny, way to make the play! Wooo!"

I turned to find Ray behind me, screaming, his arm raised in triumph.

"Aren't you on duty?"

Ray's gaze never left the field. "Yep. Think of this as community relations."

I rolled my eyes.

Danny jogged off the field with his team.

Ray high fived him. "Great play. You look good out there."

Danny's eyes lit up. "Thanks. Can we get the snacks out now?"

"Sure." I walked over to the cooler and lifted the lid. The kids crowded in, grabbing sports drinks and energy bars from the box Danny offered. I backed away to give them room, ending up next to Ray.

"Danny's got good hands. He's got speed. He reminds me of Sean."

Sean, Ray's brother, had played football in high school, a running back no less. Ray and I attended every game. Sean was a star player, never on the bench, always in the game. He dreamed of being a professional athlete, and the scouts encouraged him. But in his senior year, he got injured. His knee was shot. He lost his drive for everything. Until he discovered drugs, that is. I hoped Danny wouldn't turn out to be another Sean. "He definitely looks good out there. I think he's having fun."

As they ate, the boys replayed every moment on the field, clearly pumped after getting on the scoreboard. When the whistle blew for the third quarter, Danny hustled to the bench to watch the defense take the field.

Tired from my big night, I headed for the bleachers and took a seat about halfway up. Ray continued to follow Danny up and down the field whenever the offense was in the game, his lips moving although I couldn't hear what he said. He'd become one of those fathers, blending into the sideline masses.

The quarterback passed the ball to Danny, too high. Danny leapt into the air and caught it, landing nimbly and running for the goal.

I stood up. "Go, Danny. Go, Danny, go."

Touchdown.

Danny did his little dance again. Ray whooped and hollered, slapping Danny on the back when he ran off the field. Danny beamed. Even the coach high fived him.

With the score tied, play grew more aggressive and each team took more risks, some of which ended badly. In the last quarter, after a fumble and a turnover, Danny's team got the ball again, close to their own goal. At the signal from his coach, Danny joined the offense as they took the field.

The first pass went to the other running back, who ran for ten yards before the visiting team took him down, a little more roughly than necessary. With the second handoff, the quarterback looked for Danny, who was twenty yards down the field. The pass left the quarterback's hand, spiraling downfield. Danny got into position. He caught the ball. A player from the other team slammed him to the ground. Danny didn't get up.

I leapt to my feet and started down the bleacher stairs, my heart beating wildly as I thought, "Don't let him be hurt. Don't let him be hurt."

Danny sat up. He shook his head.

I stopped running.

Danny rose to his knees, then his feet. He jogged back to his team's huddle as the crowd cheered.

I breathed a sigh of relief and started back up the bleachers.

A man at the edge of the woods caught my eye. He was on our side of the field, way down by Danny's team's goal post, hovering just outside the tree line, well back from the field itself. A baseball cap shaded his face. He had on jeans and a T-shirt.

It was a strange place to stand and observe the game. I wondered if he lived in one of the homes on the other side of the trees.

The quarterback threw another pass to Danny, who caught it but landed with his knees on the ground.

The man pumped his fists, obviously rooting for Danny's team. He moved closer to the field and me.

I thought I saw a dark spot like a tattoo on his arm. I froze.

Danny's team fired off another play. The ball went to Danny again. He ran.

The man stepped forward eagerly. I saw the swish of his ponytail. My heart sank.

It was Danny's father.

I scanned the sidelines, looking for Ray. His attention was glued to the field, where Danny had been tackled just inside the thirty-yard line.

Why had Danny's father come to the game? Surely he realized the odds Ray would be here. Why take the risk? He was a wanted felon. Did he think Ray wouldn't recognize him?

"Go back in the woods. Go back in the woods." I willed Mr. Phillips to hear the words as I muttered them under my breath.

Ray moved down the sideline, no doubt jockeying to witness Danny's next touchdown.

The ball snapped. The quarterback caught it, jogging backward as he studied the field.

Danny darted back and forth on the ten-yard line, struggling to get open. The other running back did the same. Then he stumbled and went down.

The quarterback's focus shifted solely to Danny. He waited, then threw.

The ball flew through the air.

Danny leapt. He caught it. His feet hit the ground. He spun and raced for the goal line.

When he crossed it, our side of the field went wild, cheering, slapping each other on the back, and hugging.

Mr. Phillips pumped his fists again. He moved toward the field.

"Go back in the woods. Go back in the woods." A bead of sweat trickled off my brow.

His mouth opened.

"Don't yell out. Don't yell out." My cautions disappeared in the din.

Danny finished his victory dance and headed off the field, surrounded by his teammates, a huge grin on his face.

Mr. Phillips' lips moved.

Danny's head tipped. He spun around, looking.

I moved down the bleacher steps. "No, no." I hit the ground running, no longer able to see Danny or Mr. Phillips.

But I could see Ray. He'd stepped back from the sideline crowd, only yards from Mr. Phillips. Ray had him in his sights, his hand on his belt.

"No, Ray, no. Don't do it. Please don't do it." I brushed past another father, knocking his shoulder. He didn't even notice me; he was so buoyed by the touchdown.

Ray started walking toward Danny's father, who didn't seem to notice him, his eyes still glued on the field, his arm waving in the air.

I wondered if Danny could see him. I hoped not.

Ray kept moving.

"No, Ray, let him go. Let him go. Please, let him go."

Mr. Phillips saw Ray too late. He took a step back, but he didn't run.

Ray already had the cuffs off his belt. He slapped one around Mr. Phillips' wrist.

I stopped running. I looked at the field. The other team had the ball. They were rushing to get off a game-saving play. I couldn't see Danny.

Ray cuffed Mr. Phillips other hand and led him away.

The crowd on the sidelines didn't even notice. They were too wrapped up in the last minutes of the game, screaming out advice to the defense. A couple of the boys moved toward our cooler with wicked glints in their eyes, perhaps preparing to douse their coach with the ice.

Without another glance at the field, Ray opened the door to his patrol car and helped Mr. Phillips inside. He slammed the door and got in the driver's seat.

He drove off.

The whistle blew. The crowd on our side of the field roared.

I turned and found Danny right behind me, gazing at the parking lot with tears streaming down his face.

TWENTY

"Find him, Ray, or don't come home!" I slammed down the phone.

Maury jumped and looked at Erica for guidance. She didn't blink.

I sank into my living room couch across from their chairs. "Should we keep looking?"

Danny had run from me when I reached out to comfort him, throwing down his helmet and accelerating to a speed unequaled on the field. The last I saw of him, he disappeared into the same woods his father came out of.

After an hour of waiting, then an hour of searching on my own, I'd called Erica and Maury to help. We split our town into quadrants and drove each street at less than ten miles per hour, hoping to catch sight of Danny. Erica then checked some of her favorite old hideouts. I returned to the empty field to see if Danny had come back there. It was all to no avail. He'd now been missing for almost eight hours.

Erica examined her thumbnail. "Danny knows how to hotwire cars and he can drive. He could be in New York City by now, Jo." She chewed the corner of her thumb.

I wondered if she would rather Danny didn't come home. She'd run off and gotten married right after he arrived, as though she needed to be first in line for someone's attention and realized he'd displaced her for mine. Still, she'd leapt in the car to help me search for him. "Ray said no cars have been reported stolen." Not to mention I'd made Danny promise me a long time ago that he wouldn't drive anymore—not until he reached sixteen.

"You said no cars were left in the parking lot after the game or parked on the neighboring streets. Maybe Danny found the car his father came in."

"You're not making me feel better, Erica." My only hope was that Danny would never leave his dad, who now sat in the county jail, thanks to Ray, probably in the cell right next to Brennan Rowe, thanks to me. Ray and I were a two-person life-wreaking crew.

"Sorry. Danny'll be back. Where else has he got to go?" She got up, smoothing her tight jeans down her legs. "We're going home. I don't want to be here when Ray gets here. I've seen you two fight before. Maury can't take it."

First of all, Ray and I didn't fight. We engaged in brief skirmishes, and, in the past, most of those had been about Erica, who used to live with us. How very like her to overlook that. Ray and I had different approaches to managing her behavior, just as we did with Danny's behavior.

Maury made a face as though offended at the notion he might be too weak, but he didn't hesitate to hop up and follow Erica out the door. I couldn't blame him. I'd had nothing nice to say to Ray for the last six hours. Now it was eight o'clock and my boy was still missing, his heart broken by the one man who had promised to take care of him.

I would never forgive Ray if Danny didn't come home.

I'd checked Danny's room when I got home to make sure he hadn't already been there and packed up his stuff. Of course, when Danny had come to us, he'd brought only the clothes on his back. He might not think anything of leaving the same way. But where would he go? His father was his only living relative. They'd lived in a car and on friends' couches before his father left him with us. Danny had nowhere to go. This house was his home now. We were his family. Too bad he couldn't stand the sight of us.

Ray had called to inform me of Danny's father's arrest. I informed him that we'd had the distinct displeasure of being witnesses to it and that Danny had run off. Ray promised to find him. He'd called to update me twice. After what I said to him a few minutes ago, I didn't expect him to call again—unless he found Danny. Then they could come home together.

In the meantime, all I could do was curl up in a fetal position on the living room couch, one eye on the phone, the other on the front door. Danny always used the front door. I willed him to walk though it.

The phone rang.

I snatched it up. "Danny?"

"Cory."

"Oh."

"But I'm calling about Danny."

"You know where he is?"

"No. Is he missing?"

"Yes." I filled Cory in on the football game and the arrest. He wasn't surprised to hear about Mr. Phillips. In fact, he confirmed my suspicions.

"He's in a holding cell next to Brennan."

"Brennan called you?"

"He heard the officer call Mr. Phillips by his name. He knew he had to be Danny's father from the scar on his neck and the tattoo."

The scar on Mr. Phillips' neck looked as though someone had tried to slice it open and finish him off. According to Danny, he'd gotten attacked in prison, the very reason he never, ever wanted to go back there. The tattoo, a heart with a sword running through it and a blacked-out scroll beneath it, was a remnant of a love gone bad. The man had an unhappy past, losing his wife and then her sister, his second love, to untimely deaths. He might have given up stealing cars if not for the fact that he couldn't read and had no other significant income prospects. Of course, Ray said that was no excuse. I had to agree, albeit unwillingly.

"Brennan didn't see Ray, so he asked to make a phone call. He wanted to be sure you knew Mr. Phillips was there."

I knew all right. "Did Brennan say anything about his case?"

"Actually, he said a lot, but you don't want to hear about it now. It can wait."

"Tell me. It will take my mind off Danny." And Ray. "Was he angry at you for looking through his things?"

"He didn't say."

"What did he say?"

"His argument with Wayne wasn't about him being gay. They all found that out right after senior prom night, when Monica expected fireworks and Brennan didn't deliver. She dumped him and started dating Wayne, who had a reputation for delivering."

"Really?" I sat up. "Interesting."

"It gets better. Wayne dated a lot of girls in high school, except for Monica and her friend Elizabeth. It made Brennan sick to think of him with Monica. She was special to Brennan, even if they weren't right for each other."

"And?"

"Brennan tried to tell her what kind of guy Wayne was. She didn't care. Wayne was the right kind of guy compared to Brennan. So after graduation, Wayne, Monica, and Elizabeth were the three Musketeers. Brennan didn't really talk to them again until Monica called to invite him to go with them to the five-year reunion. He said he was so surprised to hear from her that he said 'yes' without thinking. When Wayne couldn't ride with them, he was relieved."

"Does he think that's what they argued about at the reunion? How Wayne moved in on Monica?"

"He doesn't remember, but that's his guess."

"Did he say anything about his argument with James Gleason?"

"Only that James still thought he was driving drunk and didn't care enough about Monica."

"Did he tell you anything else?"

"Not really. He ran out of time."

"You must be thrilled that he called."

"I would be if he had really wanted to talk to me. He just called me to get the message to you and Ray."

"But he confided in you. He answered the question you asked him that night you had dinner at his house. That's a good sign, Cory."

"I guess so. Listen, do you want me to help you look for Danny?"

"No thanks. Ray's got the department helping him now. I'm going to stay here and wait."

"Call me as soon as you hear anything, no matter what time."

I promised and disconnected. Feeling chilled, I headed into our bedroom to get a sweater. I flicked the light switch and walked into the closet. Chunks of mud covered the carpeted floor. "What the—?"

The biggest pile of mud lay in front of my dresses, which hung to the floor, hiding the wall behind. I shoved them aside and gasped.

"Danny."

He still had on his grass-stained and muddy uniform, his face a film of dirt. His gaze remained trained on the floor, refusing to acknowledge me.

I held out my arms. "Danny, come here, buddy. I was so worried about you."

He blinked.

"Danny, we'll work it out. It'll be okay. We'll take care of your dad, I promise." I wiggled my outstretched fingers. "Come on, it's okay."

He fell into my arms, nearly knocking me over. His body shuddered. Great sobs burst from his boney chest. "I want my dad. I want my dad."

I pulled him tight and rubbed his back, remembering those words. Danny had said them almost a year ago, the night he came to live with us. I thought we'd come a long way since then.

But now, we were back to square one.

TWENTY-ONE

MONDAY MORNING I ROLLED off the edge of the bed, where I'd spent the night trying to keep as far away from Ray as possible and wondering how to proceed from here. Ray had come home last night and lectured Danny for an hour, first about how running away from problems never solved anything, then about how crime cannot go unpunished. Danny sat through the whole talk in silence, only asking if he could go to bed when Ray finished.

I had turned on my heel and gone to bed as well, irritated Ray couldn't sense Danny's despair over his father's arrest. Ray would not be open to a little constructive criticism, especially when he undoubtedly was feeling plenty guilty already, even though he'd never admit it.

A steaming hot shower didn't ease the tension in my shoulders. Before the alarm clock woke Ray, I managed to dress in jeans and a long-sleeved lime T-shirt and head into the kitchen, where I fried bacon and scrambled eggs to serve Danny his favorite breakfast. I made enough for Ray, too.

When our bathroom shower water turned on again, I went in to wake Danny, who moaned when I shook his shoulder. "I don't feel good."

My hand flew to his forehead, automatically checking for a fever. "In what way?"

"My stomach hurts."

"You didn't eat last night. Your stomach's empty. I made you bacon and eggs. Food will make you feel better. Get up and get dressed now." I didn't wait for an answer, walking out of his room but leaving the door open. A few minutes later, I heard his bureau drawers sliding open and closed.

Danny and Ray converged on the kitchen table at the same time. They exchanged grunts. The food was on their plates. Ray dug in. Danny pushed his eggs around his plate.

I sat down with them, sipping my orange juice and not feeling all that hungry myself. Most mornings the two of them talked and joked. This morning the silence was oppressive. "Eat your breakfast, Danny. The bus will be here in ten minutes."

He obliged me by sticking a whole slice of bacon in his mouth, making his cheeks bulge.

Ray finished and carried his dishes to the sink. "I'll pick you up from practice today, Danny, and take you to see your dad."

Danny kept his face lowered to his plate, gnawing another piece of bacon. "I'm not going to practice."

"Why not?"

"I don't want to play football anymore. I'm quitting the team." He spoke around a mouthful of food, spitting tiny pieces.

Ray grimaced but chose to ignore Danny's lack of table manners to pursue the bigger issue. "You can't quit. You're committed to finish the season."

"I don't want to."

Ray laid his hand on Danny's shoulder. "We all have to do things we don't want to do. It's part of life. You made a commitment to the team. I'll pick you up after practice."

I knew that statement was the closest Ray would come to an apology for arresting his dad. I just didn't know if Danny had the maturity to grasp it.

Ray bent to kiss me. I let him peck me on the cheek, planning to call him later to ask what we were going to do to help Danny's father, who wasn't likely to have money for a lawyer.

When the front door closed behind Ray, Danny shoved the last of his eggs into his mouth and washed them down with juice. Then he let out a tremendous burp.

I half-gasped, half-giggled. "Does your tummy feel better now?"

"I guess so."

"Go brush your teeth. The bus will be here in a minute."

Danny remained seated, shoulders slumped, eyes downcast. "I don't want to go to school today. Can you take me to see my dad?"

I stood and gathered up his dishes. "You have to go to school. Ray said he'd take you after practice. I'll call and see about getting your dad an attorney today."

"Can you ask Catherine Thomas?"

Shocked, I almost dropped his plate on the floor. "How do you know about her?"

181

"Ray talks about her. He says she's a great attorney."

Once again, I tried not to let the little green monster eat at me. And once again, I failed. "She is a great attorney. I will call her. I promise. Now go brush your teeth."

I loaded the dishwasher and met Danny at the front door. He had his backpack in hand. I leaned in to kiss his cheek. Then I opened the door as the school bus puffed to a halt at the curb.

Normally, Danny would bolt out the door and onto the bus. This morning, he hesitated. "Jolene, do you think the guys on the team saw Ray arrest my dad?"

My heart broke. Poor kid, he must be embarrassed. Humiliated. "I don't think so. The other team was pushing hard to score. I'm sure they all were watching the end of the game."

"But they saw me run off."

I didn't know what to say to that. My eyes had been glued to his disappearing back. I didn't know what everyone else saw. "I think they were too busy celebrating the win. Maybe they figured you had to leave early."

The bus driver tooted his horn.

I waved to him, hoping he wouldn't pull away. "You have to go now, Danny. Everything will be all right. Don't worry."

He nodded, shouldered his backpack, and ran out the door. But for the first time ever, he failed to wave to me as the bus pulled away. I preferred to think he just forgot.

With nothing to do at home but worry, I decided to go to work, even though on Mondays Asdale Auto Imports was traditionally closed. I'd wear my jeans instead of a business suit and get a little cleaning done. Although my customers were the most meticulous people—as evidenced by the perfect condition of their precious cars—dust did build up in the corners of the showroom from time to time. Today was a perfect day to make it disappear.

Driving to work didn't keep me from worrying about the strain on Ray and Danny's relationship, not to mention Ray's and mine. Or the fact I now knew and cared about two people in the Wachobe County Jail, an all-time record which gave me acid indigestion. It also didn't help that all the questions I'd asked of Brennan's old friends had been a catalyst for murder and his subsequent incarceration or that the loss of my Ferrari had led to Mr. Phillips' arrest. Everyone I cared about was hurting, including me. Worse, I knew I'd met a murderer—and it wasn't Brennan Rowe. If only I knew who it was.

After unlocking the door and turning off the showroom alarm, I sat behind my laminated wood desk and dialed Catherine Thomas' cell phone, determined to take action where I could.

She answered on the first ring. "Jolene, I was going to call you today."

"Were you? I must be psychic." I tried for levity but fell short.

"I want to talk to you and Cory. I hired an investigator who's going to retrace your steps, and I wanted to get as much information in advance as I can before sending him to Albany and Binghamton."

Her investigator would be the third round of questions for all these people, after ours and the police's today. I doubted the investigator would get very far. "Sure, no problem, do you want us to come to you?"

"I'm on my way over to Wachobe. I'm due in court this morning for Brennan's arraignment. I can stop by your home or office afterward, around eleven o'clock."

I wondered if she'd be able to get Brennan out on bail but decided not to ask. She'd let us know when we saw her, no doubt. "Okay, I'll call Cory. Why don't you meet us at the shop?" I spoke quickly. "But I need to ask you one more thing before you hang up."

"Yes?"

"Can you handle another client?"

"Depends, who's the client?"

"Danny's father, Mr. Phillips. Ray arrested him yesterday at Danny's football game."

Catherine's gasp made the phone lines crackle. "At the game? In front of Danny?"

I explained the whole situation to Catherine, relieved I wasn't the only one who found Ray's action upsetting.

"So you think Mr. Phillips stole the Ferrari and sold it for Danny's college fund? What proof do you have that he took it?"

Here was the difficult part. "I think Danny gave his father the alarm code for my shop. I know he saw me punch it in several times. I never thought to hide it from him, but when the Ferrari disappeared, I realized Danny must have given it to him."

"He'll never admit it."

"Not now, that's for sure."

"How old is he?"

"Just twelve."

"Does Ray know?"

"I'm sure he guessed. He put Mr. Phillips at the top of the suspect list."

"How many other known car thieves were visiting Wachobe at that time?"

"None that I know of."

Catherine was silent so long I thought she'd hung up. Then she spoke. "I don't think even Ray would expect Danny to testify against his father. I'll take the case pro bono. You and I never had this conversation about Danny and the alarm code."

This time I knew she hung up. I hit the "end" button on my cell, hoping she was right about Ray.

Then I dialed Cory's number. He agreed to meet Catherine and me at the shop at eleven.

With an hour and a half to kill, I wandered into the showroom, intent on dusting and mopping and maybe even cleaning the windows.

I pulled the mop bucket from the closet and headed into the garage to fill it at the sink. With the bucket in one hand and the mop in the other, I moved to the front of the showroom and commenced work.

I hadn't mopped more than a few square feet when I looked out the window and saw Celeste Martin crossing the street. Or should I say, stopping traffic?

As she sashayed across Main Street, Celeste held her hand out toward oncoming cars like Danny did on the football field to ward off a tackle. It worked better for her. The cars all stopped, even though Celeste not only jaywalked but jaywalked in a diagonal direction from the Talbots store she managed right toward the door to my shop.

"No, no, no." I wondered if I could run to the door and lock it in time. Could she see me through the tinted showroom window? Celeste was a champion gossip and the root of our town's grapevine. I didn't think I had the strength for her today.

I was still thinking about hiding when the bells on the entry tinkled and she sailed into the showroom, not a hair out of place on her perfectly coifed blond—though not naturally blond—head. "Jolene, you poor thing."

"What?" I resisted the urge to ward her off with my mop, choosing to lean on it instead.

"I heard about Brennan's arrest. Cory must be beside himself. Is he here?" She cast her glance about in such a showy manner that I knew she knew he wasn't. "I just wanted to lend my moral support. I certainly don't think Brennan killed anyone. He has a lot of skeletons in his closet but not real ones." She held her hands clasped in front of her like a schoolgirl, a perfectly accessorized schoolgirl with a size two figure and a pricey wardrobe from Talbots, where she was the manager.

That old assertion about Brennan again. "Cory's not here." But I wished he was.

"No, of course not, it's Monday. Why are you here?"

Perhaps the real reason Celeste had crossed the street. Asdale Auto Imports hadn't been open on a Monday since my father passed away almost six years ago. It was a serious break in the routine. Celeste followed everyone's routine.

I waved my hand over the floor. "Just catching up on some mopping."

Celeste nodded. "I noticed you had the shop closed several days last week. Is everything all right?"

"It's fine." I didn't elaborate, hoping she'd take the hint and leave.

No such luck. Instead, she seemed to hunker down a bit, leaning against the Austin Healey. "How's Danny?"

"Fine, thanks."

"Really? I heard Ray arrested his father at the football game yesterday. Danny must be very concerned."

My mouth went dry. Trust Celeste to know all the gossip. I could only hope she hadn't heard it from one of Danny's teammates' parents. Would the arrest be the talk of Danny's school today, too? "Where'd you hear that?"

"One of my friend's sons works at the jail."

I nodded to acknowledge her statement, relieved Danny's friends might not be aware.

"How's Danny taking it?"

"He'll be fine. Everybody will be fine."

"You have a very positive attitude, Jolene. I've always admired that about you."

I blinked, uncertain if she spoke in jest and wondering what would come next. She was priming me for something.

"Well, I just wanted to offer my support." Celeste started to back toward the door. "Let me know if there's anything I can do to help Brennan or Danny's father. I think of you all like family."

Perhaps that was because she had dated my father once, unbeknown to me. Never mind their twenty-plus-year age gap. Maybe just once she wasn't here to fish for information. "You know, Celeste, I do have one question for you."

She stopped and smiled. "Yes?"

"That rumor about skeletons in Brennan's closet? Or what he's been hiding in the foundations of his buildings all these years. How did those get started? Where did they come from?"

"Oh. Let me think." Celeste closed her eyelids. I could almost see her move from one stop along the grapevine to the next like a ball in a pinball machine. Ding, ding, ding. Hit the paddle, keep the story going. Celeste's friends and family connections were unparalleled. Church, exercise class, the merchants association, book club, volunteer work: all excellent places to cull information. She could look through a window anywhere in this town and know exactly who lived in the house, maybe even the remaining balance on their mortgage and the last time they went to church.

I waited patiently.

Her eyelids flew open. "I started it."

My jaw dropped.

Celeste waved her hand. "I know it's hard to believe. But I think I did."

Not hard to believe, just hard to believe she'd admit it. I recovered. "How?"

"As soon as Brennan moved to Wachobe, he opened a bank account at the bank where my cousin's niece works. He wrote a check for cash every month for five thousand dollars." Celeste bugged her eyes to emphasize the amount and the oddity.

I arranged my expression to surprised and shocked, since that seemed to be the reaction she sought.

"Then he went to the grocery store with the cash. My friend at church manages the store."

I knew that. I nodded.

Celeste seemed annoyed, as though she could tell I already knew this part. "Where he would ask for a five thousand dollar money order, which he put in an envelope and mailed."

Now I gave her the jerk of surprise she'd been waiting for, and she preened. "Do you know who he mailed it to?"

Celeste pursed her lips and rolled her eyes skyward. "I don't recall the name, but it went to an Albany address."

"To the Potters?"

Her gaze shot to me. "Yes!" Celeste jumped up and down like a contestant on a quiz show. "To a William Potter."

I knew the answer but asked the question anyway. "Does Brennan still mail the money?"

"He stopped over a year ago."

"Do you know why?"

Her face dropped. "No."

Finally, something I knew that she didn't. Brennan helped pay off Elizabeth Potter's hospital bills, just like he said. Perhaps the sheriff's department could obtain the financial records to confirm it.

"But how did the rumor about Brennan burying stuff in his foundations get started?"

Celeste had the good grace to look ashamed. "I said the payment looked like he had a skeleton in his closet. Then the next time I heard it, it was that he had hidden something in the foundation of his building. You know, people never repeat things exactly the way you say them." She sniffed.

How true, not that Celeste ever worried about the truth. Like all gossips, her interest lay in the titillation, not the truth. But apparently she liked to be quoted accurately. Go figure.

I took the high road. "Thank you for sharing that story with me, Celeste. You may very well have helped Brennan."

"Wonderful!" She stepped closer to me. "I do have one question for you, though."

Ah, she'd been priming me all along. "Okay."

"Was Brennan really having an affair with the dead guy, Wayne Engle?"

TWENTY-TWO

By the time Cory and Catherine walked through the door to the showroom together at ten fifty-eight, I had considered and dismissed the theory Celeste presented dozens of times. She said it was the latest rumor around town—and not one of her own making. The source, she believed, was the wife of someone who worked at the sheriff's office. At first, she thought that might be me. After I ridiculed the rumor, she reconsidered. In fact, she stormed off in a huff, bringing the traffic on Main Street to a screeching halt as she headed back to Talbots in time to unlock the door for business.

Cory also laughed off the rumor as the three of us sat around the conference table in the showroom an hour later. "No way. Take it from me, Wayne Engle was not gay. He was a ladies' man. Didn't you see those women working in his office? They told his story."

Catherine opened a leather binder and ran her pen down a list of names. "Funny you should say that. I've got their names right here: Pam Sullivan, Missy Temple, Silvia Porter, and Elizabeth, or

Beth as she prefers, Smith. Anyone want to guess who Elizabeth Smith is?"

Cory and I exchanged puzzled glances. "We met an Elizabeth Potter." A vision of her climbing out of her Honda Accord in her driveway flashed before me, followed by a memory of the same color Accord in the parking lot at Wayne Engle's office. I recalled Mrs. Potter saying that her daughter had been married and divorced twice. "Are they the same woman?"

Catherine nodded. "It gets better. Guess the name of the witness who claimed Brennan pushed James Gleason into the street at the festival."

I gasped.

After a moment, Cory responded, "Elizabeth Smith?"

"That's right. And even though both the surname and the last name are quite common, I confirmed it's the same woman. She really gets around."

Cory frowned in my direction. "How come you didn't recognize her?"

I remembered Evie's comments about Elizabeth Smith's new hair. "She had a new hairdo, and to be perfectly honest, I didn't look at her all that carefully on the day Gleason died." Some detective I made. Ray had been right all along to dismiss my investigative efforts. "So she was blackmailing Brennan, and Wayne knew about it."

Catherine tapped her pen on the paper in front of her. "Are you referring to the five thousand dollar monthly payments to her father?"

"Yes. She must have known something Brennan didn't want anyone to know—like the fact he was drinking the night Monica

Gleason died. No wonder both Wayne and Elizabeth denied it. Wayne probably got a cut of the money."

"Actually, Jolene, I spoke to Mr. Potter last night. He claimed Elizabeth didn't know anything about the payments. Brennan arranged to help pay her medical bills years ago. Mr. Potter didn't like accepting what he referred to as 'charity', but Brennan insisted. Only her father and mother knew where the money came from to pay off all her bills. They didn't tell Elizabeth."

Cory leaned forward to rest his forearms on the table. "Okay, but why didn't Brennan recognize her? She stood right next to him and pointed her finger in his face."

Catherine reached down into her briefcase, which was on the floor beside her chair, and pulled out a book. "She went through the windshield of the car and needed reconstructive surgery on her face: her nose, her eyelids, her cheekbones. She's not the same girl she was in high school." Catherine laid the book on the table. It was another yearbook from Brennan's graduation class, but this one had an unfamiliar girl's name embossed on it. She flipped through the pages until she came to Elizabeth Potter's photo.

I recalled Elizabeth's mother's very similar words to Cory and me. "Where did you get this yearbook?"

"I graduated from Albany Law School. It's a world-renowned school. The partners recruit from there all the time. One of our associates was born and raised in Albany. She attended the same high school as Brennan and was in her freshman year when he graduated. She wanted to help with his first case. She brought in her yearbook so I could see the two other people who were in the car crash with Brennan. Now she's helping with both cases."

Cory held out his hand for the yearbook. "May I see it?"

Catherine handed it over.

He turned the pages until he found Monica Gleason's photo. He studied it a moment, then spun the yearbook to face me. "Jo, look hard at her. Who does she look like that we met?"

I studied the blond hair, the sparkling eyes and the dimples. It was the dimples that reminded me. "Matthew Gleason."

"Exactly."

Catherine glanced back and forth between us. "She was his aunt. It's not surprising he would look like her. They share a gene pool."

I leaned back in my chair. "I wish we had met or at least seen his mother. He doesn't look anything like I remember his father. He had red hair and different features."

Cory snapped his fingers. "We saw her picture at their home. He doesn't look anything like the woman in the picture. She had dark-hair and glasses, remember, Jo?"

"I do. Can a dark-haired woman and a redhead make a blond?" I looked to Catherine for an answer.

She made a face. "I've had to research questions like that before for cases involving proving parentage. Genetics for hair color are not as firm as eye color. It has to do with the amount of color in the hair as well as the two alleles each parent passes on. It's certainly possible, but I would expect some red tints to the blond hair. How blond is Matthew?"

"Very. Like white blond."

Catherine reached for the yearbook and returned to Monica Gleason's photo. "It's a black and white photo. Hard to say how blond she was."

"She was very blond. Like white blond, too. We saw the two-by-three color photo of her. It was in Brennan's yearbook, remember Cory?"

He nodded. "She was pure blond."

I tapped the yearbook cover. "So was Wayne Engle. He and Monica had a relationship after high school. Maybe Matthew resulted. Maybe he was the cause of the argument at the reunion. Maybe Wayne hadn't stepped up to his responsibilities. That wouldn't go over well with Brennan, would it, Cory?"

Cory thought for a moment before answering. "He takes the law and business ethics very seriously. That's why he hates the rumor about what he's hiding in his foundations. He doesn't like any hint of irresponsibility. He conducts his personal life the same way."

"Interesting theory." Catherine made a note. "We'll confirm Matthew's parentage. Maybe Wayne Engle was named his godfather for that reason. Matthew might have pushed him in front of the car because he was angry not to be recognized as his child. We'll consider the possibility."

I wondered if Catherine knew more about the investigation than us. Perhaps the sheriff's department had improved the resolution enough on the YouTube video to recognize him. "Do you know for a fact that Matthew was close enough to the scene to do that?"

She shook her head. "It's still early in the investigation. The sheriff's department is keeping anything they find out very tight to the vest. That's why I need to send my own investigator. I'm just surmising from the questions they asked Brennan."

And she'd surmised Matthew was a suspect, which made sense. He certainly hadn't seemed too upset by the loss of his father.

She turned to a fresh sheet of paper. "All right, I have some questions for you two. First, I want to know everything that happened while you were in Albany and Binghamton."

Cory and I retold the story together as a tag team, filling in each other's pauses. Catherine asked a few questions but mostly just let us ramble along uninterrupted.

When we finished, Catherine wrote for a few minutes, then she scanned pages of notes she must have written on a previous day. "Are you sure Matthew Gleason said he met Brennan once?"

Cory and I glanced at each other to confirm. I nodded slowly. "Positive."

She made another note. I read it upside down. It said, "Get a picture of Matthew Gleason to show Brennan."

I shifted my gaze to Cory, who seemed to be reading the same line. His eyes met mine. He opened his mouth first. "Brennan doesn't know Matthew?"

Catherine closed her notebook and gave Cory a sympathetic glance. "I know it seems unfair, but I can't tell you anything Brennan said to me. At this point, I don't recommend you ask him questions, either. I know he calls you, but you don't want to know anything about this case. You could end up being called to testify against him. You don't want that, do you?"

Cory swallowed. "Definitely not. Jolene and I wondered if we caused Wayne Engle's death by asking as many questions as we did. We wanted to help Brennan, not hurt anyone."

Catherine pulled her briefcase onto her lap and tucked her notebook and pen away inside. "If it's any consolation, I think you helped his first case. No way will any judge or jury believe Elizabeth Smith's testimony against him. She's too suspect herself. I don't even know if the DA will take it to trial once he understands all the relationships involved. We might never have uncovered them all if you hadn't asked questions. Brennan could have sat in the courtroom and watched Elizabeth testify, never realizing who she was. It's been years since they've seen each other, and she's a new woman."

I took some comfort in Catherine's words, but not enough to erase the guilt of possibly contributing to a man's death. Cory and I would carry that with us for a long time to come.

Catherine snapped me out of my reverie. "Jolene, Danny's father was arraigned this morning. He pleaded not guilty. His bail was set at five thousand dollars. He had two hundred in his pocket when he was arrested. He said he doesn't have access to more money, so he'll have to stay in jail. I got the earliest court date possible, a month from now. I may have questions for you later on regarding his case as well, but right now I have to focus on Brennan."

Catherine placed her briefcase on the table and stood, smoothing the wrinkles from her navy skirt. Once again today, she wore a stunning suit with matching heels, and I had to admire her sense of style. Sadly, I purchased all my style at Talbots, under Celeste's direction, another reason for our love-hate relationship. Catherine seemed to come by all her style naturally, as well as her talent and good looks. Everything about her said "Winner," and I had no real concerns for Brennan's future now that it rested in her capable hands.

I said as much to Cory after she left.

He hung his head dejectedly. "I went to Brennan's arraignment this morning. She got bail set for him, but he doesn't have any more money. He wouldn't take any from me, not that I have enough savings anyway. He just kept telling me not to worry. He's banking on Catherine to win, too."

"Maybe with Catherine's investigator and the sheriff's department asking questions now, Brennan will be cleared quickly. I think Elizabeth Potter makes a great suspect. She may have pushed James Gleason and tried to blame Brennan. Maybe Wayne figured that out and called her on it. Maybe he even saw her do it and that's why he's dead."

"But why would she want to kill James Gleason?"

"I can only guess. Something to do with Monica or the accident? I don't know." And I hated that I didn't, because I felt like I should. One of the people Cory and I had met was a killer.

"We'll go crazy speculating. I'll have to have faith in the investigators and Catherine for now." Cory straightened in his chair. "Listen, I saw Mr. Phillips' arraignment, too. I started to call you, but then I realized Ray was there. Did he call you?"

"No. We're all barely speaking in our house. Danny's heartbroken over his father's arrest and what he sees as Ray's betrayal. Ray's defensive, and I'm caught in the middle and, quite honestly, sympathetic to Danny, which only makes Ray more cantankerous. I came to work today to try to keep my mind off it all."

"Sorry I brought it up." Cory stood and stretched. "You want to get some lunch?"

"Sure." Maybe lunch would take my mind off Danny, Ray, and his father. I doubted it, because now all I could think about was whether or not we should pay for Mr. Phillips' bail. Would Danny expect us to? After all, I'd promised more than once to help his dad. If we didn't pay his bail, Danny would be visiting him in jail, a place a kid should never have to go, then possibly in prison afterward, a place no one ever wanted to go. If we did pay his bail, Mr. Phillips would most likely jump to avoid prison, perhaps taking Danny with him back into a life no child should lead. Of course, it was possible Mr. Phillips would want Danny to remain with us, but given the current tensions between Danny and Ray, Danny might not want to stay. Would Mr. Phillips yield to pressure from Danny? And why hadn't Ray called me after Mr. Phillips arraignment? Was he surprised to see Catherine representing him? He must have known I would call her. She represented him the last time Ray arrested him in Wachobe. She got him off, too.

Then it hit me. As the arresting officer, Ray knew Mr. Phillips' arraignment was this morning. He knew the judge would set bail for Mr. Phillips, yet he told Danny he would take him to see his father after practice today. So clearly Ray knew Mr. Phillips wouldn't be able to make bail and had no intentions of paying it himself.

And he probably wouldn't want me to, either.

TWENTY-THREE

I HAD SPAGHETTI SAUCE and pasta bubbling on the stove around seven o'clock, expecting Danny and Ray to walk through the door at any moment after Danny's visit with Mr. Phillips. As I ran a knife through a loaf of Italian bread, the phone rang. Hoping to hear Ray's voice, I tucked the phone under my chin and kept on slicing.

It was Erica. "We're going to the funeral."

"What funeral?"

"Wayne Engles."

I nicked my finger with the knife. A drop of blood blossomed on its tip. I grabbed a paper towel to wrap around it. "Why?"

"Maury and I found his body. We feel responsible for him. Maury's going to bring a huge bouquet of roses. It's good karma to see him to rest."

"I don't think that's a good idea."

"What's wrong with roses?"

"Nothing." Except Maury's obsession with them, that is. I'd thought it only extended itself to presents for women, but apparently in his book, roses were appropriate for every occasion. "It's not the roses. Wayne Engle was murdered, Erica, most likely by someone he knows well. His killer might be at the funeral. You and Maury don't need to be rubbing elbows with a killer."

"We'll be rubbing elbows with the same people you and Cory met. Maybe a few more. You two are safe enough. I'm sure we will be, too."

I couldn't think of a response to that. Instead, I tried a diversionary tactic. "How do you know when his funeral is anyway? Maybe it's for family only."

"It's Wednesday morning at ten. The medical examiner released his body today, and his office released a statement regarding the funeral. It's open to anyone. He didn't have any immediate family. Isn't that sad?"

He had a godson, Matthew Gleason, who might be a suspect in his murder. I refrained from sharing that information with Erica. It would be just like her to go to the funeral and sidle up to him first.

"Besides, isn't Ray going to attend? He was the first one to respond to the scene."

I really didn't want to get into the fact that Ray wasn't assigned to the case. "Erica, I just don't think you guys should go."

"Mom does. And last time I listened to you instead of her, and look what happened."

Mom trumped me again. Pretty good for a ghost, not that I believed in ghosts. "Okay, well, keep your eyes open." And your mouth shut. Not likely, knowing Erica.

"I will. I'm planning to get the names of everyone who attends."

She hung up before I could ask her how she intended to do that. Did I really want to know?

I went toward the guest bathroom, looking for a bandage to cover the prick in my finger. The front door opened as I passed through the living room. Danny burst through it, tossed his fleece on a wall hook, and slouched past me with his backpack in hand.

"Hi, Danny. How was your day?"

He grunted. His bedroom door closed in my face.

Ray came in and stopped when he saw me in the middle of the room. "Where's Danny?"

"In his room."

"Tell him to get out here and set the table. He needs to learn what it means to have responsibility and work for a living." Ray passed me and disappeared into the kitchen. I heard the refrigerator door open and close, then the top pop off a beer bottle.

I decided to continue into the bath and bandage my finger, hoping they'd both settle down with some breathing room. When I returned to the kitchen, Ray occupied one of the breakfast bar stools, his elbows on the bar, head cupped in his hands. His beer sat untouched in front of him.

I rubbed my hand over his back. For years, I'd rubbed this man's back almost every night. He was obviously upset and didn't know what to do. "What happened when Danny saw his father?"

Ray lifted his head from his hands and took a long pull on his beer. "I don't know. He won't tell me."

"Oh." I massaged his shoulders with both hands, feeling the knots of tension.

"He did ask me if we would pay his father's bail."

"What did you tell him?"

"I asked him if his father put him up to asking me for the money."

"And?"

"He said 'no.' Then he told me he hated me."

"Who hates you? Mr. Phillips?"

"Danny."

I let go of Ray's shoulders and headed over to stir the pots on the stove. "You've heard that before. We both have. He doesn't mean it."

Erica used to tell me all the time that she hated me, especially after I'd driven off one of the guys she rutted with on the couch or after I'd refused to give her money. No parent ever got through a kid's life without hearing it at least once or twice. Ray's brother said it to him a million times. I'd have thought he'd be insulated from the sting of the words by now. Ray must care more about Danny than Sean. Of course, Sean was his younger brother, not his child. Their mother made all the final decisions for Sean.

Ray slid off the stool. "I'm going to get changed. Tell Danny to set the table."

I resented being ordered about, as I was sure Danny would, too. Ray always got very drill sergeant-like when upset. It was his defense mechanism, but I didn't welcome or enjoy it. I liked to make my own decisions. But I'd overlook his behavior for now.

Danny didn't reply when I knocked on his door. I opened it and entered his room anyway. He lay on the bed, hands clasped behind his head.

I sat on the edge of his bed. "How's your dad?"

"Okay."

"Did you talk for a long time?"

"Not really. He said Catherine Thomas is his lawyer. He said to thank you for calling her."

"No problem. She was happy to do it."

"My dad's sharing a cell with Brennan in the regular jail."

Then they'd been moved out of holding cells after their arraignments and into the mass population, which consisted of many others from all over awaiting trial.

"Is that a problem?" I knew it might be. Danny had parroted Mr. Phillips' prejudices when he came to live with us. Cory had to win Danny's friendship. Everyone loved Cory, but Brennan and Mr. Phillips in the same cell might be awkward at best.

"No. He knows Cory and Brennan are my friends. Brennan knows he's my dad, too."

I nodded. "What else did your dad say?"

"He said Brennan talks in his sleep. He has nightmares and wakes up screaming."

"How awful. Does your dad understand anything he says?"

"Yeah, he talks about a baby and the deer and his dad and he screams a girl's name, Monica. Isn't that the girl who died in the car crash?"

"Yes, it is." I didn't know what to make of Brennan's dream. Could his hidden memories be coming back to him in his sleep? Perhaps our theory about Monica, Wayne Engle, and Matthew was correct. The deer were new. Maybe one had ventured into the road in front of them, causing the crash? It was hard to go very far on the country roads around here without seeing deer. I wondered if the reunion had been out in the countryside near Albany. Surely the crash had been if it took so long for another car to come by and find them. "Anything else?"

"My dad told Brennan what he says in his sleep. He said Brennan doesn't remember, but he can tell Brennan knows he wakes up screaming and all sweaty and feeling scared."

"That's too bad. He's under a lot of pressure right now. It probably affects his sleep." I wondered if Brennan needed a psychiatrist and if he'd gotten any counseling after the crash all those years ago. Killing a woman, especially one he cared about, and seriously injuring another, even if by accident, was a heavy burden to carry through life. It seemed like it was all coming to rain on him now.

"Yeah." Danny didn't seem to want to talk about it any further.

"Listen, can you set the table? Dinner's almost ready. We're having spaghetti and meatballs."

"Okay." Danny rolled off the bed and followed me into the kitchen where Ray had finished slicing the loaf of bread. He put it on the table and watched as Danny pulled dishes from the cupboard for the table. His intent gaze made Danny uncomfortable. I could tell by the way he kept his eyes averted from Ray. When everything was set, I dished up the spaghetti and placed it on the table along with a tossed salad.

Ray and Danny ate in silence. I tried to start a conversation a couple times, but they kept their answers to a minimum, effectively dissuading me from trying again. My bread felt like chalk in my mouth; the spaghetti repulsed me. The only thing I felt like cutting with my knife was the tension in the room.

After dinner, Ray made Danny wash the dishes. When Danny clattered the pots in the sink rebelliously, Ray lit into him, lecturing him on attitude, which only made Danny's mood just that much worse. By eight o'clock, Danny had disappeared into his room and closed the door. I hoped he was doing his homework but chose not to ask.

Tuesday morning was a repeat of Monday night. No conversation at the table. Danny scraped his dishes loudly, expressing his underlying hostility toward Ray, who responded defensively with more lectures, which only made Danny slam the door on the way out of the house. I couldn't wait to escape to work, where I shared my troubles with Cory, including what Danny learned from his father.

I felt better. But Cory exhibited some strain of his own later in the day.

"Have you seen my metric wrench set?"

My fingers stopped moving over the adding machine keys long enough for me to look Cory in the eye, conveying the ridiculousness of the question. I never touched his stuff. "No."

He cast his gaze about my office as though he didn't believe me. Absurd. I even had my own screwdriver to take plates on and off cars. We had a division of labor, and my labor never required his tools.

"I can't find them and I need them to finish Mrs. Mooney's Volkswagen. Dammit." Cory never swore. As a matter of fact, he'd tried to help me break the habit I'd learned at the feet of the master, my father, a very sweet man with a potty mouth.

"They have to be here." I got up to help him search for the wrenches.

Two minutes later I found the set in the bathroom. When I handed them to Cory and told him, he scrunched his brow, "Did I go in there? I went to … I had to … oh, crap."

"TMI, Cory. TMI."

He blushed. "That's not what I meant."

I laughed. "I know. Take a break. Come in the office and have a cup of coffee."

He poured fresh coffee into his travel mug from the pot we kept going all day in the showroom. It was for him primarily, since I didn't drink coffee and Asdale Auto Imports attracted very few walk-in customers. I wished I'd stopped to pick up donuts on the way into work, but it had been his turn. He'd forgotten, another sign he wasn't himself.

"What's bothering you, Cory? Are you worried about Brennan and his nightmares?"

He sighed. "Not exactly. But I've been thinking about what you told me this morning. I keep replaying our conversation with Catherine yesterday, about how Matthew looks like Monica Gleason. And now you told me Brennan has nightmares about a baby.

207

You know, I couldn't take my eyes off Matthew Gleason the day we met him. There's something about him…"

I waited for Cory to continue. When he gazed at the ceiling instead, I prompted him along. "I noticed you stared at him, twice. What is it about him?"

"The way he holds his head. His smile. His mannerisms. His voice."

"What about them?"

Cory set his coffee on the desk and leaned in. "He reminds me of Brennan."

I felt my jaw go slack. "Brennan?"

Cory nodded. "I think Brennan is Matthew's father."

TWENTY-FOUR

We debated visiting Brennan at the jail to ask him if Cory's theory might be even a remote possibility. Cory couldn't rule it out. Brennan had told him he and Monica didn't experience fireworks on the night of their senior prom. That didn't mean they'd experienced nothing. Brennan hadn't really specified. Cory hadn't asked.

In the end, we called Catherine Thomas, because she'd asked us not to speak to Brennan. I put her on the speakerphone.

"You want me to ask him what?"

Cory replied, "You have to ask him if it's possible he fathered a child with Monica."

Catherine took a moment to respond. "I've become Dr. Ruth. All right, I'll ask him. You know I won't share the answer with you."

Cory frowned.

I jumped in. "That's okay. Just ask. It could put a whole new slant on everything."

"That's putting it mildly." She hung up.

209

A couple of other ideas had occurred to me. I hit the button to kill the speakerphone and leaned back in my executive chair. "Let's theorize, Cory."

His brow shot up, and his eyes glittered with curiosity. He settled back in his chair. "Okay."

"Let's say Brennan and Monica created Matthew. Then they broke up. Monica moved on to Wayne, which upset Brennan. Did he know about Matthew?"

Cory shook his head vehemently. "No way. Brennan would have wanted to be Matthew's father. He and I have talked about how great it would be to have children. He would have wanted to be part of Matthew's life."

"Now he wants to be a dad. Then he was only eighteen. He might have viewed things differently at that age."

Cory shook his head again. "I'm sure, Jo. He would never have walked away from Matthew."

"Okay. So he didn't know he was a father, but did Monica know Brennan was Matthew's father?" As soon as I posed the question, I knew the answer.

Cory didn't. "Wouldn't his name be on the birth certificate if he was?"

My past problems with birth certificates returned to haunt me. Ray and I had lost out on an adoption in part due to lies written on a certificate. "I think you can say 'unknown' in place of naming a father. Either way, if Brennan's name had been on the certificate, I think he would have been contacted about Matthew's custody when Monica was killed in the crash."

Cory rubbed his forehead. "He was unconscious for days after the crash. Maybe they made the decision without him."

"They would have had to ask him when he woke up. He was an adult. No one could make the decision for him. If he is Matthew's father, I think his name's not on the certificate."

"But Wayne's is?"

"Maybe. He might have agreed it was best for James and Suzanne Gleason to raise Matthew, if they were already married by then and willing. Or maybe they knew Monica would have wanted it that way. He still got to be godfather." I weighed the theory mentally for a moment or two. I liked it. "Okay, say we're right about Matthew's parentage. Then what did the four Musketeers argue about at the reunion?"

Cory considered my question. "Brennan's never mentioned that Monica had a baby. It could have been when Monica told Brennan about Matthew. Maybe he and Wayne had words."

I weighed his theory and liked it, too. "Brennan could have been upset if Wayne hadn't married Monica or taken responsibility for the child. Or maybe that's when Monica decided to drop the bomb that Matthew was really his child. It would be incredibly upsetting to learn you fathered a child you didn't know about, upsetting enough to affect Brennan's driving on the way home."

Cory leaned forward excitedly. "Exactly. Maybe he and Monica argued in the car about why she never told him."

"Or about whether he really was the father."

"Either way, it would be almost impossible to keep his mind on the road under that kind of sudden stress."

I nodded in agreement, shivering involuntarily as I relived our recent near-brush with death when Cory was distracted at the wheel a few days ago.

Cory grimaced. "One problem."

"What?"

"Why didn't Elizabeth Potter or Beth Smith or whatever the hell her name is tell Brennan about the baby after he came out of his coma? She must have heard everything."

"Because she hated him. She must have suffered terribly after the accident with all the surgeries and therapy."

"Which is why she tried to pin James Gleason's death on Brennan. To make him suffer the way she suffered. She took advantage of the opportunity to get him in trouble when it was presented. James either stumbled into the road when the crowd surged or she pushed him. We know Brennan didn't push him."

I liked this addition to the new theory. It made sense.

Cory's knee started to bounce.

"What?"

"I like the whole theory, but I can't figure one thing out." He hesitated.

"Go on."

"We know why Brennan was at the Grand Prix festival. We know why the Gleasons were there. Wayne Engle was a gear head, so it makes sense he'd attend. But why was Elizabeth Potter or Beth Smith or whatever her name is there? What are the odds she's a big car race fan? She was seriously injured in a car accident, endured multiple surgeries, and probably suffered through hours of painful physical therapy. She should hate cars. So why was she there, right on the spot when James landed in the street?"

For the life of me, I had no answer for that.

Cory spent the rest of the afternoon finishing Mrs. Mooney's Volkswagen. I spent half of it paying invoices and bills and the other half wondering what to do about Danny and Ray. Their relationship had deteriorated rapidly. I didn't know what to do or say to improve the situation. Paying Mr. Phillips' bail money would free him to make some decisions for himself and Danny, but I feared he might make the wrong decisions regarding Danny. After losing my mother, my father, and the baby Ray and I hoped to adopt, I dreaded having another person taken away from me, one of the many reasons I overlooked Erica's nonsense all these years. She was unpredictable but she was with me, both literally and figuratively. I wanted Danny with me, too.

And I wanted the agreeable, rational, and loving Ray with me too, not the defensive, demanding, prickly one he'd become lately. No doubt he felt guilty about arresting Danny's father and angry at being so helpless to control his own relationship with Danny. Any affection displayed between Danny and I made him all the grumpier. I didn't know if he was jealous or in need of more attention from me. Maybe he wanted me to consider him first in my thoughts and actions. I know he'd felt jealous when Erica came first in the past. But in my mind, Danny and Erica were more needy and, therefore, always had to come first.

Normally, I would call Isabelle to talk through all my concerns and for advice on family issues. Today I'd reached for the phone at least three times already, then pulled my hand back, fearing she'd repeat her allegations against Jack and I'd have to tell her about the surprise party, still days away. I hoped Jack had finished his plans for that and wouldn't have any more suspicious phone calls or unexplained disappearances.

The fourth time I reached for the phone, I hit the speed dial for Isabelle. I couldn't hide from her for two weeks. I might as well call her today.

"Hi, I was going to call you. I heard about Brennan's second arrest this morning from my receptionist. She said it was on TV Saturday night. What's going on?"

I filled Isabelle in on all the news, but not our theories, which were only gossipy speculation until we had some kind of confirmation.

"Wow. How's Brennan holding up?"

"When he calls Cory, he says not to worry. Catherine's representing him, and we all know she's a winner."

"Not in the game of love."

I smiled. "True, lucky for me."

"How are Ray and Danny?"

Apparently Mr. Phillips' arrest hadn't been newsworthy. I filled her in.

"Oh my god, Ray slapped the cuffs on him right there at the game? Poor Danny. Are the kids at school teasing him?"

"He hasn't mentioned any problems at school. The problem is between him and Ray. The whole situation has destroyed their relationship. Danny is sullen, withdrawn, and uncooperative when Ray's home. Ray lectures him on responsibility and piles on the jobs. Danny resents it. They don't even speak. I don't know what to do."

"If it makes you feel any better, my father was incredibly hard on my brothers when we were growing up. They hated him then but look how productive they are now. And everyone still sits down to dinner together every Sunday night. My brothers wouldn't miss it."

"That's true, but your brothers only had one father figure. Danny has two."

"Should you bail out Mr. Phillips? Then you could all sit down and talk together."

"I'm afraid he would jump bail and take Danny with him. He doesn't ever want to go back to prison. He almost got killed there."

Isabelle clicked her tongue. "Catherine is his attorney. Can she get him off?"

I weighed the evidence against Mr. Phillips. The only real evidence against him was the fact my Ferrari disappeared the same day he did—and of course, his known history of car theft. Everything else I knew of was supposition, and only Catherine and I knew about it. "I'd like to think so."

"Then keep taking Danny to visit him and just wait out the month until his trial. Ray and Danny love each other. They'll simmer down and remember that soon enough."

"What if Catherine gets Mr. Phillips off and he takes Danny away?"

She didn't immediately reply. Eventually, she heaved a huge sigh. "Jolene, I've realized we can't control everything in our lives and there's no sense in driving yourself crazy trying. Things happen for a reason."

I wondered if she might also be referring to her own situation. "You're right. I'll sit tight and see what happens."

"Good."

"So how are you?" I closed my eyes, fearing I'd hear the worst.

"I'm doing really well. The ad I shot for the United Way came out fabulous. They love it. I love it. Donations are going to pour in this year."

"Awesome."

"Cassidy is all excited about Halloween already. She wants to be a princess. We're going to look at costumes this weekend."

"Great. She'll be adorable. Take lots of pictures." Would she ever get around to telling me about Jack?

"I decided to enroll in a Spanish class. It might help open up a new customer base for my agency."

"Great." I waited through a few moments of silence.

She sighed softly. "Jack and I are doing okay. I don't know what happened the last few months, but everything's back to normal now. It's weird, but I'm not questioning it. I'm happy."

"I'm happy to hear it. I knew you two would be okay."

"You and Ray and Danny are going to be fine, too. The three of you belong together, I know it."

As I hung up the phone, I hoped Isabelle was right.

TWENTY-FIVE

THINGS WERE NO BETTER at our house Tuesday night or Wednesday morning. Danny complied when Ray asked him to mow the lawn after dinner on Tuesday, but he broke the weed whacker. Ray thought he did it intentionally. I wasn't so sure, since the machine had been tricky at best for me to use in the past. Wednesday, Danny's cereal bowl slipped from his hand and smashed on the floor, sending shards of white Pfaltzgraff everywhere. Danny apologized immediately. Ray wanted him to sweep up the remains and wash the milk splashes off the surrounding floors and walls, but Danny would have missed his bus. I cleaned it up instead, which seemed to irritate Ray more. It was a relief to have them both out of the house. I ran off to work as quickly as I could to escape the negative vibes they left behind.

The phone rang as soon as I finished poking the code into the shop's alarm keypad. I picked up the extension on the conference table.

"Asdale Auto Imports. This is Jolene. How may I help you?"

The caller hung up.

I walked toward my office.

The phone rang again. I reached my desk, sat, and answered on the fourth ring.

Again, I heard a click after my greeting.

Cory sauntered through the front door, donuts in hand. He carried the bag into my office and deposited it on the desk with a theatrical flourish. "I remembered today."

That was good, especially since it was my turn and I'd forgotten. Ray and Danny had addled my brain.

The phone rang again. I made no move to answer.

Cory laid his jacket on the back of the chair. He eyed me. The phone continued to ring.

"Is this a new sales approach, Jo? Cuz I gotta tell you, I don't think it's going to work."

"Someone hung up on me twice today already."

"Then allow me."

He picked up the phone and said nothing, listening. After a moment, he set it down. "It's probably kids playing. They won't call back."

I didn't bother to remind him all the kids were in school, or at least, they should be. This trick was juvenile, but I doubted a kid was behind it.

The phone rang again. Cory snatched the receiver from the cradle and reeled off his standard greeting. He closed his eyes and held out the phone. "That's really annoying."

"It sure is." We sat and watched the phone for a moment or two, waiting for it to ring again. "We'll let it go to voicemail this time."

It didn't ring again.

Cory unfolded the bag of donuts and held them out to me. "Why would anyone waste time with that kind of behavior?"

I extracted a cinnamon fried cake and broke it in half. "Maybe they want to know if we're both here."

"Who would care?"

"I'm not sure." I took a bite and chewed slowly. "Erica and Maury were going to Wayne Engle's funeral this morning. It starts in an hour in Binghamton."

Cory swallowed a gulp of his coffee. "We can't get there in an hour. It would be over if we left now."

"That's my point. I wonder if someone was calling to see if we were here instead of on our way there."

"You think they're afraid we'd be forward enough to show up at the funeral and ask more questions?"

"Either that or someone is going and doesn't want us to see them there."

"Who would that be? I'm sure they've all cooperated with the sheriff's department by now."

"We never met Suzanne Gleason or saw that fourth woman who works in Wayne's office. What was her name?

Cory closed his eyes, probably trying to picture the nameplate on her desk as was I. "Silvia something."

"Silvia Porter. That's what Catherine said."

"I don't see how she could be important, but I did think it was weird Matthew's mother never called to thank you for the cookies after he made such a point of writing your number down. What number did you give him?"

"My cell. I didn't think she'd call. She doesn't know us, and we asked a lot of questions. Besides, I've given wedding presents and never received any acknowledgment. Cookies for a grieving family are relatively insignificant."

Cory swallowed his donut in two bites. "I guess. Still, I was pretty impressed with Matthew's manners. At least he made the effort to write your number down."

"True. Maybe he takes after Brennan, just like you said."

Cory stared at me. I feared I'd inadvertently said the wrong thing, but after a moment, he nodded. "I think you're right. The phone calls this morning were just a coincidence."

I tipped my head and held his gaze. "How many years have you worked here?"

"Between you and your dad, around fifteen now."

"How many times in all those years did this shop receive hang-up calls?"

"I can't think of any, but I'm sure we've had them."

"Four in a row?"

Cory ran his finger under his neckline. "Okay, not four in a row. What's that phone company code you dial to call the person back?"

"I don't know." I started pulling out my desk drawer, searching for the white pages. "I think they explain about it in the front of the phone book. Here." I yanked the book out of the desk and laid it flat, ruffling through the pages. "*66"

I lifted the receiver and dialed the code. A message responded. I hung up and repeated the words, "The caller was not in our area code."

"So they were in Binghamton?"

"Or Albany. Or Alaska, for that matter."

Cory shook his head. "You may be right. Someone does want to make sure we're not at the funeral. The question is 'why?'"

Around ten minutes to five, Cory shut off the lights in his garage and unplugged the coffee machine in the showroom, carrying the remains of the pot into the bathroom to dump in the sink.

I put away my files and stood up, ready to call it a day.

The showroom bells jingled, announcing a new arrival. It was Erica with Maury in tow. She had a huge smile on her face as she practically skipped across the showroom to greet Cory and me.

Her attire caught my attention next. A black dress and black shoes, appropriate for a funeral except for the amount of cleavage peeking through the bodice, the thigh-skimming length of the hem, and her five-inch stilettos. Her image was more appropriate for a porno video—although after seeing the women who worked in Wayne Engles' office, Wayne might have applauded her choice.

Maury's black suit said "undertaker," but the red rose with babies breath in his buttoner said "wedding."

Cory wiggled his eyebrows at me.

I ignored him.

"Jo, what a funeral. There were two hundred and forty-seven people at the service. The receiving line took forever. It's such a shame. That Wayne was a looker. The funeral director did a great job masking the gash in his forehead. I'd have never known if I hadn't seen it myself."

Cory's lips twitched.

I frowned in his direction. "How do you know it was two hundred and forty-seven people? Did you count?"

Erica waved her hand. "Oh, no, they were milling about everywhere. I never would have gotten a correct count." She reached in to her glossy vinyl shoulder bag and whipped out a black book. "I counted the names in the guest register."

I gasped. "You stole the register?"

She made a face. "Of course not, Jolene. We waited until everyone except Matthew and his mother had left. The funeral director offered them the book. They didn't want it. So I said I would take it."

"And they gave it to you?"

Maury spoke up. "They seemed to think she had worked for Wayne. I think that's because she offered to send out all the thank you notes, too. We have them in the car." He grimaced.

Erica tossed her blond hair and grinned. "I'm unemployed. What else have I got to do?" She handed the guest register to me. "Take a look. I tried to meet everyone at the lunch afterward. Go ahead, just ask me about any of them."

I scanned the pages. Cory sidled over next to me and read them over my shoulder. "I don't see the Potters. I don't see any names from the sheriff's department—"

"Max and Gumby were there. They didn't sign the book." Erica glanced at Maury. "Gumby tried to hit on me. Can you believe it?"

Maury's fists clenched but his face remained expressionless.

I could believe it. Sheriff's Deputy Steven "Gumby" Fellows was the only local man I knew taller than Ray, and the first man to hit on me after Ray and I split. He wasn't successful with me, but he had a lot of notches in his bedpost. A few years ago, he married a stripper. Neither one of them seemed to be taking the "forsaking all others" portion of their marriage vows very seriously.

I tipped my head to acknowledge I'd heard her, hoping Erica would let the subject go instead of upsetting Maury further. "The only names we recognize are Suzanne and Matthew Gleason—"

Erica cut me off again. "Suzanne Gleason was a nervous mess. Every time Gumby or Max even glanced in her direction, she shook. I asked Gumby if she was a suspect in Wayne's death. He wouldn't tell me, but after I asked, he kept a closer eye on her, which just made her that much more jumpy. She spilled coffee on her pants, poor thing. Matthew's girlfriend rubbed ice cubes on her leg to make sure she didn't get scalded. I felt sorry for Suzanne."

"I wished we'd met her. She wasn't home when Cory and I went to Binghamton." I sighed and continued reading the register. "We can name the women who really did work for Wayne: Pam Sullivan, Missy Temple, Silvia Porter, and Beth Smith."

"Oh, Beth Smith." Erica rolled her eyes in an exaggerated manner at Maury, who grinned in reply. "She's something else."

"What do you mean?"

"Her hair is freaky, but she had a big pear-shaped diamond on her finger that caught the light. It was gorgeous."

I couldn't believe I'd missed it when she and I shook hands outside her townhouse. "Do you know how long she's been engaged?"

Erica nodded. "Since Sunday. The other women she works with were whispering about her. They said she's a cradle robber. Apparently she's talking about eloping."

I thought back to her mother's statement that she'd been married twice already but was dating a boy. Evie had said she was dating a young man, too. I'd just thought their descriptions were the quaint wording of an older generation, not an accurate description of the man. "Any idea who he is?"

Erica jumped up and down, squealing. "Don't you know?"

I couldn't help but laugh at her antics. "I have no idea."

"She's engaged to Matthew Gleason."

TWENTY-SIX

"Matthew Gleason?" My stomach tightened with distaste. "Ew, that's just wrong. He's young enough to be her son. What's he doing with her? And what's she doing with him? He doesn't even have a job. Is she going to support him? Ew. That's icky."

I thought back to the day we met Wayne. We'd asked him about Elizabeth Potter or Beth Smith, as we now knew her. He'd said they weren't close anymore and I thought a flash of anger had crossed his face. Well, obviously they had been physically close enough with her desk just a few yards outside his door, but they weren't friends anymore. Could he have been angry over her relationship with Matthew? Had the two met when Matthew visited his office? Wouldn't that be ironic, especially if Wayne turned out to be Matthew's real father? He'd surrounded himself with half-dressed women and one had caught his godson's—or son's—eye.

Cory's expression spoke of his distaste. "I expected more from Matthew."

Erica reached out her hand, oblivious to the implications of her news. "I need the book back, Jolene. I have to write out all the thank you notes. You can have it when I'm done, if you want."

I gave it to her, reluctantly. "Don't lose it."

She closed her purse. "I won't. I promise." She twirled and tucked her arm through Maury's. "Take me home, baby. I got work to do."

Cory followed me into my office as I put on my suit jacket in preparation to leave. "What do you make of it, Jo?"

"I'm completely baffled why a young man would want to marry Beth Smith. She's not unattractive, but she's got mileage. I'm sure his mother doesn't approve."

"I wonder if his father didn't approve. It would be a motive for Beth to shove James Gleason in the street during the race festival. Maybe it was an added bonus for her to try to pin his death on Brennan."

"Now we know why she was at the race. He did say his girl-friend was there. Too bad we didn't ask her name sooner, not that I know what it all means anyway." I grabbed my purse. "I'm sorry, Cory. I'd like to talk about this more, but it's my turn to pick up Danny from practice. Ray's on the evening shift tonight."

"No problem. I don't know what all this means either. You go ahead. I'll set the alarm."

As I navigated the side streets of Wachobe, headed for the foot-ball fields behind the middle school, I ran through all the facts we'd learned to date. None of it made sense to me anymore. Suzanne Gleason had also been at the festival, close to the spot where her husband, James, died only moments after he was hit by the car. She'd witnessed the argument between Brennan and her husband, but allegedly not his death. Did she know something more that she feared he might tell Brennan? Or fed up with James' combative ways, had she taken the easy way out of their marriage, perhaps to spend her days with Wayne Engle, who later spurned her? Maybe that was why the sheriff's deputies made her so nervous today. Or did she think Matthew had killed his father, either to protect her from him or in anger over a possible rejection of his relationship with Beth Smith? Had Wayne figured out the truth or, worse, witnessed the act, leaving Matthew no choice but to kill him, too? Or had his mother killed him to keep him from turning in Matthew? Or could the two of them have conspired to kill both James and Wayne?

Beth Smith seemed more suspicious to me by the day. She'd pointed the finger at Brennan, which we knew couldn't be true. It was hard to believe she'd simply been mistaken. She had to have done it on purpose. But why? Did she push James Gleason into the street and blame Brennan to kill two birds with one stone? Or had she done it to protect the real killer, Matthew, her lover? Had Wayne known the truth either way and therefore needed to be eliminated?

A tooting horn snapped me out of my speculations. I'd failed to notice the light turn green. The guy behind me hadn't. He tooted again. I hit the gas, forcing myself to let the questions go for now.

A quarter mile later, I pulled into the circular drive in front of Danny's school. He sat on the low brick wall that surrounded the school with two of his friends. When he spotted me, he waved to them and trotted over with his backpack in hand, his coat slung over one shoulder. He climbed in next to me, and I caught a whiff of body odor that made my eyes water. I cracked open my window. "Hi, Danny, how was practice?"

"Good." He pitched his backpack and coat over the front seat to the back.

I pulled away from the curb. "We're having takeout for dinner. What do you prefer, Chinese or pizza?"

When he failed to respond, I glanced at him. He faced forward, his face expressionless. "Danny? What would you like for dinner?"

He blinked. "Can you take me to see my dad?"

"Um, sure, I guess so." I hoped his dad wouldn't think we had a water and deodorant shortage at our house. "Do you want to eat first, maybe shower?"

"No."

All righty then, Mr. Phillips was in for a real treat.

The half hour ride to the jail passed in silence. When I attempted conversation, Danny asked to turn on the radio. I let him, thinking the noise might take both our minds off our troubles. It worked, because Danny started to sing under his breath. I had to smile.

When we arrived, Danny signed in at the jail and waited for the guards to go through all the necessary logistics to reunite him with his dad. I considered asking to visit Brennan while Danny was with his dad but remembered Catherine's request to not talk to him. With so much swirling in my head, I couldn't wait to talk to someone.

When Danny disappeared inside with the guard, I dialed Ray.

"What's up?"

"Danny is in visiting his dad. I'm waiting for him. What are you doing?"

"I'm sitting on the county road over near Brennan's house, waiting for a semi to speed by."

The local truckers and Wachobe were at odds. The town no longer allowed semis to drive up and down Main Street, which enraged the truckers enough to hold a sit in, parking their trucks all over Main Street right before the July 4th celebration this year. The parade had to be cancelled because the police chief couldn't get them to move, even when he slapped them with fines. The town refused to revoke the new law. Lately, the truckers had taken to speeding up and down the county roads in defiance.

"Any luck yet?"

"No, it's been a quiet night."

"Well, it's been a busy day. Erica and Maury went to Wayne Engles' funeral today. They found out Matthew Gleason is engaged to marry Beth Smith. Do you think Gumby and Max know that?"

"I don't know. I can call and ask Gumby. He'll tell me."

"Do he and Max talk about Brennan's case with you?"

"Sometimes, when the sheriff isn't looking."

"Do they have any idea who killed Wayne Engle?"

"Darlin', they think Brennan did it."

"Why?"

"You know why. But I keep throwing out different ideas. They seem to listen. They're looking hard at the three wild cards from the Watkins Glen festival: Matthew and Suzanne Gleason and Elizabeth Smith. The case will crack soon. They've only been on it a couple days." Ray sucked in air. "I gotta go. I gotta guy doing about seventy-five."

The phone went dead. I pictured Ray in full pursuit and then let that image go. It was easier to not to think about his work. I just kept the faith that he did it well and safely.

I was the only person in the jail waiting room. Wednesday must be a slow night. Either that or everyone else came over after dinner. My stomach growled, and I wished we'd done the same.

Danny reappeared after fifteen minutes. He had a worried frown.

I stood up and put my arm around his shoulder, no easy feat now that he'd grown taller than me. "How's your dad?"

"Okay."

"Just okay?"

"Yeah."

"Did you happen to ask him about Brennan?"

"Brennan's good, too. He's teaching my dad how to play chess. Catherine brought them a chess board."

"She's so nice." I had to admit it. No wonder Ray had taken up with her after me. How lucky I was he'd come back. "Did your dad say anything else?"

Danny hesitated. "He said he's going to change his plea to guilty."

My jaw went slack.

Danny rushed on. "He said he stole the Ferrari and sold it. He said it was time to set the right example for me and to take responsibility for his actions."

Wow. I fumbled for the right response. "You must be very proud of him."

A tear slipped down Danny's cheek. "But what if he gets killed in prison?"

I hugged Danny closer. "Catherine and Ray will make sure everyone takes good care of him."

The frown lines didn't leave Danny's forehead but I couldn't bring myself to promise Danny that nothing would happen to his dad. I'd lost my mom young. I knew for a fact anything can happen.

"Let's go home." I squeezed him again. "I need pizza. Don't you think pizza sounds good?"

After a moment, he nodded and let me lead him out the door and into the parking lot.

But I was certain he felt the shadow of the jail looming over us, just as I did.

TWENTY-SEVEN

THURSDAY MORNING I HAD an appointment to show the Mercedes on the showroom floor to Mr. Linz, the owner of Simply Divine Burgers in Wachobe. He served up the best Black Angus burgers in the world. Apparently I wasn't the only one who thought so, either. He wanted to buy the Mercedes for his daughter, a senior in high school, to drive around town. Now, that was a lot of burgers.

"It's a 2006 Mercedes SLK 280 with just over 13,000 miles and one previous owner, a woman in her sixties."

Mr. Linz smiled enthusiastically. Women in their sixties are not known to be aggressive drivers. I happened to know this particular woman could barely see over the steering wheel, and her keys had been confiscated by her son, who feared for public safety after his mother entered an off ramp thinking it was an on ramp, narrowly missing a head-on collision with a semi.

"It's a Florida car, so there's no rust. Wachobe will be its first brush with salted roads."

The phone in the showroom rang. I ignored it, knowing Cory would answer in the garage.

"Of course, it has the red exterior your daughter wanted and a black interior." I whipped the driver's door open. "I'm sure she'll like the fact it's a convertible." It wasn't a practical car for our impending winter weather but who was I to break her heart? "Would you like to sit in it?"

I held my breath as Mr. Linz squeezed his Santa belly behind the wheel. He may have eaten a few too many of his own burgers. I hoped I wouldn't need the Jaws of Life to extract him, but he seemed content enough behind the wheel, running his hand over the dashboard.

Cory appeared in the doorway between the showroom and the garage, shrugging on his leather jacket. The weather had turned colder overnight, dropping into the high forties. Tree leaves had turned yellow and red seemingly overnight, too. Fall had arrived in the Finger Lakes.

He motioned to me.

"Excuse me just one minute, Mr. Linz." I walked over to meet Cory at the front door. He had one hand on it already, clearly eager to be off.

"Brennan called. His bail got paid. He asked me to come pick him up."

"Who paid his bail?"

"He doesn't know, but one of the guards at the jail said it was a bank check delivered by messenger. He thinks it might have been his father."

"Maybe his father wants to see him again before he passes away."

"Maybe. Anyway, I'm going to go pick him up. I don't know if I'll be back today." Cory blushed. "I know we're not supposed to talk about the case, but I'd like to at least spend some time with him."

"Of course. No problem. Tell Brennan I said hi."

A half hour later, I had a signed contract on the desk for $27,500. After a test drive, Mr. Linz had decided the Mercedes was perfect for his princess, and he was on his way over to the bank to get me a check right now. This sale meant Asdale Auto Imports was in the black for the year, months before year end, a first ever. Quite an accomplishment and one I had to share.

I called Ray.

"Hey, darlin'. What's up?"

I told him the good news.

"Congratulations. We'll have to celebrate tonight. Do you want to go out to dinner?"

"Maybe we could celebrate at home. Danny might want to visit his father, and I'm sure he'll have homework."

"That's true. We can pick something up on the way home after he visits his dad. What would you like?"

I'd like for the two of them to get along again, but I didn't know how to phrase that tactfully. "Surprise me. Hey, did you know Brennan's bail got paid?"

"No. Who paid it?"

"They're not sure. Brennan thought maybe his father."

"Gumby said the guy is going to die any day now. He could barely answer the questions they had for him. I guess he got teary, too. Maybe he did have a change of heart about Brennan."

"Is Brennan still Gumby and Max's number one suspect?"

"The evidence points to him, but they're looking hard at Matthew, his mother, or Elizabeth's involvement in possibly both James Gleason's and Wayne Engles' deaths. They're meeting with Ken today to compare notes and look at his timeline for Gleason's death. None of them have alibis for the night Wayne was killed, and, of course, we know all three of them were at the Glen when James Gleason died. But then, so was Brennan. Gumby and Max didn't really know Brennan before, but after questioning him, they don't figure him for a killer, either. They're looking for a motive and opportunity with the other three. I've got to go, but, darlin', your dad would be proud of you."

I hung up the phone and looked around my shop. My dad had run it as a general garage for years, but when he passed away, I'd turned it into a foreign pre-owned but pristine sports car boutique, an image more in keeping with Wachobe's upscale population and tourist trade, not to mention my knowledge of cars and business. It had been touch and go for the last five years or so. Today, with Mr. Linz's check in hand, I finally felt like I had made it.

I hoped Ray was right. I hoped my dad knew and was proud of me.

Ray and Danny arrived home with takeout from my favorite Italian restaurant, located in an old carriage house in the village. They brought me lasagna, Ray gnocchi and sausage, and Danny a wood-fired pizza with sausage, plus chocolate-covered cannolis for dessert. Ray knew me well.

Ray and Danny toasted my success over dinner, and we ate, chatting about our days. Their relationship seemed relaxed and back to normal. After dinner, they went outside to toss the football around while I read by the fire Ray built in our stone fireplace. Danny even wanted Ray to tuck him in, which hadn't happened in days. Ray and I went to bed early—but not to sleep.

In the middle of the night, I awoke. The clock read three twenty a.m. Ray snored softly beside me, and for a moment, I thought that was what had awakened me. Then I heard crying. I swung my feet to the floor and moved through our bedroom, past the kitchen, across the living room, and toward Danny's room. When I reached his door, the sobbing grew louder. I went inside, feeling for the side of his bed.

I banged my knee on the bed frame. "Oh, oh. Ow, ow."

The crying ceased. "Jolene?"

"Yes?" I reached down to rub my throbbing knee and managed to sit on the edge of Danny's bed.

"Are you okay?"

"I hit my knee. It'll be all right. Why are you crying?"

"I'm worried about my dad."

"Why?"

"They put someone new in the cell with him. A big guy. He's a freak."

"Your dad told you this?"

"I saw him. The guy had a visitor while I was with my dad. He said something to my dad when he passed him."

"What?"

"I don't know, but my dad looked scared."

I would have to ask Ray to find out more tomorrow about all this when he went to work. Maybe he could pull a few strings and get Mr. Phillips moved somewhere safe. "Ray will look into it tomorrow, okay? It's the county's job to keep your dad safe."

"Okay."

I found his head in the dark and smoothed his hair with my hand. "Go to sleep now. Everything will be all right, don't worry."

But even though I'd put Danny's fears to rest, I couldn't go back to sleep myself. I spent the night awake, pondering Mr. Phillips' fate.

TWENTY-EIGHT

CORY REPORTED TO WORK on Friday with a smile on his face and a spring in his step, the kind I only saw when one of two things happened for him. Since he hadn't tried out for a part at the local Broadway-quality theater recently, I knew he was in love. Of course, he'd been in love with Brennan for a while now but reluctant to admit it, given his history of bad luck.

Cory dropped into the chair across from me and reached for the donut bag. "I have news."

"Do tell."

"I know Catherine said not to talk about the case, but Brennan told me a few things. First, he did meet Matthew Gleason when Matthew applied for a job with Brennan's construction crew six months ago. Brennan just didn't remember him, because his foreman spent most of the time talking to the kid. They didn't offer him a job, because he didn't have any experience and they really didn't have any openings. Matthew seemed to take the rejection in stride, though. He thanked them very politely for their time."

Cory popped the second half of a donut in his mouth and gulped it down. "He also said Matthew called him more recently."

"Really?"

"Remember the night Brennan got the call and wouldn't tell me who it was?"

I nodded.

"It was Matthew. He called to ask Brennan questions about Monica Gleason. Matthew said she was his mother, and he wanted to know more about her death."

"Did he say who his father was?"

"No, and Brennan had no idea until Catherine told him what I thought. He asked me a lot of questions about Matthew."

Cory brushed the cinnamon sugar dust from his hands into the trash. "He does not remember the night of the reunion at all. He said it's possible Monica told him about Matthew. He said he would have wanted Matthew, just like I thought."

"Did he say anything else?"

"He thought he might visit his father before it's too late."

"Really?"

Cory sipped from his coffee mug. "I don't think it's a good idea, but Brennan didn't know until now that his father was dying. He doesn't want him to go without at least saying goodbye."

"Did he tell you anything else?"

A flush started at the base of Cory's neck, crept upward, and suffused his face. "He said he wants to spend the rest of his life with me."

Tears burned the corner of my eye. "Oh, Cory. That's wonderful. Congratulations."

"Thank you. I wanted you to be the first to know."

A tear escaped and trickled down my cheek. "I'm honored. Oh, man, I'm so happy for you." I hopped out of my chair and ran around the desk to hug Cory, who almost cracked one of my ribs with his enthusiasm.

He turned his head to swipe at his eyes then wiped his hand on his pants. "Okay, enough talking. I'm way behind on Mr. Belzer's Jaguar. I gotta get to work."

I sat in my chair and tried to do a little work myself, locating a new automobile for my showroom floor. When Mr. Linz picked up his Mercedes next week, I would have a gap to fill. None of the cars sitting outside in my parking lot merited being showcased inside the shop, at least not until Cory worked some magic restoring them. Another hot car to catch the eye of the passers-by was what I needed.

Two hours of surfing the Internet turned up a handful of possibilities to run past Cory. I walked into the garage and stopped next to his feet. He lay on his mechanic's creeper under Mr. Belzer's silver Jaguar. I could hear the wrench clinking against the car's undercarriage as he worked.

"Cory, I sold the SLK 280 to Mr. Linz yesterday. I need an inventory replacement. What do you think of—"

The phone rang. I started around the front end of the Jag.

Cory slid out from under it faster, blocking my path. "I'll get it. Brennan said he was going to call me this morning." He stripped the surgical gloves from his hands and grabbed the extension.

I could tell from the smile on his face that the caller was Brennan. I headed back to my office to give Cory some privacy.

A couple minutes later, he appeared in my doorway. He leaned on the jam, frowning.

"Something wrong?"

"Brennan's father died last night."

"That's too bad. How's Brennan taking it?"

"Okay. He said his father's lawyer called him earlier this morning to let him know. The lawyer is making all the funeral arrangements per his father's last wishes. The funeral will be on Monday."

"Should we go?"

Cory nodded. "We can ride with Brennan. He said his father would roll over in his grave to see Brennan and me there together."

"I'll bet."

"His father did pay his bail, though. The lawyer said he wanted Brennan to be able to hear his will. He read it to him over the phone."

"I thought he wrote Brennan out of the will. Did he have a change of heart?"

Cory came into the office and sat. "No."

"He left Brennan nothing."

"Exactly."

"So why did Brennan need to hear the will read?"

Cory curled his lip. "Because his father left his money to Brennan's progeny, if—and I'm quoting here—he ever manages to be a real man."

"Ouch. What a jerk."

"That's putting it mildly. Brennan knew his father had put the progeny clause in the will when he wrote Brennan out years ago, but he didn't know the exact wording of it. He said it was better that his father passed now before we know if Matthew is his grandson. He wouldn't have wanted to give his father the satisfaction of knowing his line was carried on past Brennan."

"Any idea how much Matthew will inherit if he is Brennan's son?"

"About two million, plus property. Brennan's father lost a ton of money when the stock market dropped."

"Wow, that's a lot of dough, almost too much for a young guy like Matthew. It could be overwhelming."

"Brennan said Catherine is still trying to find out if Matthew is his son. Her investigator got the door slammed in his face at the Gleason house by Suzanne. He's in Albany now, combing through birth and adoption records."

"So we have to wait and see."

Cory flexed his fingers, cracking a knuckle. "Brennan said he also got a call from the hospice in Albany at nine a.m. One of the caregivers said she had some personal things his father wanted to give him. She offered to drive up here to drop them off. Brennan almost told her not to bother."

I knew hospice care meant peace, comfort, and dignity with quality individualized care. I didn't realize they provided a delivery service, too. Hard to believe the old man inspired such loyal service.

"She said she was headed this way anyway to visit her daughter. She was leaving the hospice right after she called. He said she'd be here by noon at the latest. He's going to call me afterward and let me know what she dropped off."

I glanced at the clock. It read eleven a.m. One hour to wait to find out what the old man wanted delivered to Brennan. Hopefully, it wouldn't be hurtful like his will.

I grabbed the sheet of printouts from my desk. "Do you have a minute for me to run through a few of these purchase options with you? I found a handful that look promising to replace the Benz."

Cory settled back in his chair. "Go ahead."

I read the highlights for a Mercedes, a Jaguar, a BMW, and a Maserati, located in Albany. Cory groaned at the mere suggestion he would have to drive that route again to look at the vehicle. "Pick something closer to home, Jo."

I clicked through the screens on the computer. "The Porsche's in Buffalo. The ad says it's pristine." Of course, they all say that, which was why Cory had to go look the cars over before we made a purchase decision. "Never seen winter. Silver on black leather. 66,000 km. Heated seats, traction control, alarm, dual air bags and side air bags, windstop, Xeon lights with washers, five-speed manual, clear 3M chip protector. Even includes a Porsche car cover."

"I like that one. I can visit my parents at the same time. Maybe Brennan can ride along. I can introduce them."

"Great. I'll call and see if I can get you an appointment for next week. Is Tuesday okay?"

"Make it Friday or Saturday. I'll spend the weekend."

"Done." I picked up the phone and dialed.

Ten minutes later Cory had an appointment for Friday night at seven o'clock. I didn't like the time. It would be dark by then, and it was always best to look at a car in the daylight. Maybe Cory could stop in again the next morning if he liked what he saw at night.

My stomach growled. I glanced at the clock. Was eleven forty-five too early to think about lunch? The little donuts we ate each morning tasted delicious but they didn't last long in the tummy.

I wondered if Brennan was waiting anxiously for the hospice worker to arrive. If she stopped for lunch, she'd be that much later. Was Brennan as curious as me to learn what she was bringing? It was awfully nice of her to drive the five hours from Albany to drop it off. Cory and I drove there twice in the last week. Now we never wanted to make the drive again.

My heels tapped the showroom floor as I headed into the garage.

I got halfway there when I stopped. It was almost five and a half hours from Wachobe to Albany, taking the most direct route the GPS provided. Yet the hospice worker who called Brennan said she would be here in less than three.

I raced into the garage, grabbed Cory by the ankles, and yanked him out from under the car.

He appeared, flat on his back, wrench in hand, a stunned expression on his face. "Jo, are you crazy?"

"You said the hospice was in Albany, right?"

His brow furrowed. "Yes. So?"

"According to Brennan, the hospice worker left there at nine a.m., right?"

"Yes."

"She's supposed to be here by noon, right?"

"Yes." The light dawned in his eyes. "She can't get here that fast, not driving anyway."

He jumped to his feet. "Where's she coming from, Jo?"

"Binghamton is doable in less than three hours."

"We should have known a hospice worker wouldn't drive all the way here. Who do you think it is?"

"I think it's Beth Smith. She must know about the money. No wonder she's in a hurry to elope with Matthew. She must know he's Brennan's son and she must know about the will."

Cory stripped the gloves from his hands and picked up the phone. "Let me call Brennan."

I watched his face as he waited for Brennan to pick up. And the fear that washed across it when he didn't.

"Try his cell."

Cory punched in the number and waited. "Still no answer."

"I don't like it, Cory. Let's go over there. The worst thing that can happen is Brennan will laugh at us."

We rushed out the side door from the garage to the parking lot, leaving the building unlocked in our haste.

A gust of wind hit me in the face. The day had turned cold, the skies overcast. I climbed into the passenger seat of Cory's BMW and struggled against the wind to close the door. As soon as I got it shut, he hit the gas, jolting us backward into the lot. He threw the car in drive and took off.

He pulled out of the parking lot onto Main Street, tires squealing, nearly colliding with a laundry service truck trying to parallel park. Too late I remembered how Cory's driving deteriorated under duress.

I grabbed the seat belt and pulled it tight over my chest, clicking it in place. Then I braced myself against the dashboard as Cory blew through a red light. Thankfully it was a T intersection and the traffic was coming from the other side. They had time to stop, horns blowing, as Cory's BMW brushed in front of them.

I wished I'd thought to bring my cell phone with me so I could call Ray to meet us. Of course, with the way Cory was driving, someone was bound to report us to the authorities anyway.

He hung a hard right onto the county lake road where Brennan built his cottage. A semi blew past us from the oncoming lane, no doubt on its way around Wachobe. Cory's BMW rocked in its wake and I feared we might turn over.

We didn't.

Cory hit the gas. We fishtailed. I clung to the door handle as he powered through it.

Swaying bushes, bent trees, vacant cottages, and glimpses of white caps on the lake flew past my window as I tried to hold onto my stomach contents. Thank god I'd only eaten one of those tiny donuts.

Cory accelerated. I glanced at the speedometer. He was going eighty and driving up the middle of the road instead of staying in his lane. We might not get a chance to look like fools in front of Brennan if we came face to face with another semi at this speed.

Three miles passed in a minute. He slammed on the brakes and we swung wide, narrowly missing Brennan's mailbox.

I stifled a scream.

Cory roared up the driveway and hit the brakes.

My head almost collided with the windshield.

He flung open his door and raced onto the deck surrounding Brennan's stunning cedar cottage.

I chased after Cory, thinking we should proceed more cautiously.

But his fear for Brennan overcame his common sense. He tried the front door and found it locked. He rang the doorbell wildly.

I heard it ringing inside the house over the wind, which gusted around the side of the house, pushing me off balance and swirling the new fallen leaves into mini tornadoes.

Cory started around the side of the house. "I'll try the back door. Wait here."

A few seconds passed. I wrapped my suit jacket more tightly about my chest and peeked in the etched windows alongside the gold trimmed oak door, noticing nothing amiss. Then I glanced back toward the road and spotted a Honda Accord parked in the county road past Brennan's driveway.

Beth Smith was here.

A chill unrelated to the wind flowed through me.

Hurried footsteps approached from inside the house. The door flew open.

I turned to see who had opened the door.

And found myself face to face with the barrel of a gun.

TWENTY-NINE

My GAZE MOVED UP the gun past the sparkling pear-shaped diamond and black leather-clad arm to the shoulders and white turtleneck beyond. Then I stared at her face. Hatred, pure hatred. That's all I saw.

Beth Smith motioned for me to enter the house by wagging the end of the gun. "Come on in. I know I can't keep you out."

I stepped inside, staying clear of the gun barrel, and scanned the area.

Brennan's home had an open floor plan. I saw gleaming hardwood floors, a floor-to-ceiling grey stone fireplace, chocolate-colored leather couches, chrome and glass tables, the television broadcasting the midday news, and a panoramic view of the lake from the windows. No one was visible in the living room, nor in the dining area beyond. The granite kitchen countertops jutted into the living room, forming a breakfast bar over a line of stools, but I couldn't see inside the kitchen. A few leaves followed me inside on a gust of wind to swirl in the foyer.

"Brennan's in the kitchen. So's your friend Cory. Why don't we join them?" Beth used the gun again to point.

She moved away from the door, leaving it ajar.

I walked ahead of her, looking for a weapon—or at least a phone—and finding neither.

We entered the cherry kitchen with its black granite counter-tops and stainless steel appliances. Brennan stood in front of the stove where a tea kettle whistled softly as though he'd been ready to brew a pot. It would be hard for him to do now because hand-cuffs kept his right hand locked to the handle of the stove. They weren't regulation like Ray's but they seemed sturdy enough to do the trick. A file box sat nearby on the countertop. I wondered what, if anything, of interest it held.

A second scan of the room revealed Cory lying facedown on the floor, just inside the back door, immobile. I didn't see any blood, although only his head and shoulders were visible.

Brennan tipped his head in my direction, acknowledging my arrival. He must have read the concern for Cory on my face. "She hit him in the forehead with the butt of the gun when he came through the door. I think he's unconscious."

I moved closer to check if Cory's back rose and fell to prove he still breathed. It did.

Something poked me in the shoulder. "Stand over next to him, facing me."

I crossed the floor and turned to face Beth.

She kept the gun trained on me as she rummaged in Brennan's kitchen drawers with her other hand. "Don't you have any cords in your drawers, Brennan? I need to tie your friends up. Otherwise, I'll have to shoot them now."

Brennan didn't respond.

She yanked open the drawer next to the refrigerator. "Ah hah. Everyone has cords."

She yanked out what looked to be a cell phone charging cord and threw it at me. It fell at my feet. "Tie up Cory with his hands behind him."

When I made no move to pick up the cord, she stamped her foot, "Tie him up or I'll shoot him."

I stooped and picked up the cord. Then I loosely wrapped it around Cory's wrists.

"Tighter."

I tied it tight enough to satisfy her but not tight enough to hold Cory for too long if he came to. He hadn't even reflexively twitched when I touched him, not a good sign he'd wake anytime soon.

Beth motioned toward the nearby kitchen table. "Sit down."

I took a seat on one of the wrought iron chairs and studied her.

She moved back to the far side of the room. Her hand dropped a bit as she held the gun, perhaps from the weight of it. Aside from the gun and the ugly twist to her expression, she appeared calm and determined. Brennan probably hadn't recognized her with the funky new hairdo when she knocked at his door. He would naturally offer her refreshment after her long drive.

Brennan broke into my thoughts. "Now what, Elizabeth?"

"It's Beth. Not that you care. Not that you ever cared."

"We were friends once, Beth. I cared."

"You never came to visit me after the crash, even when you were still in the hospital recovering from your coma. You never came once to visit me."

"I tried. Your father wouldn't let me. He thought I'd upset you."

Beth's brow wrinkled as though this were news to her. Her eyes glittered like a wild animal's.

Brennan continued to talk as if he didn't notice, although I had no doubt he did. "I'm sorry about the accident, Beth. I never would have hurt you intentionally."

Her arm dropped ever so slightly. Now the gun pointed at Brennan's kneecaps. I tried to judge the distance across the room to her and knew I would never make it if I attempted to overwhelm her.

I looked for a weapon as Brennan talked on. "What can I do to make it up to you, Beth?"

She raised the gun to his face. "I'm going to kill you."

My gaze shot from the knife block on the countertop by the stove to Brennan's face.

His expression never wavered from compassionate and kind. "Why?"

"Because you ruined everything."

"In what way?"

"In high school, it was all about you. Monica couldn't go anywhere or do anything without you. I was the tagalong to make a foursome with Wayne. Nobody cared about me."

Brennan shook his head. "We cared. We were the four Musketeers, remember?"

"I remember when you broke up with Monica. She went to Wayne for comfort, not me. He would never even look at me. Then she got pregnant. I was the first one she told. She didn't even know if it was your baby or his. Disgusting."

Brennan winced. "What did she do?"

"She counted the weeks and decided Matthew had to be Wayne's. He didn't know any different, but when I met Matthew a few months ago, it was obvious to me."

"Why didn't Wayne take custody of Matthew after Monica died?"

"No father was named on the birth certificate because Monica wasn't absolutely sure. James said he was Matthew's closest living relative. He and Suzanne were married. They all decided a family environment would be better for Matthew. Wayne became his godfather, but he didn't really pay too much attention to Matthew. Wayne never paid too much attention to anyone but himself. The Gleasons never told Matthew about Monica being his mother. He thinks Suzanne and James are his real parents."

Brennan's head jerked at those words. He opened his mouth then closed it again.

I knew he was thinking about the phone call from Matthew, who knew Monica was his mother. How did he know? Apparently Brennan thought it best not to tell Beth that Matthew knew more than she thought. And if Matthew knew about Monica, did he know about Brennan, too?

Brennan cleared his throat. "I know I didn't push James Gleason into the road. Did you push him, Beth?"

She grinned wickedly and stamped her foot again, this time with glee. "I shoved him. No one noticed, including you. Everyone was looking at the cars."

"Why did you kill James?"

"He didn't want Matthew with me. He was going to ruin everything."

"But why blame me?"

"You walked right up to my wheelchair that day. I can't walk very long so I still need my chair for events like the festival. You looked right at me and you didn't even recognize me. I got out of the chair to follow you to tell you off for all the years of pain. Then James showed up. He was going to tell you about Matthew. See, he knew Matthew was your son, too. The older the kid got, the more obvious the resemblance became. James wanted money from you."

"And you want money from Matthew?"

Her smile was twisted. "You told Monica in the car that night all about your father's will. You wanted her to have Matthew tested to see if he was yours. She didn't want to. You were arguing with her when the deer crossed the road. You swerved to avoid the deer, lost control of the car, and hit the tree.

"Poor Monica." Beth said her name as if it left a bad taste in her mouth.

Brennan sagged against the stove, a lost and bewildered expression on his face. "When did you decide to go after Matthew and the money?"

"When he came knocking on my door six months ago, asking about Monica. He'd found her diary and he suspected she was his mother. I'd got by on nothing for years. And no men ever wanted me for long once they got a peek at my scars. But Matthew couldn't wait to spend time with me. I was the link to his mother. And I played him just right. I told him he reminded me of her and how much I loved her. It was the perfect time to move in on him, when he felt so betrayed by James and Suzanne."

Bile crept into the back of my throat. Beth was venomous.

Brennan cleared his throat. "But why kill Wayne?"

She waggled the gun in my direction. "When she showed up in his office asking questions about me, Wayne had a few of his own. He talked to me, and then he decided to get in touch with you. I knew the two of you would figure it out. I needed to marry Matthew first. So I called in the message from you and Wayne went running. All I had to do was beat him here."

Brennan closed his eyes.

I felt something touch my ankle and recoiled. It was Cory's hand. He'd gotten loose from the cord while Beth talked.

He lowered his hand back flat to the floor. His other hand moved to the same position as though he was ready to push up to his feet, but he remained motionless, perhaps waiting for the ideal moment.

Beth didn't seem to notice his movements or the fact he wasn't tied up anymore.

Brennan's chin had sunk to his chest. He seemed speechless at this point in the face of Beth's brutality.

I knew he wouldn't be any help overcoming her chained to the stove as he was. I couldn't count on Cory, even though he'd managed to untie himself. After a blow to the head, he might not get on his feet fast enough to be of help.

My gaze slid back to the knife block, then dismissed the notion. Guns trump knives every time. Although Beth's hand drooped from the weight of the weapon every once in awhile, she could still get it in position fast enough to kill me. Even if I threw the knife block at her, she could duck and shoot me at the same time.

I had no idea what to do.

Brennan's eyes were closed. I didn't know if he was grieving for his lost friends, thinking about how to save us, or simply praying for a miracle.

Beth glanced at Brennan and curled her lip in distaste. Then her gaze slid to me. I looked away, knowing animals always felt threatened by eye contact. And Beth seemed like an angry tigress to me.

Her gaze dropped to Cory. Her eyes narrowed and she took a few steps forward to train the gun on him.

A loud crash came from the front of the house. Startled, I jumped in my chair. The front door must have slammed against the wall from the wind.

Beth twirled around to investigate, leaving her back to me. I leapt to my feet and shoved her as hard as I could. She fell to her knees, dropping the gun, which skittered across the wood floor and came to rest under the kitchen cabinets.

"Cory, get the gun."

I heard him scrambling behind me as Beth crawled across the floor, her hand outstretched, reaching for the gun.

She was much closer to the gun than Cory and completely blocking both our paths to it, so I jumped and planted my butt in her back like a wrestler, slamming her to the floor and knocking the wind out of her.

Cory tumbled over us and fell next to the gun. He got it in his hand and clambered to his feet. He threw the gun inside a drawer and stood with his back to the closed drawer, shaking.

Before I got off Beth, I felt around in her pockets. The right pocket of her leather jacket held a keychain, plus one single key. I pulled them all out and stepped over to Brennan, unlocking the handcuffs with the single key. He massaged his wrist as he stared down at Beth, who lay sobbing on the floor, kicking her legs and pounding the floor like a spoiled child.

"I'll call 911." I moved to the phone mounted on the kitchen wall. As I dialed, Brennan stepped over Beth to examine Cory's forehead.

The dispatcher said she would send the nearest patrol car as well as contact Ray.

I hung up the phone and turned around.

Now Beth stood in the middle of the kitchen, blood spattered on her chin from where she'd hit the floor.

Seeing her, Brennan reached for a paper towel from the dispenser next to the sink.

She took off, throwing open the back door and disappearing into the wind.

"Aw, shit." Ray would never forgive me if I let her get away now. I ran after her, Brennan and Cory close on my heels.

We rounded the back corner of the house in time to see her step off the front porch and run across the grass toward her car.

I started after her, the wind buffeting and trying to push me back toward the house. Brennan and Cory passed me, closing in on her.

When they were halfway across the lawn, Beth reached her car door, flinging it open and jumping inside.

I stopped. "Cory, Cory."

He turned to look at me over his shoulder.

I dangled Beth's car keys in the air.

Cory put an arm out to stop Brennan as I walked toward them. "She's not going anywhere."

Beth got out of the car and started screaming and yelling, a whirlwind of fury in the middle of the road. Like a thwarted child, she shook her hands at the sky and stamped her feet. The wind carried her words away from us, but I could still make out the enraged sound.

I could also hear sirens.

And the roar of an oncoming semi.

"Beth, Beth." I started running for the road again, passing Brennan and Cory. "Get out of the road, Beth. Get out of the road."

She didn't seem to hear me. But she saw me coming toward her. And she ran.

Right into the path of the semi.

THIRTY

On the night of Isabelle's surprise party, Ray and I got dressed in the closet together. He put on a pair of tan chinos, a light blue shirt, a multicolored blue tie, and his navy blazer. I put on a ruffled hot pink off-the-shoulder dress with a neckline that skimmed the swell of my breasts.

"Ray, can you zip me up?"

He took hold of the zipper pull, swiped my hair away, and leaned down to run his lips over the back of my bare neck, sending shivers down my spine. "Do I have to?"

I playfully swatted him away. "Yes, we're going to be late. I don't want to miss the look on Isabelle's face when we all yell 'surprise.'"

Danny waited for us in the living room, watching his beloved SpongeBob and wearing a pair of tan chinos, loafers, and a yellow dress shirt. He looked handsome—and annoyed to have to be going to this party. He'd been very quiet since he got home from visiting his dad with Ray today.

"Do I have to go?"

I thought once again of how much he and Ray were alike. "Yes. We're all going and we're going to have a good time." So help me.

Danny passed the hour-long drive to Isabelle's party by listening to his iPod.

Ray kept my Lexus at an even sixty miles per hour, five over the speed limit and six under the radar. "Are Erica and Maury coming tonight?"

Erica and I used to have Thanksgiving dinner every year with Isabelle's family when Ray and I were separated. Their family knew us both well. "They were invited, but Erica's taking sewing lessons at the quilt shop. She didn't want to miss class tonight. They're learning how to make buttonholes."

Ray snorted.

"Don't belittle her. She's using her time constructively. I'm proud of her."

"Did you pay for her lessons?"

I looked out the window and changed the subject. "Matthew called Brennan this week. Brennan asked him to when they saw each other at Beth's funeral. Matthew said he wants to get to know him. He's coming to Brennan's house tomorrow."

"Is Cory going to be there?"

"No, he thought the two of them should get acquainted first." It would be a relief if one positive event ensued after all these deaths. Cory's and my morning donut discussions were a lot quieter lately. We both knew we'd been the catalysts for two people's deaths. Even though we'd been in the pursuit of truth, the fact never got less painful.

"That's a good idea." Ray hit the left-hand turn signal, waited for an oncoming car, then made his turn.

"Cory said Beth's parents were heartbroken at the funeral. Her mother couldn't stop sobbing, and the doctor had apparently given her a tranquilizer."

"They went through a lot with her, only to have her throw it all away."

My secret fear was that could happen to even the most attentive and loving parents. "Well, at least Brennan and Matthew will have each other."

"Matthew's an adult. He doesn't need a father anymore."

"Then maybe they can be friends. That would be just as nice, wouldn't it?"

"Sure."

I glanced over my shoulder into the back seat. Danny's eyes were closed, listening to the iPod. He didn't seem to hear our conversation. "Danny's been awfully quiet since he got home today. Did anything happen when he visited his dad?"

Ray glanced in the rearview mirror. "His dad has a black eye."

"How did he get it?"

"He won't say. I'm sure one of the other prisoners hit him."

Frustration boiled in me. "Can't you guys keep him safe? It's the county jail. You work for the county."

Ray frowned. "The guards do what they can, Jolene. They don't have the manpower to watch him every second. He might get roughed up a little."

"And you don't care. He could get killed."

Ray checked the mirror again. "I care, but I can't control the situation."

"We could pay Mr. Phillips' bail and get him out of there."

"And he might take off with Danny, especially now that he's had a taste of jail again. Do you want to take that chance?"

I couldn't answer Ray—because I didn't know. Mr. Phillips had entrusted his son to us. Had his faith in our abilities changed? His situation certainly hadn't. He was still a homeless car thief, as far as we knew. Danny was a well-behaved seventh grader with good marks who played on the football team. He couldn't have any of that if his dad took him away. Mr. Phillips had made it clear Danny's education was important to him when he stole my Ferrari to start Danny's college fund—or so he said. Would he sacrifice his own needs for Danny's?

Forty-five minutes later, I still didn't have an answer when we pulled into the parking lot for the party house, which was so full Ray almost gave up and went home. He finally found one remaining spot at the far side of the parking lot.

We slid out of the car and headed toward the brightly lit portico.

Inside the lobby we left our coats with the attendant and entered the party room.

A wave of heat hit me in the face. Guests dressed in all their finery filled the room as bow-tied, white-shirted waitresses roamed, offering hors d'oeuvres and flutes of champagne. A band dressed in navy tuxedos played jazz softly. White Christmas lights glittered on topiaries placed strategically around the room, and magnificent bouquets of fall flowers graced every table, set off by flickering vanilla scented candles.

Jack must have invited every person he and Isabelle knew. I didn't see either of them anywhere, but Jack's brother stood on a dais, speaking into a whining microphone that pierced my eardrums.

"Everybody, can I have it quiet please?"

All the heads in the room turned toward him.

"Jack just texted. They'll be here in a few minutes. We'd like everyone to form a line around the perimeter of the room. Then we'll dim the lights. When they walk in, we'll all yell 'Happy Anniversary,' okay?"

Everyone started to jockey for position around the perimeter. Since we were still in the doorway, we only had to move a few steps to stay close to the entrance yet out of the way.

The lights dimmed. We waited.

And waited.

A few people giggled nervously. Some started to whisper.

A man by the window called out, "They're here. Shush."

Moments later the doors flew open. The lights went up.

Isabelle stood in the doorway on Jack's arm, wearing a stunning red satin dress with matching shoes and a diamond necklace that caught the light. Her eyes bugged out when we yelled.

A tentative smile—then a broader one lit up her face and spread to her eyes. She fanned herself with her clutch as her gaze moved around the room.

Jack, looking dapper in a black tuxedo, unhooked his arm from hers and stepped to the side. "Surprise, honey. Happy anniversary."

Tears glittered in the corners of Isabelle's eyes. She shook her head in wonder and disbelief before moving to kiss him.

Everyone applauded.

Cassidy ran forward from where she had been waiting at her grandmother's side, her curls bouncing and her crinoline and taffeta rustling. She stopped in front of Isabelle, pressing her palms together. "Are you surprised, Mommy? Are you surprised?"

"I sure am, baby." Isabelle crouched and hugged Cassidy tight. "I sure am."

The three of them started around the room to greet the guests. Everyone stayed in place, waiting to be received. Isabelle and Jack made it around to us at last.

Jack shook Ray's and Danny's hands. "Good to see you. Thanks for coming."

He leaned in to kiss my cheek. "Thanks for keeping the secret. I know it must have killed you."

That was putting it mildly.

Isabelle's eyes met mine. She started to cry.

I hugged her.

She whispered in my ear, "I'm such an idiot."

"No, no. He must have been planning this for months. He was keeping a secret from you, just not the one you thought."

"Let me steal Jolene for a moment, Ray." She took me by the hand and led me toward the bar. "I feel so stupid. You know, when you and Ray split, it was right around your ten-year anniversary. I was so sure you two were meant to be together forever. Your separation rocked my confidence. Then when Jack started acting secretive, I assumed…"

She pressed her hand to her nose and sniffed.

I tried to ease the moment. "Well, you know what happens when you assume."

She laughed. "I do now."

The band started to play "From This Moment On," Shania Twain's big hit from the late nineties, and the song Jack and

Isabelle had chosen for their first dance at their wedding. Jack approached from across the room, took Isabelle by the hand, and swept her onto the dance floor in front of the band. Her smile was radiant.

Ray appeared next to me. "Nice party. Isabelle looks stunning."

I sighed with happiness. "Yes, she does. Where's Danny?"

Ray waved vaguely over his shoulder. "He's discussing the merits of about a hundred different Playstation 3 games with Isabelle's nephew."

Other couples moved to join Isabelle and Jack on the dance floor. Ray crooked his arm. "Care to dance, Mrs. Parker?"

"I'd be delighted, Mr. Parker."

The evening passed in a whirl of filet mignon, wine, and chocolate mousse cake. By ten, I felt bloated but satisfied. Danny, finished with his Playstation discussions and bored to tears by the music and dancing, agitated to go home. The party seemed like it was just getting started, but I told him to wait by the front door while I bid Isabelle goodnight and rounded up Ray from his conversation with the men by the bar.

Isabelle hugged me tight. "This was amazing. I'm so glad you came."

I squeezed her back. "Me, too. Where's Jack? I want to compliment him for a job well done."

Isabelle waved toward the men's room. "He's making room for more wine."

"Oh. Well, tell him the party was wonderful."

Ray and I found Danny slumped on a bench in the lobby. The coatroom attendant had disappeared. She must have been taking a break because her tip jar sat unguarded on the ledge. We waited a few minutes but she failed to return to her post.

Ray gazed at the claim tickets in his hand. "What coat did you wear?"

"My white one. I'll help you look."

We entered the coatroom and started up the first aisle, checking the hanger numbers against our tickets. We rounded the bend into the back aisle.

And came upon Jack in a clench with another woman.

She spotted us first and tapped him on the shoulder. He spun to look at us.

Ray looked at the tickets in his hand. "I think those are our coats you're leaning on. Could you pass them this way, Jack?"

Jack swallowed and obeyed.

I gazed at him, my mouth hanging open. He couldn't meet my eyes. The woman appeared unrepentant. I had no idea who she was.

Ray put his arm around my shoulder and nudged me toward the door. "Great party, Jack. Take care."

He pushed me along. I resisted, tempted to go back and claw Jack's eyes out. "Keep moving, Jolene. It's not our affair."

A poor choice of words on Ray's part.

He moved me into the lobby and placed my coat around my shoulders. "Danny, let's go, buddy. Time to go home."

I stared at the coatroom then tried to locate Isabelle in the party room, willing her to come and witness this for herself. I didn't want to be the one to tell her and break her heart.

Ray swept me out the door. He whispered in my ear as we crossed the parking lot, "Isabelle knows. The wife always knows."

On the way home, I analyzed Isabelle's crazed behavior over the last few weeks and her admitted suspicions regarding Jack's behavior. She'd been acting completely out-of-character, emotional, irrational, like she'd lost her identity.

And I realized Ray was right.

I kissed Danny goodnight and went into our bedroom to change while Ray tucked him into bed. After washing off my makeup and brushing my teeth, I climbed into bed, welcoming sleep.

Ray appeared in our bedroom doorway, loosening his tie. "Hey, don't go to sleep yet. Danny wants you to tuck him in, too."

I threw back the bedcovers and padded across the cold wood floor in my bare feet. It was nice to be wanted, but sometimes it was okay to be left out, too.

"Good night, Danny." I brushed the hair from his forehead and kissed him.

He lifted up on his elbows. "Can we talk for a second?"

"Sure." I sat on the edge of his bed.

"My dad has a black eye."

"I know. Ray told me."

"He won't tell me how he got it. He just said not to worry."

"But you're worried."

Danny swallowed and nodded. A tear ran down his cheek. "You promised to help him. Can you bail him out of jail?"

"I could, Danny. I have the money." I hesitated, then decided to go with the truth. "I'm afraid he'll run and take you with him. I couldn't bear to think of you living out of a car again."

I expected Danny to protest, to claim this would never happen. He said nothing. Instead, he lay back down on the bed. "I understand."

His calm acceptance broke my heart. I pulled the covers over his shoulders and kissed him again. "I love you, Danny."

He turned his head away and the covers muffled his reply. "I love you, too, Jolene."

I thought he might be crying.

In the living room, I curled up on the couch, pulling an afghan around my shoulders as I hugged Erica's pillow to my chest. When Danny said he understood, did he mean that he thought his father would run? Did he mean his father would take him away, too? Or did he simply mean that he knew I'd break my promise and never take a chance by paying Mr. Phillips' bail?

How could a twelve-year-old understand when I didn't?

I read the words on Erica's pillow again. "I smile because you're my sister. I laugh because there is nothing you can do about it."

Such a stupid gift shop saying. But it made me feel better. As her surrogate mother, I had taken every one of her failures and setbacks to heart, wondering what I could have done or what I should have done. In the end, did she really turn out so bad?

Soft sobs filtered through Danny's door. Although my heart broke, what more could I say to him? Words, in this case, were worthless.

Danny needed to know he was loved, that he'd come first always. Ray put him second when he did his job and arrested Mr. Phillips. He wasn't wrong to do his job. He just wasn't right. Mr. Phillips had done the right thing by changing his plea to guilty and put himself at risk for it. Danny had felt lost after the arrest, pulled between us and his loyalty and love for his father. Now he felt afraid for his father's safety. It wasn't right.

Another one of the stupid gift shop sayings popped into my head. While Erica's chosen saying showed up on pillows and plaques, this one usually appeared on wall hangings with seagulls and beach scenes and read something like, "If you love something, set it free. If it comes back to you, it was meant to be."

Stupid. Yet profound.

All night I tossed and turned in bed, sleepless. Ray threw his arm over me again around three a.m. He muttered, "Don't worry about Isabelle. Everything will be all right. Go to sleep."

But I wasn't worried about Isabelle. I was a little worried about him and me—and whether he'd forgive me. Or if he'd even need to.

In the morning, I got in my Lexus and drove to the bank, where I withdrew five thousand dollars. Half an hour later at the county jail, I laid it on the counter to pay Mr. Phillips' bail.

And I set Danny free.

THE END

Book Discussion Questions

1. Jolene and Ray had different approaches to dealing with Danny. Do you agree with one more than the other? What did you think of Jolene's final decision to bail out Danny's father? What do you think will happen to Danny and his father?

2. Both Isabelle and Cory investigate their partners. What do you think of snooping and spying on a partner?

3. In the end, Jolene and Ray believe Isabelle knew about her husband's cheating. What would you do if you were Isabelle? What did you think of her husband throwing a grand anniversary party for her?

4. What did you think of Brennan's father's reported behavior?

5. Gossip and innuendo swirled around Brennan Rowe, most of it painting him in a negative, false light. Have you ever experienced or witnessed the same? How should it be handled? Why do people generate gossip and innuendo?

6. What do you think of Jolene's and Ray's marriage? Erica's and Maury's? How are the two marriages alike and different? What do you think their futures hold?

7. Some murder mystery readers prefer the dead body to appear in the first chapter. Some expect two bodies per story. Some enjoy a mystery that delves into the past and reveals secrets. What elements of a murder mystery appeal to you most?

ABOUT THE AUTHOR

Lisa Bork lives in western New York and loves to spend time in the Finger Lakes region. Married and the mother of two children, she worked in human resources and marketing before becoming a writer. Bork belongs to her neighborhood book club, the Thursday Evening Literary Society. Her debut novel, *For Better, For Murder*, was a 2009 Agatha Award finalist for Best First Novel. The second book in her Broken Vows mystery series, *For Richer, For Danger*, was released in September 2010, and the third book, *In Sickness and in Death*, was released in September 2011. For more information, please visit her website at www .LisaBork.com.

WWW.MIDNIGHTINKBOOKS.COM

From the gritty streets of New York City to sacred tombs in the Middle East, it's always midnight somewhere. Join us online at any hour for fresh new voices in mystery fiction.

At midnightinkbooks.com you'll also find our author blog, new and upcoming books, events, book club questions, excerpts, mystery resources, and more.

MIDNIGHT INK ORDERING INFORMATION

Order Online:

• Visit our website www.midnightinkbooks.com, select your books, and order them on our secure server.

Order by Phone:

• Call toll-free within the U.S. and Canada at
1-888-NITE-INK (1-888-648-3465)
• We accept VISA, MasterCard, and American Express

Order by Mail:

Send the full price of your order (MN residents add 6.875% sales tax) in U.S. funds, plus postage & handling to:

Midnight Ink
2143 Wooddale Drive
Woodbury, MN 55125-2989

Postage & Handling:

Standard (U.S. & Canada). If your order is:
$25.00 and under, add $4.00
$25.01 and over, FREE STANDARD SHIPPING

AK, HI, PR: $16.00 for one book plus $2.00 for each additional book.

International Orders (airmail only):
$16.00 for one book plus $3.00 for each additional book

Orders are processed within 12 business days. Please allow for normal shipping time.
Postage and handling rates subject to change.

*If you enjoy the "A Broken Vows Mystery" series,
check out "A Darby Farr Mystery"
by Vicki Doudera!*

A House To Die For

A Darby Farr Mystery

VICKI DOUDERA

Red-hot realtor Darby Farr escaped her stifling hometown of Hurricane Harbor, Maine, to build a new life in California, free of painful memories and her controlling aunt. But when Darby gets a shocking phone call from her elderly aunt's assistant, it sends her back to the Maine island to close a multimillion-dollar sale — her dying aunt's last wish.

Fairview, a breathtaking waterfront estate, seems like a simple deal…until a malicious local scuttles the sale by digging up an obscure deed restriction, and the back-up buyer is found hacked to death. Facing a desperate buyer, a dangerous ex-Navy SEAL, and a storm surging up the coast, Darby must salvage the deal, piece together this deadly puzzle, and somehow stay alive.

978-0-7387-1950-4, 336 pp., 5³/₁₆ x 8   **$14.95**

Killer Listing
A Darby Farr Mystery
Vicki Doudera

Million-dollar listings and hefty commissions come easily for Kyle Cameron, South Florida's star broker. But her career ends abruptly when she is fatally stabbed at an open house. Because of a family friend's longstanding ties to the Cameron clan, realtor Darby Farr gets pulled into the investigation and learns that Kyle had a shocking secret—one that could've sealed her violent fate. Suspects abound, including Kyle's estranged suicidal husband; her ex-lover, Foster McFarlin, a ruthless billionaire developer; and Foster's resentful, politically ambitious wife. And Darby's investigating puts her next on the killer's hit list.

978-0-7387-1979-5, 336pp., 5³/₁₆ x 8   **$14.95**

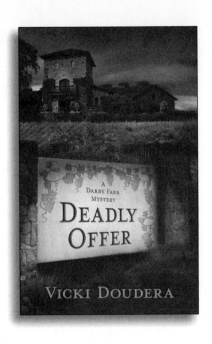

Deadly Offer
A Darby Farr Mystery
VICKI DOUDERA

When Darby Farr's assistant, E. T., learns that his sister, Selena, has suddenly (and suspiciously) died in her hot tub, Darby and E. T. travel to Selena's magnificent vineyard estate nestled in the heart of California wine country. There, Darby discovers that Selena was entertaining offers from three different prospective buyers—each one of whom is desperate to be the new owner of the winery. As a saboteur wreaks havoc on the property, Darby risks her life to crack the case and close the sale in a valley ripe with jealousy, greed, and danger.

978-0-7387-1980-1, 312pp., 5³/₁₆ x 8   **$14.95**